D1519037

Ghosts

Beneath us

The 3rd Spookie Town Murder Mystery

~

*Sequel to **Scraps of Paper** and
All Things Slip Away; prequel to **Witches Among
Us**, **What Lies Beneath the Graves**, **All Those Who
Came Before**; and out in December 2020, **When
the Fireflies Returned.***

~

By Kathryn Meyer Griffith

Ghosts Beneath Us

by Kathryn Meyer Griffith

Cover art by: Dawné Dominique
Copyright 2015 Kathryn Meyer Griffith

All rights reserved. No part of this book may be reproduced, scanned or distributed in any form, including digital and electronic or mechanical, including photocopying, recording, or by any information storage and retrieval system, without the prior written consent of the author, except for brief quotes for use in reviews.

This book is a work of fiction. Characters, names, places and incidents either are the product of the author's imagination or are used fictitiously, and any resemblance to any actual persons, living or dead, events, or locales is entirely coincidental.

For my family, as always, with love…
Other books by Kathryn Meyer Griffith:
Evil Stalks the Night
The Heart of the Rose
Blood Forge
Vampire Blood
The Last Vampire (2012 Epic EBook Awards Finalist)
Witches
Witches II: Apocalypse
The Calling
Scraps of Paper-*1st Spookie Town Murder Mystery*
All Things Slip Away- *2nd Spookie Town Mystery*
Ghosts Beneath Us- *3rd Spookie Town Mystery*
Witches Among Us- *4th Spookie Town Mystery*
What Lies Beneath the Graves-*5th Spookie Town*
All Those Who Came Before-*6th Spookie Town*
When the Fireflies Returned-*7th out in Dec. 2020*
Egyptian Heart
Winter's Journey
The Ice Bridge
Don't Look Back, Agnes
A Time of Demons
The Woman in Crimson
Four Spooky Short Stories
Human No Longer
Night Carnival
Forever and Always
Dinosaur Lake (2014 Epic EBook Awards Finalist)
Dinosaur Lake II: Dinosaurs Arising
Dinosaur Lake III: Infestation
Dinosaur Lake IV: Dinosaur Wars
Dinosaur Lake V: Survivors
***All Kathryn Meyer Griffith's books can be found
here:**
http://tinyurl.com/ld4jlow

*All her Audible.com audio books here:
http://tinyurl.com/oz7c4or

Chapter 1
Abigail

Abigail Sutton had a premonition that something out of the ordinary was about to happen. Her skin itched and a chill tickled along her spine. Her fingertips tingled. The last time she felt that combination of sensations a serial killer came to town. When he left, three people were dead and in their graves.

A chilly breeze brought goosebumps to her exposed flesh. *Trouble...trouble coming.*

She usually loved this time of day, early in the morning with a new sun in the sky above; the world tinted in a golden light that made everything look magical and made her feel peaceful. It meant a new day, a fresh start. But today, she had the feeling, it wouldn't be so.

Walking out onto her porch in her pajamas and robe, and with a sigh of contentment, she relaxed on the porch swing. A cup of her homemade chocolate coffee steamed from the cup in her hands and she sipped it as her eyes roamed the yard. As usual there was the Spookie town fog sneaking in from the woods and swirling along the fringe of the yard

1

surrounding her house. It was a gray mist full of mysterious shapes and figures she didn't dare let her eyes linger on too long because she often saw unexpected things–people or animals–in it. That was the artist in her, always trying to make sense of haphazard patterns.

Shivering, she tugged her robe closer around her because for the first day of April it was chilly. Two weeks away, Easter would be late this year. It'd be such fun, though, with the children and Abigail looked forward to it. Everything was different since Laura and Nick had come to live with her a year ago. They were a responsibility but an even greater joy.

Abigail was the happiest she'd been in years.

Her green eyes took in the birdhouses she'd hung around the edge of her porch and they stopped on the new one she'd gotten the week before. It was a miniature blue painted gourd with a crimson feathered fake bird in its opening. A pretty thing. It'd been a present from her boyfriend Frank Lester.

Boyfriend. Oh, she could have called him her lover, but boyfriend sounded nicer. They'd been dating for over a year, she'd known him now for three, and she'd finally accepted how deeply they cared for each other. Their relationship had been on a slow simmer for years and she'd enjoyed every moment of it. Getting to know him and letting the love in. They'd taken their time because when she'd first moved to Spookie and met Frank her heart had been broken. Time had been what she'd needed.

It'd been five years since her husband Joel had come up missing, a murder victim of a mugging gone wrong; three years since she'd known what had happened to him. Those years when he'd been missing had been terrible times. It felt like a lifetime ago when she'd lived in the crowded city, had toiled thanklessly at a job she'd hated and been so lonely. But now her life and her heart had basically mended. Frank, her two foster children and a town full of friendly but quirky characters had helped to heal her. She'd always remember and love her husband Joel but it was time to move on. It was way past time.

A smile touched her face. She was supposed to meet Frank at ten that morning at Stella's Diner in the heart of town for breakfast and the latest gossip. They did that at least once a week after the kids had left for school. But she had two hours before that and she was enjoying every moment of it. Alone. She'd seen Laura and Nick off and she was lounging on her porch admiring her house and appreciating her life. These days she was a lucky woman and how well she knew it.

Her brown hair had grown long and she'd tied it back in a braid so it'd stay away from her face. Frank liked her hair long and the longer the better.

She'd been a free-lance artist–a lifelong dream of hers–the last three years and had already built a reputation as a fairly good one because of the paintings she'd completed for the townspeople and the murals for the library and city hall. Right now she was working on a massive courthouse mural of Lady Justice standing outside the building and holding up her weighing scales. It was the most difficult job she'd attempted so far. The painting was twice as large, covering two walls, as the one she'd done for either the library or the city hall but she was nearly done and she was pleased with it. She'd be going there today after breakfast to put on the finishing touches and collect her check. Her smile grew wider and she took another sip of coffee.

Ah, things were good.

Her cat Snowball came bounding out from the house, shoving the screen door open with her nose and slipping through, and ran past her out into the yard. Looking for birds to chase, catch and devour. But the wild creatures weren't awake yet, probably still sleeping in their nests protecting unhatched eggs in the limbs of the trees around the house. Snowball was out of luck again. Abigail didn't feel in the least sorry for her. She cared about birds, too, and as much as she loved her cat, she hated its predatory traits. Yet a cat was a cat. It could no more stop hunting than a lion could out in the wild.

Above her the birds began to squawk so she wasn't surprised when Myrtle came up beside her on the porch, sat down on the swing and said, "Humph, I knew you'd be out here getting the sun, Abigail, so I decided to mosey on over and visit. I got some interesting news for ya."

Myrtle Schmidt was the town eccentric wagon-lady and a terrible secret keeper. Today she was wearing her typical garishly flowered sundress with the hem unraveling, too large for her tiny frame, and her silver permed hair was a wild halo about her wrinkled face. Abigail doubted if she ever combed it. The old woman wasn't smiling but her sapphire colored eyes were sparkling with barely contained excitement.

"You don't happen to have any more of that coffee do ya, Abby girl? A couple of cookies or donuts to go with it? Now that would taste so good. I haven't had a thing to eat yet and I need my strength to tell you what I have to tell ya."

"Well, good morning to you, too, Myrtle." Abigail turned and looked at her friend and neighbor. Over the years she'd lived in town Abigail had come to care about the old lady, idiosyncrasies and all. Myrtle might be a bit peculiar, but she was an interestingly feisty individual. A person was never bored when Myrtle was around, and at least once Myrtle had literally saved her life. She owed her.

"I imagine there's coffee left in the pot and I'll see if I can come up with a stale donut or something." She always kept a box of donuts or cookies in the house, if not for herself and the kids, then for Myrtle. The old lady was forever coming over and mooching food. That was her trademark.

She rose from the swing and went into the house, Myrtle hobbling behind her.

They made their way through the living room with the walls covered with Abigail's original artwork, a round tapestry rug in vibrant colors on the floor, and filled with comfortably overstuffed furniture. The house had changed since she'd bought it as a dilapidated fixer-upper and performed her magic on it. She'd painted and decorated both floors, filled them with color and then with people and love. The year before she'd taken the roomy rear hallway and had made it into a bedroom for Laura. Frank and a couple of their friends had helped her build on a room in the back for Nicolaus. So now both children had their own rooms, small, but all theirs.

Abigail cherished her house now. It was home. She felt safe and happy there.

"You know if you pop those donuts in the microwave for ten, fifteen seconds they'll be as fresh as the day you bought them," Myrtle advised. "Just saying."

The laugh Abigail released was muffled. "I'll do that."

"You're still in your pajamas, Abigail. Is it that early?"

"Really early. The sun just came up. Didn't you notice?" They were in the kitchen now. The table was covered with empty cereal bowls and dirty utensils from the kids. She'd clean everything up once Myrtle left.

"I noticed. Sorry. But when you're my

ancient age, day and night don't seem to matter. Sometimes I sleep all day and stay up all night or vice-versa. It's hell getting old, let me tell you. Schedules and sleep times go out the window. I saw you sitting outside on the swing and thought you wouldn't mind a little company. I mean since you were already awake and all."

"Uh,huh." Abigail poured coffee into a mug and handed it to her.

"I would have come earlier but, you know, those ghosts that live in the woods can be awful scary before dawn lights things up. They want to jump all over me and scream obscenities in my ears. Tell me their secrets I don't want to hear. They're such pests. Stupid ghosts."

She gave the old woman a bemused look over her shoulder as she grabbed a box off the counter and pulled out two power-sugared donuts, put them on a napkin, then added two more for herself, and slid them into the microwave. Ten seconds. "Ah, so those ghosts are still hounding you?"

"More than ever lately. What's new, huh? I can't leave my trailer longer than a minute before a mess of them gang up on me with their demands and their perpetual whining. Some of them are just lonely but some of them are just downright mean. As you know, I don't ever dare go out into or through the woods after dark. They're even worse then. They'd be hiding behind trees or big rocks. Always waiting. Popping up when you least expect them…they can scare a few years off a person with their wasting away bodies and sunken in faces. Not to mention their smell. Whooie. Most of them stink like year old garbage." Myrtle shuddered, her fingers pinching her nose as if to demonstrate what she was speaking of.

"That wouldn't be pleasant."

"It sure ain't."

The ghost thing was a chronic problem of Myrtle's. She'd been going on about them ever since Abigail had met her. She didn't know if Myrtle really could see ghosts or if it was in the old woman's imagination. Not that Abigail actually believed in ghosts. Not completely anyway. Yet too many strange things had occurred in Spookie since she'd moved there for her to be a total cynic. So she tried to keep an open mind by choosing not to think about random spirits floating around. It was easier that way.

With coffee and donuts in hand she led Myrtle back out to the porch and placing the snacks on a side table, the women took their seats. Myrtle snatched two of the circle cakes and stuffed them in her mouth. She was so short when she sat on the swing her feet didn't touch the porch floor.

"Okay Myrtle, I know you too well. I recognize that look on your face. There's a reason you're here so early, besides the donuts, that is. How about telling me what it is?"

The woman grinned. She had nice even white teeth for her age. "I promised Beatrice–

she's an old friend of mine who lives down the road from me and I'm sure I've spoken about her before–I'd talk to you on her behalf about a sort of, er, trouble she's been having. Beatrice Utley?"

"No, I don't recall you mentioning her before, but then you talk so much about so many people, I tend to forget some of what you say." A quick teasing smile. "We live in a small town, but it's not that small. There are plenty of people I haven't met yet."

Myrtle threw her an exasperated look. "Very funny about me talking too much. I don't think I do. I just have a lot to say that needs saying. That's all."

"Uh, huh. If you say so."

"I do." Myrtle's face was pouting.

"So this Beatrice friend of yours has a problem?" Her eyes on her swing mate, Abigail ate one of the donuts as crumbs and white powder drifted down the front of her robe. She brushed them off. "Why are you bringing it to me?"

Myrtle had gobbled up both her donuts and was gulping down her coffee. Then she'd ask for another cup. She was so predictable. "*Because* you and Frank did so well on the last couple *problems* we had in town I thought you'd two be just the ones to fix this one, too. If there's a mystery to be solved, a wrong to be righted, a murderer to catch, you two are the ones to do it. Him being an ex-cop and a mystery novelist and all and you…being you."

"Being me?"

"Because, *you know?* You've got the magic gene that helps you find missing people and murderers. You care. You having had a missing husband who turned out murdered and all. It's your special gift."

Abigail sighed softly. She could almost sense this was something she didn't want to become involved with, but Myrtle could be extremely persuasive. She wondered if she jumped up right now, ran into the house and locked the door, told Myrtle to go home because she wasn't going to help, if she could escape Myrtle's request? Nah, the old woman would probably only return and keep bugging her until she agreed to help. That was her way. "What does all that have to do with Beatrice Utley's problem?"

Myrtle fixed her eyes on her and they were suddenly dead serious. "Because Beatrice's house is haunted. Or so she says. She has this great big monstrosity of a place down near that cul-de-sac at the end of my road. You know the house…the white one with metal Americana stars on the front and a flagpole in the yard with daffodils around it? Her grandmother left her the house so it's real run down and full of old threadbare furniture, too. That woman never cleans or dusts and the house needs a paint job and a roof bad, if you ask me."

"I know the house." No one in town could miss it, as large as it was, and with those silver stars on the front gleaming in the sunlight, it was distinctive. Abigail had driven by it a couple of times and thought: *Such a curious looking old house...it'd make a magnificent painting. It's so full of character. It's like a worn and aged aristocratic lady who's seen better days. Scary looking trees encircling it as if they're guarding and protecting it. It truly looks like a haunted house. I wonder who lives there?* But she'd never found out until now.

"Well, she's got ghosts in the basement that are making such an ungodly racket and doing so many mean tricks on her it's driving her nuts. Her words, not mine." Myrtle snickered. "As far as I see it, Beatrice is nuts without the spooks. She always has been. I mean with her cuckoo obsession with collecting stuff, especially dolls. She's got rooms of the creepy things with their pale faces and staring glass eyes. Their tiny hands and feet."

Myrtle visibly shivered, shaking her head. "Not to mention the other weird stuff she's crammed into that place. Needless stuff, I say, in every room to the roofs. The whole house is like a messy storage shed. You can hardly move about in it. It's a wonder she doesn't trip over some of it and break her neck or some of it doesn't fall on her head and squash her flat. Good grief."

"Ghosts in the basement?" Abigail suppressed a giggle. "Really?"

"Really. They're beneath her making trouble. She claims they also sneak upstairs when she's on the third floor sleeping and they make messes, move objects, smash or even take things."

A bird was chirping in the tree above them and another one on a nearby limb returned its call. Cardinals, she mused. She could see glimpses of red between the leaves. It was a lovely spring day and it was hard to think about ghosts and haunted houses on such a morning. The swing moved leisurely back and forth. The sun was beaming down on the grass.

"How does she know they're ghosts? She could have trespassers, intruders, in her house or criminals looking to steal things. Sometimes teenagers take advantage of the elderly with big run-down houses. They find a way in, through a broken basement window or something, and do whatever mischief they want to do, then sneak out."

Myrtle had tilted up her mug and was draining the final drops, making smacking noises with her lips. "Could I have one more cup of that coffee, sweetie, and maybe a few more of those tasty donuts?"

"This time help yourself. You know where everything is," she said, stopping the swing's movement. "I'll wait here for you."

Somewhere in the distance Abigail heard a cat meowing. It didn't sound like Snowball. It must be one of the felines that belonged to the animal hoarder who lived behind her in the woods. Myrtle's sister Evelyn. That woman was as odd as Myrtle but in different ways. Last count Evelyn had over fifty dogs and cats squatting in and around her house. Some nights Abigail could hear every one of them.

The old woman wasn't gone long. This time she had a handful of donuts clutched in a napkin and her refilled mug in the other. She plopped down and picked up in their conversation where they'd left off. "You asked how Beatrice knows they are ghosts? Oh, she swears they are. She saw one of them last night in the basement when she went down there to see about the commotion."

"She really saw a ghost?"

"Tall white wispy thing that stared at her and then," Myrtle snapped her sugar-covered fingers in the air, "*poof* dematerialized! Beatrice said she nearly had a heart attack. The thing was definitely not friendly. She said the apparition, looking like a transparent starved ship-wrecked survivor, wailed at her and tried to knock her down. It went right through her like air."

Yeah, sure. Tackled by a ghost. "Yet you think Beatrice is nuts, right?"

"Nuts about some things, not this. I believe she saw what she says she saw. She doesn't have enough imagination to make up something like that. Just my opinion, mind you."

"So you believe her?"

"Of course. Heck, I see spooks all the time. You know that. They're all shapes and sizes, some good, some bad and some just plain evil. They're here all right. Everywhere."

"Okay, what exactly am I supposed to do about these manifestations? I'm not a ghost whisperer or a ghost buster and neither is Frank. Shouldn't she call a priest or an exorcist or something?"

"Beatrice isn't a religious person, if you know what I mean. She wants you and Frank to come over to her house and check it out. Solve the mystery and find a way to get rid of them spirits. She's expecting you. Evenings is best, but no later than eight o'clock because that's when she goes to bed. Most nights anyway. I have her telephone number. Here." She pulled a scrap of paper from a pocket in her dress and gave it to Abigail. "Call her. Soon. Otherwise she'll keep on bugging the jeepers out of me."

Abigail knew better than to argue with her. Once Myrtle got something, no matter how bizarre, in her head nothing would change her mind. Just wait until she told Frank about this. Myrtle wanted them to scare some ghosts away or arrest them or something. He'd get a good laugh out of it.

"I have to get going. It's trash day at the Tranquility Nursing Home and I always take a look to see if anyone's died there. When any of those old folks croak the families sometimes toss all their valuables out in the trash, not wanting to bother with them. You should see the treasures I pull out of those dumpsters. What a waste. So I make sure I go there before the trash trucks come by."

Myrtle stood up. "Be sure to call Beatrice. She's one frightened old lady. I know you and Frank will get to the bottom of it, whatever the problem is. See you later Abigail." Myrtle was up and shuffling across the front yard, reclaiming the battered wagon she'd left in the driveway. Then the morning silence was filled with her raspy voice singing an old Sinatra song, *Fools Rush In*, as she dragged the wagon away. Off to dumpster dive.

Shaking her head, Abigail watched her leave. The old woman was a character but she had a good heart and an uncanny knack for rooting out mysteries or injustices. The problem was she kept laying them at Abigail's feet and after the last horrendous escapade dealing with that serial killer Abigail hadn't been looking to solve anyone else's problems any time soon.

So much for that.

She just wanted to be happy, enjoy her life and her family. Was that too much to ask?

Apparently it was

Ghosts in the basement, *p-l-e-a-s-e!*

*****

An hour and a half later Abigail was strolling towards town in the dappled sunshine, enjoying every moment. She'd always liked the fact her house was near enough to town she could easily walk it. With the sun over her, her light jacket was all she'd needed.

She stepped from the grass onto the sidewalk lining Main Street's businesses and smiled as she peeked into the merchant's windows. Easter decorations had sprung up everywhere and pale pink, blue and green crepe paper framed most of the storefront displays.

The book store, Tattered Corners, had a window presentation of famous children's bunny books surrounded in Easter basket grass and multi-hued plastic eggs. A giant smiling stuffed rabbit was perched in the corner with baskets hanging on his front paws.

The Bakery had a window crowded with pink-iced bunny donuts and cakes with tiny chocolate eggs on them. In the middle of it all was a plate of cream puffs in the shapes of rabbits. Lulu, the owner and baker, made them every year.

Even Stella's Diner was decked out in its Easter best. Someone had strung egg shaped lights around the door and windows in typical pastel hues. It was real festive, those lights twinkling everywhere. Real welcoming.

Abigail looked around, up and down the street, before she went through the diner's door. It appeared the whole town was dressed up for Easter in ribbons and bows. Every storefront either had decorated its windows or had Easter adornments outside on the sidewalks. Tall cardboard rabbits or Easter scenes were propped up against the storefronts.

The hardware store had a glorious pot of silk snow-white lilies bordering its entrance and someone, probably a high school art student, had fashioned paper mache Easter eggs and stacked them up in miniature wagons. Fat chubby bunnies and yummy looking baskets filled with goodies, ran along the glass front. Whoever had painted the windows wasn't half bad. But then she couldn't help but think if her daughter, Laura, had done them they'd look even better. With her guidance over the last year, Laura was becoming a skillful artist and Abigail was proud of her.

Spookie sure did love its holidays. Every business went out of its way to dress up for the season. It was one of the reasons Abigail cherished the town so much. That and the people were unique; most of them were interesting, generous and kind.

She walked into the diner. For that time of the morning it wasn't very crowded. She must have caught it during one of its lulls.

A woman Abigail recognized as someone who worked at the IGA and her young daughter were there on stools at the counter and gabbing in low tones about something or other. The girl didn't look happy. There were blueberry smears around her lips.

An elderly couple was at a corner table reading newspapers and eating bacon and eggs. Abigail had often seen them around town, though she didn't know their names. The man was very frail looking and so thin Abigail thought he might be ill. He looked worse every time she saw them. A walker was snuggled against the wall at his side. The woman had to be his wife. She had the most beautiful long silvery hair worn piled on top of her head in a coiled bun. She possessed exceptional bone structure and always seemed so elegant. The way she dressed, impeccably with matching outfits and accessories, pegged her as a woman who cared about her looks. She was attractive for her age. Abigail observed the way the two interacted. The woman often reaching out to touch the man's withered hands or he smiling thoughtfully at her. They appeared to truly love each other and that touched Abigail. As she passed by them she caught a fragment of their conversation.

"It's a good price, Henry. Perhaps it is time we sell the old place and retire to California? We could be nearer the kids?" the woman was saying.

"Ah, Athena, sweetheart, you don't mean that. You hate California. You love living here. All our friends are here, our past and our lives. And the kids have their own lives and families. They don't want to bother with us. So what if someone offers us a good price for our home, it makes no difference. We're not selling." A coughing bout stopped the man from speaking further and his wife put her hand softly over his. The gentle look she gave him said it all. She'd do what he wanted her to do.

Frank was waving at Abigail from their favorite booth along the opposite wall, in his other hand a cup of coffee halfway to his mouth. Their friend Martha was sitting across from him and she waved, too.

Frank's gray streaked hair was tied back with a rubber band. It'd gotten a lot longer since she'd first met him. He liked it that length saying, now that he was no longer a cop, he was never going to cut it ever again. Though she had to admit, because he kept it clean and combed, with his intense blue eyes and sharp angled nose and face, long hair looked good on him. Not many men could carry off the look or the tiny silver earring in his ear, but Frank could. Sometimes he sported a mustache and had for the last year or so. Abigail liked the mustache as well. It made him look scholarly. He could have been a college professor or something.

"Good morning, Abigail," Martha addressed her as Abigail scooted in beside Frank. She grinned when Frank and Abigail kissed each other hello and Frank pulled her close. Martha got a kick out of the two dating and being in love. But that was because she'd been pushing them together since the beginning. Martha was the town's matchmaker and pleased to be.

"So you got the kids off to school and you're footloose and fancy free, huh?" Frank reached over and slid his hand down her cheek in a gesture so tender no one who saw it could deny he loved her.

"They're at school, but I can't say I'm totally footloose and fancy free…I've got to put the finishing touches on that courthouse mural after I leave here and hopefully after that I'll collect a nice big fat check." Abigail felt a sense of contentment sitting there with her two friends. Being with Frank and Martha in a place she'd come to think of as a second home, with great food, made her happy. But then small things, a good cup of coffee on a cold day, a decent cheeseburger when she was hungry, money to pay the bills in her bank account, a day with sunshine and true friends around her, always made her happy. She never asked for more than the world or life could give her and was grateful for every tiny good thing that came her way. She smiled at the handsome man next to her as he took her hand.

She'd been officially dating Frank Lester for a year and in the last few months they'd finally become lovers in every sense of the word. He'd already told her he loved her and had since the first time he'd met her three years ago in Stella's Diner, but he'd taken his time wooing her until the ghost of her first husband, Joel, had released her heart. Frank was a good man who cared deeply for her and she had finally let herself care for him. That morning as she sat there eating, talking and laughing with her boyfriend and her friend her future looked as sunny as the day outside.

"How's the book coming, Frank?"

"Slow. I'm stuck somewhere two-thirds in and have no idea where it's going. I rarely have writer's block, but whatever this is it's stopping me cold. I think it could have something to do with how odious the perpetrator's crimes were. My mind and heart hates going back there, if you know what I mean?"

"You're writing another murder mystery based on one of your old cases again, I take it?" Martha grilled Frank.

"It's more of a true crime novel. And it is

based on a notorious case I investigated and solved in Chicago the last year I was working homicide. It was a real nasty one. I've never been able to get it or the victims out of my mind so I'm hoping this will help. I thought writing about it would be good therapy. It frequently is."

"You want to tell me what it's about? The book, I mean," Martha pried, always wanting to know everything.

"I prefer not to talk about it as I'm writing the story. Just one of my little eccentricities. No offense. But you can read the book when it's finished."

"Great, you know how I hate waiting," Martha complained. "When will that be?"

"When it's out in the bookstores. It won't be long. I'll even give you an advance eBook or paperback copy when it's done. I'll even autograph it if you'd like."

"I'll hold you to that, friend."

Martha turned her attention to Abigail. "So your courthouse commission is almost completed? Nadine, who works there in the office, says it's beautiful. You've done a fantastic job. And she's not easily impressed. I was planning on stopping by later today to see it."

"Come on by. But if you want to see me there don't wait too long because I'm wrapping it up early; getting paid and celebrating. Maybe I'll go on a shopping spree."

"I might join you. I will stop by early then."

"So Abby, you finish the mural this morning?" Frank was motioning at their waitress, Stella, so they could put their orders in. "Wow that was fast."

"It came together easier than I had even expected." Abigail squeezed his hand. "I think it's kind of good, too."

"Everything you do is splendid, Abigail," Martha chimed in. "And I should know, I have enough of your work on my walls at home to prove it."

"Ah, you're biased, being my friend and all."

"No, I'm just someone who can tell outstanding art when I see it." Martha grinned as Stella came up to their table, order tablet in hand.

"What are you three having this morning?" Stella tapped her pencil on the tablet. "Blueberry pancakes is the special. My grandson makes the best pancakes in the state." Stella always said that every time Abigail came in for breakfast. She ought to have it embroidered on her uniform's apron.

Stella hadn't changed much since Abigail had moved into town. Her hair was still old-lady white and badly cut. This morning her blue eyes were bored–they often held that expression–and her lipstick was a vivid shade of pink instead of the normal cherry red. She was still grumpy, though. The woman, at times, reminded Abigail of that grumpy cat that was all over the Internet and television these days. Their faces had the same exact expression. But with Stella it was all put on and bluster. Underneath she was a kind-hearted, thoughtful lady. Abigail had grown quite fond of her, too.

"Then it's the pancakes for me," Frank capitulated. "Extra syrup and butter on top, like always, of course. Thank you Stella."

"Me too, the pancakes," Martha and Abigail spoke at the same time.

"You three are like three little lemmings that usually eat the same things. Well, who am I to moan about it if it makes it easier for me. It'll be a few minutes," Stella grumbled and sashayed away to put their orders in.

Abigail, Frank and Martha stared at each other and busted out laughing. Not too loud, though. Stella didn't like being laughed at.

"So, besides completing the mural, what else is new?" Martha questioned Abigail after the waitress had left. "You look like you have something else you want to tell us."

Stella was back at their side pouring Abigail a cup of coffee, which she was grateful for, and had scurried away again. Abigail added cream and sugar and took a large gulp. Stella made the best coffee in town hands down. It was strong but never bitter. Abigail sometimes just came in for the coffee alone and wished she could duplicate its exceptional flavor at home, but she never could.

"Funny you should say that." She directed her words to Frank then. "I had a visitor very early this morning, right after dawn really, with a strange request."

"And I'd bet a hundred bucks it was that nutty old busybody Myrtle." Martha made a grimacing face. "She's strange as they come and is the only person I know who wanders around at such god-awful times of the morning or night brewing up trouble of some sort or another. She's not happy unless she's in the thick of some chaos or something. What is she up to now?"

Martha had had a long running feud with Myrtle, yet in a good-natured way, since Abigail had first met them. Martha thought the old lady was touched in the head and openly disapproved of her. Yet in the last year or so her opinion of the old woman had softened somewhat, for Abigail knew, contrary to what she said or how she behaved, Martha no longer disliked Myrtle, merely questioned her sanity at times.

Abigail glanced at the realtor and at Frank again. "Of course it was Myrtle. Who else would be meandering around at sunrise pestering people? She visited me this morning and does she have a project for us. You're not going to believe this when I tell you."

"A project for us?" Frank looked amused, but not disgruntled. Unlike Martha, he genuinely liked Myrtle. "That old lady never ceases to confound me. What is it now?"

Abigail told him and Martha what the old woman had wanted.

Martha laughed sarcastically when she was done, but Frank didn't. His eyes reflected instant interest. "Beatrice must be eighty if she's a day. She's been rambling around in that old barn of hers for years. Loneliness can do weird things to a person. This could all be in her mind or she's seeking attention."

"Beatrice has ghosts in her basement? Is that like bats in your belfry? Except below?" Martha covered her mouth and snickered behind her hand, her eyes dancing. "Well, that's a new one. I thought it was Myrtle the dead were always after? I mean, she's always going on about the ghosts following and tormenting her. So the madness has spread, hey? I'd better be careful if it's really that contagious."

Abigail threw her a stern look and Martha stopped snickering.

"What does she want you and Frank to do about it? Oh, I know...she wants you two to eradicate or capture them? Clean out the basement so Beatrice has more room for her collections. Those dolls take up a lot of space." More laughter.

Abigail gave Martha another sharp glance. "No, she wants us to help Beatrice get to the bottom of it one way or another. She's afraid Beatrice might be in real danger."

"From ghosts?" Martha exclaimed. "What's the matter with the old people around here lately? Are they all insane?"

Frank ignored Martha's outburst. "And because we've cleared up a few other mysteries Myrtle thinks we can figure out this one, right?" Frank had that intrigued glint in his eyes, the one he got when there was a case to investigate. He might not be a detective anymore but he still loved to solve puzzles or crimes and to help people. It was in his blood and always would be.

"I suppose that's her thinking."

Stella had arrived with a tray full of blueberry pancakes and with a practiced flourish known only to waitresses had them all on the table and was gone before Abigail could hardly blink.

"Thanks Stella!" she called after the waitress, who tossed back a *you're welcome*.

The pancakes were covered in syrup and butter and instantly began to disappear. The three continued to discuss the ghost situation as they ate.

"Beatrice could just be lonely and, as you said Frank, she's claiming to see ghosts to get people to come over and visit her?" Martha proposed between bites. "Old people do that. Try to get attention, I mean, in any way they can. As a realtor I've seen that often enough. They'll keep you there talking away for hours if they can do it. Bribe you with cake or outrageous stories. Some hate to see you leave. I wouldn't put much stake in what they say."

"It could be for attention. That's possible," Frank was thinking aloud. "I know Beatrice fairly well, though. She was a friend of my mother's a long time ago. I still stop by once and a while to check on her. But I'm sad to say I haven't done that in a long time. My bad."

"She doesn't have any family to visit her?"

Abigail was busy stuffing her face with pancakes and talked when she wasn't chewing. As always the pancakes were perfect, not too dry or soggy, but light as a feather.

"Not really. Her husband, Arthur, died twenty years ago. She had no siblings that I know of anyway. She has one son, Lucas. He was the love of her life. She doted on the boy. Let's see he should be about fifty years or so old now."

"He doesn't go see her or help care for her?" Abigail posed the question.

"Sad story that," Frank supplied. "The two had a falling out. I have no idea what it was over. Something he thought she did wrong, said wrong–I don't know. Something she said to his wife and his wife told him. Stirred up the pot, I'd say, on purpose. The wife always wanted him to just be there for her and their kids and *her* family. She resented any time he spent with his mother. Beatrice's son got mad at her and refused to talk to or see her; hasn't in over a decade, as far as I recall. I don't know what that boy's problem is, but he's been a terrible son. You don't disown your mother just because she said something or did something you didn't like. That's not love. The son has a cold heart, is soulless or something, is what I think.

"Anyway, he broke Beatrice's heart, shattered it and she's never been the same. That's when she began hoarding that stuff in her house. That's when she started with the dolls. As if all that was filling some emptiness losing her son had created."

"That is sad," Abigail agreed, sipping her coffee. Now she had instant sympathy for the old woman in the ramshackle house with the stars on the front. Was it any different than when her husband had gone and disappeared years ago and never returned, alive that is? Wasn't what Beatrice was going through missing a son she never saw a little like a death…a little like what Abigail has suffered when Joel had never come back? Yes, it was like that. Poor old woman.

Then she had a thought. "Maybe her son has his own side of the story. Those dolls of hers? Her hoarding? Those problems, as well as other emotional ones, could go way back. She might not have been as good a mother as she'd believed she had been. We don't know, only he does. You have to admit, she sounds somewhat unconventional. And it's not easy to live with someone who has such obsessions. Her son might have legitimate reasons for not wanting to be part of her life."

"I never thought of it that way, but you might have a point. And only the mother and son know the truth," Frank said. "It is unfortunate, though. When someone gets up there in years, they need their family. I still feel sorry for her.

"Anyway, what else did Myrtle say?" He had eaten his breakfast and shoved the plate away. The man had a healthy appetite for someone so slim. But Abigail knew he'd probably go home and take a long walk or a run to work the calories off. He usually did. His doctor had warned him the year before he needed to exercise more and worry less if he wanted to stay healthy. Then afterwards Frank would sit down at his laptop and work a couple hours on the novel, his fourth, he was writing. His third book, a straight murder mystery, was due to come out in less than two months. He made a respectable second income with his murder mysteries.

"That Beatrice is expecting us to pay her a visit. She's counting on it. This evening to be exact. We should call her no later than seven and visit no later than eight because that's when she goes to bed. If you're available that is, Frank?"

"I am. Let's make it earlier though."

"About six? I have her telephone number. Myrtle gave it to me."

Martha was staring at both of them. "You two are actually going over there to look for ghosts? Really?"

"Really," Frank bantered back with a crafty grin. "You never know, we might find a cache of Caspers. Might even be my next book."

"You two have cracks in your head. So you should get along just fine with the there-are-ghosts-in-my-basement lady," Martha groused. "Just don't let the spooks get you. I don't have that many friends and I'd hate to lose you two."

Frank stood up. "Call her, Abby, and I'll be over at your house about six. We'll drive over there. I'd been meaning to visit her anyway and see how she is doing. This evening is as good as any other."

Martha rolled her eyes, getting up, too. It was time to go. "So you both are going to become ghost hunters now, huh?"

"No such things as ghosts," Frank mumbled as he took Abigail's hand and ushered her to the cash register to pay their bills. "I'm sure it's only Beatrice being Beatrice. Could be she's forgotten to take her meds or is taking too many of them. We'll find out. She's as odd in her own way as Myrtle, but we'll get to the bottom of it."

"I bet. Remember, let me know how it turns out." Martha went with them to the pay counter. "I'm off to an appointment. I have a family looking at a superb Tudor home about twenty miles away from here. They've already been preapproved and this is the second time looking at this house. I can tell they really want it. I'm going to close the deal today if I know anything about selling houses. Cha-ching!"

"Good luck," Abigail encouraged her.

They paid their bills and went their separate ways down Main Street with the stuffed bunnies and Easter decorations behind shop windows observing them parade by.

*****

Frank was at her door twenty minutes before six that evening. She'd finished up the courthouse mural job, collected her pay and had spent the afternoon shopping for her and the kids. She'd purchased nothing extravagant, merely small gifts for both children and a new blouse for herself, rewards for a job well done. She sometimes did that when she got paid. It'd turned into a ritual.

For some reason Martha hadn't made an appearance. She'd probably gotten caught up with another house showing or sale or something. Abigail hadn't minded. She saw Martha all the time and would see her again soon enough somewhere.

"Reporting for ghost hunting duties." Frank had a playful grin on his face and gave her a salute as she let him in. "Does Beatrice know we're coming?"

"I telephoned her earlier and she's expecting us. When I talked to her she was distraught. Apparently the ghost showed up again after Myrtle left this morning and, as she conveyed to me, tried to kill her this time. Imagine that? Not only a haunting but a killer ghost. My, my. Wait until you hear her story. It sounds like something someone would put in a book of fictional ghost tales. But I'll let you hear it straight from her mouth. You might pick up on something I missed."

"I'm already intrigued. Though I've never believed in apparitions and hauntings I've always been fascinated with them. Haunted houses are my favorite.

"You know, I've been playing with a new idea for my next novel. I've always wanted to write a classic haunted house story. It'd be a little different than my last three murder mysteries and the crime drama I'm working on now; more in the horror genre than mystery."

"You want to write a straight horror novel? Now that's interesting. I never would have thought you'd want to try that genre. Hmm. We have time for a cup of coffee if you'd like one?"

"Sure I would." He shadowed her into the kitchen where he helped himself to a cup. "Where are the kids?"

"Nick is at school working on an afterschool science project with some classmates and Laura's at her friend Jessica's house, supposedly doing homework but I suspect they're gossiping and gushing over their newest boyfriends. They won't be home until nine. That's curfew on school nights. It'll give us plenty of time to visit Beatrice."

"Laura has a boyfriend? When did that happen? Laura's too young to have boyfriends."

"She's almost sixteen. Not too young. I think the current boyfriend is someone called Taylor. This month anyway. It'll be someone else next month. He sounds like a nice boy. Well, or as nice as a sixteen year old boy can be. Don't worry. I won't allow her to date, except in a group, until she's sixteen."

"If you say so. But if Taylor sticks around longer than that I'll have to do a background check on him. I'll have to meet him and set down some rules."

"You're so protective. But I don't think that will be necessary."

"We'll see."

He set his empty cup down on the sink counter. "You ready to go?"

She nodded, slipping her jacket on. "Whose car do you want to take?"

"We'll take my truck. You know I like to drive."

"Typical man thing, right?"

"I don't know. No reflection on your driving at all. You're a competent driver. I just like to drive."

Abigail had driven past Beatrice Utley's house many times but now she'd get to meet the person who lived there and see the inside. It was way out at the end of Myrtle's road in a circle drive encompassing six houses surrounded by woods. All of them seemed to be from another time. They were antiquated, sprawling run-down monstrosities with tons of ginger-bread trim and lattice work, drive under carports leading to garages and numerous out buildings. Beatrice's house sat on one end of the circle and its paint was a peeling dull ivory, its windows dirt glazed. The other houses around hers were in just as bad disrepair. Two were a beige color, one light and one dark, and the other three were pale yellow, green and blue. The six of them at one time, in their heyday, must have been a sight to behold. There was money here, but it was easy to see the money had died or left. The houses needed serious renovations.

They pulled into Beatrice's driveway. It was one of those lengthy concrete ones that wound up to and behind the main structure.

"Yikes, this place has definitely seen better days and could really use a new paint job or siding," Abigail declared as she got out of the truck and Frank came around to meet her. She gazed up at the mansion before her. "I've never been this close to it before. It's huge. It looks like there are stables behind it. I don't see any horses, though it must have once had them." The stables were empty now, barely standing, and the buildings were rotten wood. There was a flourishing under and overgrowth of shrubs and weeds everywhere and it appeared as if the grass hadn't been cut in years. "It must have once been a grand place. What a shame."

"I imagine it was magnificent in its time," Frank spoke as his eyes scanned across the house and grounds. "It is a shame. I feel so sorry for a home, any home, to be this neglected."

"The owner is elderly and that's what happens when time and money are gone." Abigail was still gawking at what was around them as they walked up to the front door. Frank rang the bell. It didn't work so he knocked. Then he knocked again, louder this time.

The old woman who answered wasn't anything like Abigail had pictured her as being. A small woman, she had the whitest hair shaped into one of those old lady hairdos, like a cap on her head, but soft and feathery; a wizened face with alert eyes the color of peridot gems, a little tasteful makeup, and an emerald print dress that looked as if it had been bought in the nineteen fifties, but hadn't been much worn. She had to be about eighty years old but had held on to her looks well.

Abigail thought: *She dressed up for us*.

The woman didn't *look* crazy.

"Hi Beatrice. I'm Frank Lester, remember me? And this is Abigail."

"Hello. I remember you, Frank. Of course I do." The woman sent a delighted look Frank's way and bobbed her head slightly at Abigail. She stood back and opened the door wide. "You're Abigail Sutton, right? I know who you are. Myrtle has told me all about your…adventures. She said you can help me with my problem. You and Frank can, that is. Please, come in."

The inside of the house was sparsely furnished. There was a damask sofa with matching chairs and oak end tables on an oval rug, but there were personal belongings setting, stacked and piled everywhere up to the ceiling. At first glance they looked like cardboard boxes and Tupperware storage containers full of stuff. Heaven only knew what. It was dark in the house's interior because heavy burgundy drapes were drawn closed along the windows and kept the light out. With the dimness and the stacked containers it was hard to even get through to the sofa; the cleared paths were so narrow.

And as Myrtle had warned her, there were the dolls, of every kind and every size everywhere in normal doll clothes or fancy doll party gowns like the women once wore in the nineteen-forties and fifties. There were wife, nurse, and rich girl dolls; there were country, city and foreign dolls. Some were ceramic, porcelain, cloth or plastic. All female, though. They sat on the sofa and chairs, dressers, on the older television set, and wall shelves; and the dolls *stared* at them. The glints from their glassy eyes sent slivers of faint light in every direction.

Myrtle had been right. It was creepy. Who'd want these many dolls? Someone awfully lonely, Abigail supposed, or someone who was trying to fill up their life with inanimate objects because there were so few flesh-and-blood people in it. And dolls never talked back, never hurt or left someone. They were a captive audience, captive friends.

Beatrice led them into the living room and with a wave of her hand around them, said, "Sit anywhere you'd like."

Yeah, sure, on a doll's lap? There wasn't a place to walk through much less sit on.

"Just move some of them, shove them out of the way if you have to." Beatrice was speaking of the dolls. "They won't mind." And the old lady gave the humans a timid smile.

She and Frank ended up squeezing in on the sofa beside each other and packed in between the dolls. Frank, sending Abigail a furtive look of amusement, simply picked some of the toys up and set them on top of other ones at the end of the couch. Three or four fell noiselessly to the carpeted floor. Beatrice didn't seem to notice their plight. Or if she did she didn't say anything.

"Can I get either of you something to drink? Coffee or tea?" Beatrice offered. "I have a pitcher of lemonade ready in the fridge, if you'd prefer that?"

Abigail had the feeling to turn down the woman's hospitality would be hurtful to her. Beatrice was that sort of woman. The old rules of courtesy applied. She seemed delicate, overly-sensitive. "The lemonade sounds good. I'll help you get it." She got up and trailed Beatrice into the kitchen.

The hallway was so full of stuff Abigail almost tripped but caught herself at the last moment, her hands supporting her against the wall. How did the old woman manage living in such a place? It couldn't be easy. She was aware lots of people hoarded things but every time she encountered one, like Beatrice, she never knew how to take it or them. All this stuff lying around everywhere would drive her insane. But that was her. She was a neat freak.

As they got out the glasses and put them on a tray, Abigail looked around. The kitchen appliances were extremely out of date. The sink was one of those old steel double basin varieties that had been so popular in the fifties. The refrigerator, too, was old. Its motor made a rumbling noise as it chugged along. One could probably hear it all through the house at night. There was a gray Formica table with matching chairs around it before a large window overlooking more weeds and lush trees. There were artificial flowers everywhere in pots and in baskets which looked so real Abigail had to actually touch a bloom, a leaf, to be sure they weren't. So they must be expensive fakery.

And then, of course, there were more dolls, propped on the kitchen chairs and table; looking down at her from the top of the cabinets, counters and a crowded kitchen hutch. There were more dolls behind glass and stuffed in every nook and cranny. Abigail had never seen so many dolls in one place, unless it'd been in a doll museum. She had to force herself not to stare too openly, though it was hard. There were dolls in the sink. Were they also in the refrigerator? At least there was no rotting food setting out to lure the bugs. Or perhaps the dolls scared them away?

"You sure do have a lot of dolls, Beatrice," she couldn't help herself and blurted out.

The woman raised her eyes. "Thank you. I know. I've been collecting them for years and years. They keep me company. I have quite an assortment and I imagine some of them are rather valuable, especially the older ones. I don't get many visitors these days. My son lives far away in Florida and I haven't seen him and my grandkids in years. They're so busy and you know how children are these days? Got their jobs, the children's activities and all. They're too busy to visit grandma." Abigail heard a resigned and deep melancholy in the woman's voice.

Abigail only lowered her head. She didn't know what else to say. She kept waiting for the dolls to start chattering at her because some of them were so lifelike. She forced herself to look at anything else but them. It was hard. She could feel their blank eyes on her.

Beatrice saw her taking everything in. "My Arthur, he was my husband, helped build this house back in nineteen sixty-five or so. He fashioned it after this old mansion I once saw in a fancy home magazine. Nineteen sixty-five is when we got married, you know. Over fifty years ago. It's been my home ever since. I love it. I'll never leave it. Arthur died about three years back. But," her gaze moved around the cluttered kitchen with fondness, "he'll always be here. He never left. He loved this place almost as much as he loved me. When I get especially lonely, I speak to him sometimes. Or to his memory anyway. Then I don't feel so lonely. I'll never leave this place because how could I leave Arthur?"

The old lady seemed to expect an answer, so Abigail responded, "You can't." She understood exactly what Beatrice was saying. She'd used to talk to her dead husband sometimes, too. For a long while after Joel had disappeared, she'd sensed him with her, at her side, at times. Once he'd even saved her life with a phantom telephone call. For the first time, no matter what she'd thought about this whole ghost thing, Abigail was glad she'd come. It was heartbreaking to see how hungry for company the old woman was. If nothing else, this was her good deed for the week: visiting someone who needed visiting.

Beatrice removed the lemonade pitcher from the refrigerator. There were no dolls inside, yet it was crammed with unidentifiable food and moldy looking containers. The smell was pretty bad. Abigail hoped Beatrice didn't offer her something to eat out of it. Discourteous or not, she'd have to decline. Even the lemonade was suspect and she probably wouldn't drink too much of it. She'd have to find some way to warn Frank, as well. *Don't drink the yellow stuff...the small things floating in it may not be lemon pieces.*

They carried the drinks into the living room and Beatrice sat in the chair nearest them. Abigail noticed how she carefully scooted the dolls over to make room, except for one Raggedy Ann doll she put in her lap and held loosely.

Frank picked up his glass and took a swallow. *Oops, too late.* Abigail had to give it to him. His face didn't change. The lemonade was barely drinkable. It had a bitter aftertaste to it. *Maybe the unidentified creatures in it?*

"Tell me what's been happening here, Beatrice," he probed gently. "Everything. Don't leave even the smallest detail out. You never know what might help us figure this all out."

They listened as Beatrice unfolded her story.

"I guess it started about two weeks ago. At night," the old woman began. She had a husky voice with a soft expressive edge. She was huddled in her chair like a frightened child, holding the Raggedy Ann, and she looked so small. She almost could have been one of her dolls. "I heard strange noises somewhere in the house but I couldn't pinpoint where they were. I'd be sleeping upstairs in my bed and be awakened by a loud thumping. Like someone had dropped something real heavy somewhere in the house. I'd get up and take a look and there'd be nothing. No one."

She met Abigail's eyes with nervous ones of her own. Her aged hands were holding the doll, her back was stiff. "Since Arthur died I sometimes get a little frightened being alone here, especially during storms. You know?"

"I know," Abigail replied in a sympathetic voice. "I hate storms, too."

"I used to have a dog. Freddie. A big black lab. But he died a few weeks ago. Suddenly. Another odd occurrence if you ask me. One day he was as normal and healthy as could be and the next I found him dead in the kitchen. It broke my heart. He was a good dog and good company.

"Anyway, the weird noises went on like that for a couple of nights. I'd hear something and get up to see what was making it. It was always nothing and no one. Then, oh, starting about a week past, I'd get up in the morning and notice things down here had been moved or had simply been taken. Small items at first: a vase, a book or a magazine, some curio or other. My salt and pepper shakers–and they were real silver, too. My dolls were even being moved around. One morning when I got up I discovered some of my food in the fridge was scattered all across the floor. What a mess.

"That's when the noises–in the basement this time–really got loud. But every time I went down there the basement was empty and nothing was touched as far as I could tell. It mystified me to what was making the commotion. Then last night was the worst. I woke up about two in the morning and the ruckus was so awful I was too scared to even go down there."

"What sort of noises?" Frank inquired. He was leaning forward, taking in every word. His cop senses on high alert.

"They sounded to me as if someone was in the basement knocking over and smashing things and it frightened me so much I called Myrtle down the street to come over and keep me company for the remainder of the night. I was a basket case. But she wouldn't come until right before dawn. The ghosts, you know?"

Frank smiled. "I know. Did you go down to see about it?"

"When Myrtle got here we did. But again…nothing was down there. Nothing was disturbed. Have I finally become senile? Gone round the bend? I'm terrified now of night coming again."

Abigail felt sorry for the old lady, and reaching over, touched her shoulder in a gesture of sympathetic comfort. "Myrtle said that you thought you saw your husband's ghost?"

Beatrice avoided her gaze, turned her head away, and her voice was soft when she responded, "I've seen him in the house before, yes, or I think it's him. It's hard to tell, he's so wispy. I feel his presence more than I see him, though. You know what I mean?"

Abigail nodded.

"But he's not the one making all the commotion or causing me trouble, I know it. He wouldn't frighten me like that. He loves me." The woman looked at them again and met Frank's eyes. "This haunting isn't Arthur. It's something else. And I'm scared. Really scared."

Frank came to his feet. "Can we go down there now? I'd like to take a look around."

For a moment Beatrice's expression reminded Abigail of a bird facing a cat. Then, to the woman's credit, she straightened up and stood, too. "All righty. If you two are with me I don't suppose anything could hurt me."

"Then let's go," Frank said.

They followed her down thirteen rickety stairs into a dank and dark basement. Even when Beatrice turned the lights on it still gave Abigail a shiver of uneasiness. The first thing she noticed when they hit the bottom step was the basement, too, was full to the rafters with a life's collection of stuff. Thank goodness though, no dolls. Perhaps the basement was too dirty for them, or Beatrice liked them upstairs with her. The second thing she noticed was that, even for Beatrice, the basement appeared especially messy. Then she realized it was much

43

more than that.

The basement looked as if a tornado had gone through it. It wasn't only the untidiness but things were broken and tossed in piles everywhere. Glass glittered over everything from broken windows and the shelves along the cement walls were now laying in pieces on top of everything else. The mess wasn't a normal mess.

"Whoa! Someone's been down here and done some real damage." Frank was trolling through the wreckage inspecting things. "I thought you said nothing had been touched?"

"It wasn't like this last time I was down here!" Beatrice had one hand touching the side of her face, her eyes shocked, mouth open. "I swear it. When Myrtle and I came down here it looked as it always did. A bit cluttered, but an ordinary basement. But this–I don't know what to make of this. Why would ghosts destroy my basement? Why? What do they want?" Her eyes were a mirror of alarm. She'd brought the Raggedy Ann doll downstairs, holding it tightly, and she was trembling. Abigail moved down a step and put her arms around her, again feeling sorry for her. How upsetting this must be to an old woman who lived alone.

"Why would ghosts do this?" Beatrice repeated.

Abigail exchanged a caustic look with Frank. This wasn't the work of ghosts and they both knew it. Someone solid and human had done this. Thing was, as Beatrice had asked, why?

"I'm sure it wasn't ghosts," Frank stated firmly. "There are no such things as ghosts–and anyway I doubt if this was done by any poltergeist–if this happened after you and Myrtle were down here, why didn't you hear anything? This should have woken up half the neighborhood."

Beatrice shook her head. "I didn't hear anything. But then," she confessed hesitantly, "sometimes I don't hear so well. My left ear goes out sometimes. Wax or something clogs it up." The fingers of one hand caressed the offending ear.

Abigail didn't think that'd be enough to not hear the basement being trashed, but she didn't say anything. Beatrice and Myrtle might have heard something and had been too afraid to say so.

"Does someone have a grudge against you?" Frank inquired. "Can you think of anyone who would do this?"

"No! As far as I know I don't have any enemies. I'm only an old lady living out the few years I have left. I can't understand why the ghost would do this, but I know it's not Arthur."

Frank sighed, "There are no such things as ghosts, Beatrice," and kept poking around in the wreckage.

"That's what you think. Are you in for a surprise if one decides to show himself to you. You just wait." The old woman went back up the stairs. She didn't appear too worried about

45

the chaos on the lower floor; considering what the rest of her house looked like, Abigail thought, *well, one mess was as good as another*.

Abigail went with her upstairs and the two women waited for Frank to return to the kitchen. When he did, he posed three or four more questions to Beatrice, told her they'd look into it for her best they could but she also needed to call the sheriff's department, report the harassment and the damage and have them come out to see it themselves, make it official, and she and Frank left.

The old lady stood in the doorway, doll cradled in her arms, her lined face confused, as they drove away.

*****

In the truck once they left the driveway Frank looked at her. "Oh my God, those dolls!" He slowly shook his head. "Those things gave me the creeps. I don't know why but I could have sworn some of them appeared demonic. I had the urge to sprinkle holy water on them and watch my back with every step. As if when I wasn't looking they'd lunge after me with a knife."

Abigail laughed. "Some of them certainly did look menacing. You know I don't believe I've ever seen that many dolls in one place anywhere before. That woman sure loves her dolls."

"That she does." The steering wheel in Frank's hands rotated a notch or two. They were on the highway and the day's light was fading around them. There were crickets and frogs humming on the air, and the scent of spring was everywhere. The normalcy of it made what they'd left behind harder to accept.

"I think I'll put a call into the sheriff's department myself about this. I don't think we can count on Beatrice to do it, do you?"

"No I don't. She seemed so sure it was supernatural she won't call the sheriff. What do you think about that destruction in the basement? We both know unhappy spirits didn't do that." Abigail had her eyes on the windshield as a tiny rock pinged the window. Fortunately the glass didn't crack.

"I think she needs to clean it up, for one thing, but I don't expect she will. I told her to at least get the windows fixed. Told her Luke at the hardware store would come out and put in new windows for a fair price. She said she'd call him."

"No, I meant, who or what do you think did it? And why?"

Frank shrugged. "As you said, not spooks. When we first got there I sort of believed Beatrice had lost a few more of her marbles since I'd seen her last, with the dolls and the hoarding and all, but after seeing that basement," he paused, "I think someone's trying to scare her or worse. But for what reason I can't fathom. Not yet anyway. I'm working on a motive. Got a couple possibilities but nothing that makes any sense at the moment."

"Hmm, I also think someone's trying to

scare her and I don't buy the ghost explanation, either. So what do we do now?"

"That's a valid question. All we can do is wait and see what else happens. I gave Beatrice my cellphone number and asked her to call me immediately next time she hears anything weird in her house–anytime–and I'll zip over and check it out. In the meantime, after further thinking about it, I'm going to visit Sheriff Mearl in person, not just call him; have a chat with him and see if he'll provide an extra police patrol in Beatrice's neighborhood, particularly at night. There should be some surveillance on her house for a while."

"Sounds like a plan."

"What do you make of Beatrice's story about seeing her husband the ghost?" He drove up in front of her house.

"I don't know. Beatrice believes she's seen a ghost. She isn't sure it's her husband. She just wants it to be. It's not so frightening to her if she knows the ghost. But someone is tricking her."

"So you think the haunting is part of the game that's being played on her?"

"It could be." The truck had come to a full stop in her driveway and Abigail had her hand on the door handle ready to get out. She sent a smile Frank's way. "If you don't have anything else scheduled for the evening, would you want to come in and have supper with me? I defrosted a container of homemade chili earlier and we're having it tonight. The kids will eat later when they get home."

"Sure. I'll take you up on that. I can't pass up your chili. But let me go have that talk with the sheriff first and I'll be back here as soon as I get done."

"I'll wait for you. I might even make corn muffins to go with the chili."

"Yum. I love corn muffins, too. See you in a bit then." He drove away and Abigail went inside.

As she baked in the kitchen, put supper on the table, and Frank returned from seeing the sheriff, darkness fell over the town.

And she couldn't help but wonder what that darkness would be hiding.

Chapter 2
Abigail

Abigail didn't see or hear from Frank for days after that because they were both busy. He was working on his new novel; she with the kids and searching for more freelance jobs. She'd had a lead from Samantha her reporter friend at The Weekly Journal that a new bakery had been asking around for an artist or a painter to do some work. All she had to do was go talk to the proprietor and Samantha gave her the address.

So that morning she was headed towards the address for a meeting with its owner, Kate Greenway. Now Spookie would have not one bakery, but two, and she was delighted. Variety was good, especially since she was as addicted to bakery goods as she was.

The operating bakery in town, called appropriately The Bakery, had the best cakes and pies in the county, but she'd grown tired of their donut selection, which hadn't changed in years. And it'd be great to have another job so soon after she'd ended the last one. With two children in the house she needed to keep a steady income coming in. As a foster mother, she did get a state stipend every month but it wasn't near enough to give the kids all she wanted them to have. She had to make money to do that.

The location the new bakery was going to occupy was where a previous mom and pop barbeque place had once been. It'd been closed before she had come to Spookie and the building had been empty a long time. In the heart of town, it was squeezed in between the ice cream shop and the Tattered Corners bookstore and not far from Stella's Diner. It was close to everything, which made it a perfect location.

As she parked and strolled up to the storefront she could see someone behind the dirty windows working inside. Abigail knocked on the door and waited until the person noticed her and came over to open it. It was a woman.

"Hello. Are you Kate?"

"That's me. Kate Greenway." The woman smiled and laid the broom she'd been using against the wall. "You must be Abigail Sutton. Come on in." She was a little thing with long dark hair, a delicate face and green eyes, wearing a T shirt and faded jeans. She could have been in her late-forties, maybe fifty. She must have been working hard because her clothes were grimy and her face was sweaty. There was a yellow bandana tied over and covering her hair. She put her hand out and Abigail shook it. "I know it's a mess in here but you should have seen it before I started clearing and cleaning it out. It was an absolute disaster."

Kate led her into the shop and she looked around at the dirty walls, remnants of left behind tables and chairs, and filthy floors. Everything was covered with a thick layer of grime. "Uh, it looks like you're just starting the renovations. I was under the impression you wanted to commission some artwork from me?"

"I do." Kate sat down in a chair and gestured Abigail to take one beside her. "But I had a lot more in mind than that. I have a different sort of proposition for you. A bit unusual from what you've done so far, but I believe you could tackle it. I saw those murals you did for city hall and the library–they were great, so creative, by the way–and I had this idea." The woman seemed excited.

"Go ahead then and tell me what it is. I'll listen."

"I know donuts. I know how to bake and sell them. I worked for twenty-years at a bakery in Waterloo, that's about thirty miles from here, and I learned the business from bottom to top. I always wanted my own place, though. So for years I saved every dollar I earned and here I am." Kate's arms spread and included where they were and her gaze traveled around the room. "I got this place dirt cheap but it is so run down it's going to take a lot of work to decorate and open it. I need more than pictures or a mural. I thought that being a creative person, as well as an artist, you might be able to help me with that, too."

"You mean you want me to help you decorate and put together the whole place?" Now Abigail was looking around.

"Yes. Everything it will need. I might be an expert at baking, but I know absolutely nothing about design, fabrics for curtains, carpets, the right furniture and color combinations for the walls and floors. I want the shop when it's done to look beautiful. Then after the place is furnished I'd like you to paint pictures of my donuts on the walls. What do you think?"

"But I'm not a professional decorator, Kate."

"I don't think you'd need to be. You know color and what looks good. I'm awful with that remodeling stuff and I'm basically color blind. The person, I don't know who it was because I didn't catch their name, who told me about you mentioned that besides your usual artwork and those stunning murals you've painted all over town, they'd seen your house and what you've done with it. They said you completely renovated it yourself and you have a real eye for that sort of thing. They were sure you could handle this project.

"Now don't worry. You won't have to actually do the labor, merely advise me on how to decorate, what type of furniture and stuff would look good in here…and paint the donut wall pictures. I think I'd like them somewhat large, but realistic looking, you know? Good enough to eat.

"I'll be truthful with you. I can't afford to

pay you a lot. I'm on a tight budget. But, besides what I can pay you," and here she smiled, "you could have free donuts for the rest of your life."

Abigail laughed. "Well, that's a real deal breaker for me. Donuts are as good as money, sometimes better. And my monetary fee? We can work that out. I like the idea of designing a bakery so I'll cut you a break. When do you plan on opening?"

"I hope in two months around the end of May or early June. I have workmen coming in tomorrow to begin the construction. I'm having them tear out all the old counters, rugs and that wall over there." She pointed to a section of wall along the rear of the room. "It'll open up this space here so there's more room. If you'd like you could come by tomorrow morning any time after nine if you want to be here for that. You don't have to. For the first part, the renovations, I could pay you per hour but the paintings we'll discuss further and set a flat price for. I calculate the walls will be ready for those pictures around the middle of May."

Abigail had decided. The thought of renovating the bakery intrigued her. And it was work. Work was good. Free donuts for life! That alone was worth it, though donuts wouldn't pay the electric or water bill, but the cash would.

"All right, I accept." Abigail put her hand out for the other woman to shake and she did. "I already have some notions on what you might do in here to make it a showplace. I have ideas on color combinations, too. Did you want people to simply come and buy your donuts and leave or would you want to have a counter, barstools, table and chairs for them to stay and eat here as well?"

"Oh, I want them to stay if they'd want to. Sit at the counter or a table and linger over my donuts and coffee. Visit and chat with everyone. Like they do at Stella's Diner. I want this to be a welcoming, social place. I like people." She was smiling wider now, her expression enthusiastic.

"I'll do my best to help you make it such a communal oasis. I'll start mulling over possible renovations right away and let you know what I come up with. Perhaps as soon as tomorrow. I'll also be here in the morning to watch construction begin. I can't wait." And she couldn't. Studying the room in her mind she could already see its possibilities and how charming it could look when it was done. It was a new adventure. Imagine that. She was going to try her hand at being a decorator.

The women swapped proposals about colors, tables, floors, barstools and counters. What might look good and what might not. Abigail took pictures on her new cell phone–expensive or not, because of the children, she'd finally gotten one–of the space so she could plan the remodeling layout. The women exchanged telephone and email numbers.

"I'll see you tomorrow then," Abigail said before she left.

"Tomorrow," Kate replied.

Abigail was walking away from the shop, shading her eyes from the glaring sun, when Myrtle came around the corner, her rusty red wagon bumping along behind her. She was wearing the same exact clothes as two days before and a tattered straw hat on her head. The wagon was full of junk, or it looked like junk to Abigail. The old woman nearly ran into her. No apologies, though. That wasn't Myrtle's way.

"Why good morning Abigail." The old woman's eyes looked at where Abigail had just exited. "I see you met Kate Greenway, the newest addition to our town?"

"I have. In fact she's asked me to help her remodel the new bakery and paint some pictures on its walls. She's opening the donut shop before June and she'd going to live above it."

Myrtle's face cheered up at the mention of donuts and she licked her lips. "Another bakery and more donuts. There can't never be enough pastries for me. Yippie. By June, you say?"

"By June."

Myrtle glanced once more at the shop. Kate had resumed her sweeping. She stopped for a moment and waved at them through the window's glass. It looked as if she was waving directly at Myrtle.

"You know Kate?" Abigail walked beside her friend in the direction of her car.

"I know the girl. I know her mother far better, you could say. We're old classmates and sometime friends. Clementine Kitteridge. She lives out there in that haunted cul-de-sac where

Beatrice lives."

Abigail was surprised. "Kate is Clementine's daughter?" She knew of Clementine Kitteridge. Everyone in town did. The woman had such a tragic past. Frank had told her about it. Clementine had had a happy family forty years ago until her beloved husband, Abe, and three of her four children had died in a terrible auto accident. A snowy, icy January night and the car had run off the bridge into Turner's Creek. There'd only be one survivor from that crash and the child, about five years old, had been badly injured.

"Yep, Kate is the one that lived. But she does have some chronic medical problems and a bum leg. She still walks with a limp. Clementine said she was moving back here from another town to help take care of her. Clementine's really up there in years, awful lonely these days, and not feeling so well. The daughter's returned to help her out. I've met Kate a few times. I'll have to go in and see her. Though I didn't know she was opening a bakery. Great news all around then."

"I would say it is. Kate seems like a nice person. A hard worker. I look forward to collaborating with her and making the bakery a place people will love to gather and eat what Kate bakes." Abigail hadn't noticed any of Kate's chronic conditions or her limp, but then she hadn't seen her moving around. They'd both sat on stools most of the time. Then again Myrtle didn't always get things straight. She liked to embellish her stories, whether they were true or not.

They were at Abigail's car. She was anxious to get home and draw out remodeling ideas for Kate and the bakery. She didn't want to hurt Myrtle's feelings, but she had to get going. She had so much to do before the kids came home from school. Then there'd be super to make and time with the children.

"Are you up to going to Stella's for a piece of her pie of the day?" Myrtle suggested hopefully. "I think today it's chocolate. My favorite."

Yeah, any kind of pie was Myrtle's favorite and Abigail would end up paying for it as she always did. She was about to turn the old lady down, too busy she'd use as an excuse, then glimpsed the loneliness in the old woman's face she tried so hard to hide and Abigail gave in.

"Sure, I have a half hour or so I can waste…for chocolate pie. Let's go."

"Good. I can fill you in on all the heartbreaking details of Clementine's life. It's quite the story. And tell you about the cruise I'm going on."

The two aimed themselves towards Stella's Diner, Myrtle chattering all the way like a magpie and Abigail listening. Well, half-listening. Her mind was already busy with the donut shop makeover.

They sat in a booth at Stella's and over pieces of pie Myrtle told her what she knew about Clementine, her life, and her daughter. It was a sad story and it made Abigail look at Kate in a different way. Kate was a true survivor. All that tragedy so early in her life could have turned the woman bitter, but, as far as Abigail could see, it hadn't.

When the sad story was over Myrtle gushed about her cruise and the fun she was going to have.

"So, Myrtle, you're going on a sea trip?" Stella had brought them their pie and coffee and Abigail was spying on the other diners around them. There were a couple of locals and several people who must just be passing through town because she didn't recognize them. "When and where are you going?'

"Leaving tomorrow morning with my friend Tina and we're going to the Bahamas. It won't be a long cruise, only seven days, but I'm looking forward to it. You sure can have fun on one of those fancy boats. There are activities and entertainments galore. Singers and dancers. Every night. Gambling even. As you know I do love cards. You stop at these ports and get to stretch your legs in an exotic town you've never been to where you can buy souvenirs to your heart's content. The best thing? The food, exquisite and never ending buffets of it, is *free* and it's fantastic." Her mouth went up into a grin as her fork dug into the pie.

"Well, the food isn't exactly free. You pay for it with your ticket fee."

Myrtle ignored that comment and yammered on, "I stay up every night and play dominos, pinochle or rummy with all sorts of fascinating people and eat all the scrumptious buffet food. They have crab legs and shrimp every night! And in the mornings, whoa, those breakfast spreads are out of this world.

"Did I ever tell you about the last cruise I went on? Oh, back a couple years me and Tina went to the Caribbean. On a gigantic ship called The Princess. I bet there were a hundred thousand people on that tour. Now that was a hoot."

"A hundred thousand?" Abigail tried not to smile but it was hard not to.

"Yep. Maybe more. Let me tell you what happened on our first island stopover…."

Soon she had Abigail laughing over her on-board antics and hilarious anecdotes.

And, before they parted ways, she revealed another case of a haunting she'd uncovered in town. "My friend Alfred–that's Alfred Loring who lives on Doris Street in what I'd call a run-down shack with holes for windows–like Beatrice is being haunted by ghosts. He relayed to me this morning when I bumped into him at the IGA that spooks have been knocking at his windows and breaking in, taking and moving stuff, the last week. He's heard them. I told him to come and talk to you and Frank. That you already are on the case and you'd help him get to the bottom of it."

Oh great, what were they now, the town's new ghost investigators?

"Truth is," she leaned over the table and

gave Abigail a penetrating look, "that's the main reason I'm taking off on the cruise. Too damn many spirits floating around for my liking. I'm hoping that by the time I return, things will have calmed down and gotten back to normal. The spooks will be gone. Moved on as they always do. They don't like staying in one place too long. You know I'm sick of them bothering me and my friends. They need to shove off." Myrtle made a shooing gesture with her hands.

"Alfred Loring is being haunted, too?" Abigail couldn't believe the problem was spreading.

"So he says. But he hasn't been right in the head, either, since the early nineteen-seventies. He's smoked too much of that marijuana weed, you know?" She winked. "I always take everything he says with a grain of salt, a big one, as I believe he's still smoking it quite regularly. That could be why he thinks he's seeing apparitions. It's most likely that crazy smoke."

"But you see ghosts all the time?"

Myrtle gave her a piercing look. "That's because I'm like one of those mediums, you'd call it. I've seen dead souls since I was a child. It's rare. Now these other two don't have the calling like I do. You know ghosts just don't show themselves to anybody. You got to be special to see them." Myrtle cocked her head and her expression was one of smugness.

"You and Frank got any leads yet? I haven't been to see Beatrice lately so I don't know what's going on with her."

"No, not yet. We're working on it, though."
Frank was anyway. Abigail had almost
forgotten about the incident, what with the new
job and everyday life. "Frank and I might drop
in on Beatrice and see how she's doing,
though."

"Good. She needs looking after. Then go see
Alfred." Myrtle scribbled something down on
her napkin with a pencil she pulled from her
pocket and pushed it across the table at her.
"That's his address. I already told him you were
coming to see him. Soon."

"Thanks a lot." But it did strike Abigail as
strange that now a second elderly person was
claiming to be haunted. That couldn't be a
coincidence, could it?

An hour later they parted ways, Abigail paid
for both their pie and coffee, and drove home to
begin Kate's sketches.

*****

After supper Laura entered the kitchen
where, on the table, Abigail was finishing up the
last of the sketches and settled in a chair beside
her. Nick was in the living room watching one
of his favorite shows, *Supernatural*. Snowball
was curled up in his cat bed by the stove,
sleeping.

"Abby, my sister Charlene called me earlier
and she wants to know if Nick and I can spend
the weekend with her at our cousin Sheila's?
We're having a family reunion. All my brothers
and sisters will be there. I told her, of course, it

was okay? Is it? Can you drive Nick and me to Sheila's house on Friday after school? It's been weeks since we've seen the other kids. I miss them. Even Giles is going to be there. He's on leave until next week and has been visiting everyone a couple days each. He'll be at Sheila's by Friday and if we go there he can spend more time with all of us."

The year before Laura and her other siblings had become orphans but none of their other relatives had had room for all six children together, so they had been split up between cousins and aging aunts and uncles across the state. Giles, the oldest, was in the army.

Abigail had taken in Laura and Nick because there'd been an instant and undeniable bond between the three from the first morning Abigail had met them at the library while she'd been painting a mural. She'd felt bad the children had had to be split up, but these days they all seemed to be flourishing. Whenever she could, though, she made sure the sisters and brothers saw each other, even if it meant driving across the state for them to do it. At least Sheila's house, at a hundred and fifty miles, wasn't that far away. She could drive there and back easily in three or four hours and often did. She'd do anything for Laura and Nick and their siblings. They were such sweet kids.

Abigail peered up from her drawing. "Of course it's okay. Whenever you or Nick want to see your brothers and sisters, anywhere, anytime, I'll take you. You know that. Friday, huh? And then I'll pick you up on Sunday evening?"

"Yes." Now Laura was smiling. She was nearly unrecognizable from the rail thin, bereft urchin that Abigail had originally taken in as a foster child, along with her brother, after their father had been murdered by the Mud People Killer and her mother had died from illness. She was now a pretty and happy thriving sixteen year old who smiled easily. Her artwork had continued to improve and if she kept making high grades, in two years she would be up for a full scholarship to any art college she'd want to attend. Abigail was proud of her and Nick.

"I can't wait to see Giles. It's been almost a year since he had leave."

"So it'll be quite the celebration. I bet you're thrilled?" Abigail put her pencil down and looked at the girl. Giles, almost twenty, had been in Afghanistan the last eight months and everyone had been worried sick over his safety. Laura and Nick had spent a lot of time emailing him to keep him updated on things and packing off care packages for him. He'd made it back in one piece and everyone was relieved.

"You know Sheila's invited you to stay, too, if you'd like?"

"Oh, sure…where would she put me? Outside in the front yard on a cot? If everyone's coming there won't be room for me. Thank you but no thank you." Sheila's house was tiny. It was more like an overgrown garage.

"Besides," she tapped her fingers on the

drawing beneath her hand, "I have this new commission, a full decorating job, and major construction begins on it tomorrow. Kate, my new boss, really wants me to be there. There's so much we have to decide even before my real work begins. She needs my help so I need to be here."

"That's okay." Laura stood up. "You can stay and visit for a while on Friday with us, though, can't you? A few hours? You can have supper with us?"

"Of course I can. It'll be great to see your brother and sisters again." Abigail had by then thought of asking Frank to drive up there with her and the kids. It'd be a nice get away and after they dropped them off they'd have rare alone time. In fact, they'd have the whole weekend alone and she was already planning for that. She and Frank might even go out on a real date Saturday night.

"Fantastic!" Laura gave her a quick hug before she joined Nick in the other room. She enjoyed *Supernatural*, too.

Abigail brewed a cup of tea and returned to her sketches. She wanted to present them to Kate the next day. Amazingly she'd come up with floor plans without even trying. Just being there that morning with Kate had given her the ideas.

*****

After the kids had gone to bed there was a knock on the door. It was Frank. He often dropped by once the children were tucked in.

He gathered her into his arms and kissed her.

"And to what do I owe this visit?" she asked when she was set free.

"Do I need a reason?" he said that every time. It was a sort of running joke between them.

"Not really." They smiled at each other.

"I have some news for you and, heck, I wanted to see you. It's been days."

"I know. And perfect timing, too," she said. "Come on in. I just put my work away and the kids are in bed. I have a new job and I've been dying to tell you about it. Now I can. Among other things."

"And," Frank added, trailing her into the living room. "I also thought since it's a gorgeous spring night you might want to sit out on the porch swing, stare up at the night sky, the stars and the moon, and talk about…wraiths and apparitions."

"Wraiths and apparitions?" Then she made the intended connection. "You've heard something more from Beatrice, haven't you?"

"I sure have. She telephoned me this afternoon. I just left there. She claims she saw her husband's ghost again. Oh, and someone or something trashed her basement again."

"It was already trashed." Abigail had gone to the closet and grabbed a jacket. It was chilly outside.

Frank didn't answer until they were on the porch sitting on the swing. "She hired two neighborhood boys she knew to straighten it up after we left. Last night someone or something snuck in and undid it all. I saw the end results. It's worse than the first time. Not only did someone destroy the basement, they broke some of the house's windows and tried to burn down her garage. They didn't succeed, though. Fire trucks got there in time and put the fire out.

"I called Luke from the hardware store and he and his part-time helper, Jeff, are fixing the windows for the second time in three days. Beatrice is a wreck. She's scared to death." He took her hand and the swing gently moved back and forth. The sky was alight with stars and the world was full of the perfume of flowers. There was no wind at all.

"More vandalism? That's disturbing all right. Who would do this to her? She's just an old lady. It doesn't make any sense."

"You're telling me. I've been trying to fill in the blanks now for days. I can't. Yet. But there is *something* going on. I feel it. I do believe her son should be contacted. He needs to be aware of what's happening to his mother. They have been estranged for years and it hurts her. I did have an early suspicion that in some way she might be doing this to get his attention. Until today. Now I don't think so. There's too much damage. She couldn't have done it herself."

"I agree. I don't believe it, either. Something else is going on here."

"Well anyway, I'm about ready to call her son up and scold him for neglecting his mother.

Tell him to get his butt down here and visit her. She's old. Lonely. She needs her son." He shook his head in disgust. "If my son ever treated me like that, I'd be all over him."

"That's you. But I can't imagine you and Kyle not being close."

"Oh, we've had our disagreements over the years, but the older he gets the more he seems to appreciate me. What can I say? I raised a good kid."

"Lucky you. I've known so many children who leave their parents behind. They go off to find their own lives far away and never look back. It's so sad.

"So…you said Beatrice saw her husband's ghost again?" There was a faint meow. Snowball was sitting inside framed in the window. Getting up from the swing she let the cat out. The animal bounded into the yard and careened around the side of the house. Abigail reclaimed her spot beside Frank.

"So she swears." Frank picked up where they'd left off.

"Did he say anything to her?"

Frank flashed her an odd look. "You know I asked her that same question but she couldn't give me a decent answer. All she said was he was really upset about something but she couldn't understand what it was."

"I guess she doesn't speak ghost."

"They have their own language, huh?" Frank put his arm around her and drew her closer. "Okay. You mentioned you had something else to tell me?"

"Oh, you're going to love this. Myrtle informed me today at Stella's that now we have another mysterious haunting of an old person."

"Who?"

"Someone called Alfred–"

"Loring. I know him. I see him around town all the time. He's a kooky old bird, and a veteran, real patriotic, but in my opinion these days missing a few brain cells. What happened?"

"According to Myrtle it sounds a lot like what Beatrice is experiencing. He's hearing suspicious noises in the night. Pounding on the walls. Someone tromping around his house when no one's really there. Unseen intruders. Small vandalisms."

"He seeing ghosts, too?"

"You know Myrtle did say something about ghosts, but not if Alfred had seen any.

"She's going on a cruise, you know."

"Really. That woman sure does like to travel."

"And gamble."

"That, too," Frank said. "And you know she wins more times than not."

"She does seem to have the magic touch when it comes to making money."

"That she does."

They sat there in a comfortable silence for a while, gazing up at the sky. An owl hooted somewhere in the trees above and the sound of wings could be heard.

"Something just occurred to me, Abby."

"Uh, huh?" Abigail was content sitting with him listening to the night, though the old peoples' troubles were bothering her. She still had that uneasy feeling she got when trouble was heading her way, their way, big trouble, and it had grown.

"If I remember correctly, Alfred lives not far from Beatrice."

"Myrtle gave me his address. He lives on Doris."

"Oh my," Frank mumbled softly. "That's a side road off of Beatrice's street. They're practically next door neighbors."

"And you think that coincidence means something?"

"My cop sense says so, because in my world there are no coincidences."

"Myrtle told Alfred we'd take care of everything. He's expecting to see us. Soon."

"I'm already ahead of you, Abby. What are you doing tomorrow morning?"

She squeezed his hand. "I'm going to visit old Alfred with you. See what he has to say."

"Ten o'clock fine with you?"

"How about nine? I need to be somewhere tomorrow morning and don't want to be too late. We can swing by and see Beatrice as well. I have a couple of questions for her myself."

He groaned. "So early?"

"That's not early for you, Frank Lester. Aren't you the writer who gets up at the crack of dawn to work on his novels?"

"I am. Oh, all right, nine it is. Now where do you have to be tomorrow morning and what was the other news you had for me?"

Tucked up close to him, she told him about her new commission and the bakery and, as she knew he would be, he was happy for her. It wasn't until after she'd said goodnight to him she remembered she'd forgotten to ask him about going with her when she took the kids to Shelia's on Friday. No problem. She'd ask him when she saw him in the morning.

After he was gone, she finished up the sketches she'd promised Kate. Even in her critical opinion they'd turned out good. Then an hour later she switched off the lights and went up to bed. She'd come up with three suitable layout designs for the bakery and couldn't wait to show them to her.

Yet in the recesses of her mind, the ghost mystery, as she'd begun calling it, churned and gnawed at her thoughts and the uneasy feelings grew.

Was Beatrice's dead husband really haunting her? Ridiculous. It had to be someone playing mean tricks on her. But why? Now with Alfred Loring also being on the hit list, the answer might mean so much more. All she knew was that something wasn't right.

Attacking, destructive ghosts. Yeah, sure.

Chapter 3
Abigail

Alfred Loring's house, if one could call it that, was, as Myrtle has so whimsically tagged it, little more than a shack. It didn't belong in the same neighborhood as Beatrice's wilted mansion, but it was. It was hidden in a thicket of trees further away from the road. Small, dilapidated and surrounded by castoff items like wash machines, rusted cars, broken furniture and trash, it was an eyesore.

"I hate to say this," Abigail whispered to Frank as they waited for someone to answer the door, "but I've never seen a house like this. It's so modest. And what's around it reminds me of a —"

"Junkyard?"

"Or rubbish dump." Her gaze slid in his direction as she held her nose. He was grinning. "How does anyone live like this?"

"Alfred is a weird old duck. He's a collector of sorts. Very resourceful though. He served in the Viet Nam war and was awarded a Purple Heart or two. He came from a family of carpenters and built this place himself in the nineteen seventies after his parents died and left him this piece of land. It's a sizeable amount of acreage, too." Frank rapped at the door again and someone inside could be heard yelling at them to keep their clothes on, he was coming.

"That explains it then."

"Explains what?"

"His house in this neighborhood. Weren't there any housing codes in the nineteen seventies?"

"Not in Spookie evidently. But the house has been here for as long as I can remember and no one's going to tell Alfred to update it. If he could even afford to do it. He lives on a pension and veteran's disability. But, beyond all that, there have been rumors he's sick; that he's dying. So no one's going to bother him about the decrepit state of his homestead."

"Oh, that's so sad." Now she felt dreadful for thinking badly of him and his home.

The door burst open and a grizzled man somewhere in his seventies was scowling at them. "What do you want?" His voice was somewhere near a growl.

"I'm Frank Lester and this is Abigail Sutton."

The man's face and shoulders relaxed and a faint smile emerged. "Ah, the ghost busters Myrtle said would be visiting. Frank and Abigail. Howdy. I feel like Scrooge in that Christmas movie. You know when he was told to expect three visitors? The police were the first and you're the second. I wonder who will be the third? I'm thinking it could be the Easter Bunny, with Easter so near and all." He chuckled. "Enter."

"Yeah, that's us," Frank quipped with a cynical smile as he reached out and shook the man's hand. "We're ghost busters, whether we like it or not."

"Not that I believe that crap about my problem being ghosts and such," the old man griped as he led them into his home. "That's Myrtle's foolishness. Myself? I believe it's a bunch of miscreants causing the troubles, but that Myrtle wouldn't take no for an answer and had to bother you both. It is humans pestering me. If I catch those damn scallywags making their mischief I'll fill their butts full of buckshot. I have the guns here to do it. Those &#%@ !!#!& better stay away if they know what's good for them. Buckshot isn't easy to get out."

The inside of the shack wasn't what Abigail was expecting. It was neat, sparse, but clean and nothing like the outside. Though it was humble, it seemed to be of sturdy construction. Frank had said the man lived a simple life. He didn't have a computer, the Internet or even Cable. There was aluminum foil on his old TV's bunny ears and there was a conversion box on top of the set. So he was only getting the basic local channels. Well, that was simple.

Sitting at the wooden table with mismatched chairs they heard a story fairly similar to the one Beatrice had related to them days before. For weeks Alfred had been tormented with knocking at his windows, disturbances in the basement, things going missing in the house and other petty crimes against his property. But, unlike Beatrice, he swore it wasn't supernatural, but man made.

They journeyed down into his basement and, sure enough, it'd been trashed the same as Beatrice's. There were windows broken, objects turned over and cans of paint and varnish spilt. The lower level was in complete disarray. There wasn't really much in the basement, but what was there was smashed, spilled and tossed about.

For crying out loud, Abigail thought, who would do such a thing to an old person?

Somewhere during their later conversation, peppered generously with cuss words provided by Alfred, Frank asked, "Alfred, is there anyone mad at you? Have you had any disagreements lately with anyone?"

Frank had also mentioned Alfred could be a hothead at times and over the years had had feuds with just about everyone in town over one thing or another. Delayed PTSD, no doubt. The old man had had a terrible experience in Viet Nam and it hadn't only been the fighting. He'd been captured and had been a prisoner of war for years before he'd been released at the end of the conflict. He'd been tortured and abused and it'd left horrendous scars, both physical and psychological.

"Not that I can recall." Alfred's face

scrunched up and his brown eyes clouded. He made a dismissive gesture with a hand that more resembled a claw. "Oh, wait a minute. I did piss off these two pesky realtors, a man and a woman, or I think they were realtors, who wanted to know what I'd sell my house and land for. The man was an irritatingly creepy dude with a head of hair like a Brillo pad and eyes that couldn't stay still. He just wouldn't take no. Third time he came by himself and I told him no way in hell was I going to sell to the likes of him or anybody for that matter. I scared him off with my shotgun and warned him never to come back. I took care of him all right. You should have seen the look of panic on his weasel face before he scrambled off." Alfred laughed deep in his throat. Frank laughed with him.

"Uh," Abigail weighed in, "you often have people just show up at your door trying to buy your property?"

"More than a few over the years, come to think on it." Alfred scratched the side of his neck for about the tenth time where there was an angry looking rash. At times he moved as if he were in pain. Arthritis most likely or it was old wounds. "The woman who'd accompanied the man the first time, she was a looker I have to say that for her, offered me a hundred thousand a couple of weeks back. I told her, too, I wasn't interested."

Abigail remarked, "Whew, that's a lot of money."

"It is. But this is my home and this is where

I plan on dying. Under this roof in my own bed with my mementos and memories. Nobody is going to scare me off, either."

Abigail had the thought that Alfred's demise wasn't far off. The man was very ill, even she could see that.

"Did the damage we saw in the basement happen last night then?" Frank spoke to the man in a friendly voice and the veteran seemed to be warming up to him. Alfred's scowl was gone.

"No, it happened oh, three, four nights ago, I reckon. I just went down there and noticed it yesterday, though. But the disturbances have been waking me up at night now for over a week. It's getting tiresome. I need my sleep. Somebody or something was lobbing rocks at my roof last night and because of the noise I couldn't sleep."

"Have you called the sheriff about this?"

"I have. Sheriff Mearl was out here yesterday. Took the report, huffed and puffed like usual, told me he'd keep his ears and peepers open and I wasn't to use my gun again. He was as much help as he always is. Which is to say, not much. And if someone comes on my land uninvited, I darn well will get out my gun and use it. This is my land, my home and I can do what I want on it."

Abigail thought Frank would say something to that, but he didn't. As one gun owner to another, she imagined the two men thought the same about self and home protection.

"Alfred, do you know Beatrice Utley?" A

tall man, Frank looked uncomfortable in the cramped house at the small table. The chair he sat in squeaked when he moved as if it would collapse at any moment and deposit him on the floor.

"Sure I do. She's my neighbor over there." His thumb cocked in the direction of Beatrice's house. "I holler at her sometimes when I see her somewhere, but she don't holler back. We don't socialize much. She's a little hoity-toity, if you know what I mean? She has money and I don't. Also, she's not my type. And, oh lordy, I heard about those crazy dolls of hers. I don't do crazy. I have enough issues of my own."

By the looks of him, the way he lived and what was happening to him, Abigail agreed. Alfred had his own problems.

She and Frank stayed another half hour but learned nothing else that could have helped them. Alfred was as in the dark about what was going on as Beatrice had been.

And after leaving him, Frank and Abby drove over to Beatrice's to see how she was doing. She was fine. She'd had the basement straightened up again and the police patrol had kept anything else from occurring. So Far. Frank had telephoned her son the night before after he'd left Abigail's house and had explained to him what was going on. The son seemed like he cared about what was happening to his mother on the phone, but so far hadn't shown up or called her. It made Abigail feel bad for her.

"Well, that's done," Frank had exhaled when they were heading towards Abigail's house so she could pick up her car and get to town. She wanted to get to the bakery. Her new job waited.

"I pray everything is okay with those old folks now and nothing else happens to either one of them. I still can't believe someone would torment them like that."

"Me either. I'm not giving up yet on finding who did it and making them pay for it."

"You're not going to stake out their houses every night, are you?" He'd done that for her when the Mud People Killer had been after her the year before.

"I might. I have the strong suspicion it isn't over yet."

"So do I."

"And I have a hunch or two," he said, "I'm following up on. I can't help but think what's happening to Beatrice and now Alfred isn't somehow linked. As I said, there's no such thing as coincidences."

"Let me know how that goes, will you?"

"You know I will, Abby."

"Now on to something less mysterious and cheerier. I'm driving the children to Shelia's on Friday, they're going for a weekend reunion with their brothers and sisters, and wanted to know if you'd like to tag along? We wouldn't be staying long and then we'd have the rest of the night to ourselves."

"The weekend?"

"You can have some of that, too. But remember I have that new commission and I'm supposed to be at the bakery Saturday morning to see how the construction is coming along. But you can have Friday and Saturday night."

"Fair enough. We'll have to go out to the movies or something Saturday after you're through at the bakery."

"Hey, that's an excellent idea. There's a film or two I've wanted to see and one of them is being shown in Imax."

"I know you've been dying to try Imax, so pick the movie and a time Saturday and we'll go. My treat."

"Of course your treat. You're the wealthy author here, not me."

"I'm not wealthy," Frank bantered. "My books are doing fairly well, but I'm no Arthur Conan Doyle. I'm not rich."

"Yet. You get a couple more novels out there and your fame will spread. I expect you to be a millionaire one day."

"Ah, so that's why you're going out with me? Because you think I'll be rich someday?"

She gently squeezed his arm as he was driving. "Yep, that's it. It's all about the money." And they both laughed.

He dropped her off at the house and drove away. She knew she'd see him later because she'd invited him for dinner.

*****

Abigail was hurrying down the sidewalk towards the bakery, her portfolio clasped in her arms, when she almost bumped into Samantha.

"Whoa, Abigail, where are you going in such a hurry?" the editor exclaimed, putting her hands out to cushion the collision and then bringing one of them up to shove her thick glasses higher on her nose. Today she had her vibrant red hair in a ponytail and was wearing blue jeans and a T-shirt that had the words *I Write the News* on it.

"To my job at the new bakery. I'm going to help the owner, Kate Greenway, decorate it from floor to ceiling, and then paint donuts on the walls. Thanks for the tip the other day."

"Ah, you're welcome. I just heard the prospective owner was looking for an artist or a painter from someone else, can't even recall who now. I didn't even know the owner's name…so it's Kate Greenway?"

"It is. She's Clementine Kitteridge's daughter."

"Really? I know Clementine, of course, but I've never met her daughter. I'll have to introduce myself to her when it's ready to open and run a story on her business. I do that with all the start-up shops in town. Like a *welcome to Spookie* kind of piece. Donuts, huh?"

"All donuts. But, according to Kate, of many exotic varieties. She's a donut wizard. She showed me some pictures of them she had in a scrapbook and they looked delicious. Which by the way is what she's calling the place. The Delicious Circle." They'd arrived at the bakery's door. Abigail could see Kate inside fussing with something behind the counter. Probably sorting out what was to go and what was to stay.

"I can't wait until she opens then. Late May or early June, huh? That's not far off."

"I know, but that's what she's aiming for. I mean, we're aiming for. You want to come in and meet her?"

"Not now, she looks busy, and I'm on my way to meet someone for an interview." Samantha smiled and looked into the shop. She wiggled her hand at the occupant, who returned the wave. "Tell her I'll stop by nearer to her opening date and get her story and photos. Tell her I'm thrilled she's opening her business here in Spookie. We can always use another bakery."

"I will." Something in Samantha's tone when she'd said she was going to an interview had tipped Abigail off. "What interview?"

"I don't know much about it as of yet. It concerns more local vandalism. There seems to be a wave of it going around lately."

"Vandalism?"

"I've labeled it that for convenience," Samantha explained, "though it sounds more to me like a bunch of malicious teenage mischief against elderly people."

"What do you mean?"

Samantha sighed and shifted from one foot to another. The sun was glowing on her face and highlighted the scarlet in her hair. "I've spoken to three citizens in the last two weeks, older people, who have had windows shattered, damage done to their property and their houses broken into. They've had things stolen and have been just generally harassed. In some instances terrorized in their own homes with nightly–and one of them put it exactly in these words–wraithlike intruders that have scared the heck out of them."

"Wraithlike intruders…you mean ghosts?" Something prickled up along Abigail's neck. What was going on in Spookie anyway?

"I'm not going to say that out loud or they'll drag me off to the looney bin. But yes, that's what it sounds like. I'm going to do a cautionary editorial on these incidents because I feel as if the town should know these crimes are going on. We need to be more vigilant and we need to catch these hooligans terrorizing our old folks."

"You know Frank and I are investigating a couple of occurrences that sound similar to what you're reporting on."

"You are, huh? Now that's curious."

"So you might go talk to Beatrice Utley and Alfred Loring, as well. They've also been recently and repeatedly targeted. Same events as what you've mentioned. Frank is looking into it."

"You mean you and Frank are investigating it like you did the Summer's disappearances thirty years ago and the crimes last winter?" The editor gave her a slight smile.

"I guess we are."

"I know both of them. Okay, I'll go see them, too. Thanks for the tip." There was a troubled look on her friend's face. She'd taken a small notebook out of her jacket pocket and had written the names down.

Before they parted ways, Abigail requested, "Can you keep me up to date on what happens to those old people and their situations? And let me know what else you find out after you interview them? Give me a call?"

"Sure. But you'll be able to read about it in next week's edition. Now it's beginning to look as if it'll be a front page story as well an editorial. There's been so many incidents reported."

"Unfortunately."

"I got to run, but I'll call you later and we'll catch up more. Let's have lunch one day soon?"

"We can do that. I'll talk to you later."

Samantha scurried down the sidewalk towards her appointment and Abigail, her mind still on what Samantha had disclosed, entered the bakery.

Kate, in dusty jeans and sleeveless shirt, came up to her. "I saw you out there chatting to the town reporter. I've yet to meet her but someone pointed her out to me the other day so I know who she is."

"Samantha Westerly. You will be meeting her soon enough. She'll be in to do a story on you and your business when you open the doors. She always does a nice spread with photos and it also goes up on the Internet. It could really help kick off your business."

"Free publicity. My favorite kind. She

knows we're opening around the beginning of June?"

"She knows. Now…wait until you see the plans I drew up last night for the bakery."

Abigail spread out her drawings on the counter and they spent time discussing them. Kate liked two of them, but loved the third one where the room was painted in shades of red and pink and milk chocolate. "I incorporated the colors of those donut pictures you showed me.

"And here," she gestured to the area behind them, "there will be small round tables with wire-backed chairs for people to sit and drink coffee at with their pastries. I know you said you were keeping this counter, but we can spruce it up with warmer colors. I can paint the menu or donuts on it and we can cover it with a layer of clear coat. And the donut theme will continue on the table tops and along that back wall. That's where one of the murals will be. I also know where you can get some beautiful glass display cases for your pastries dirt cheap. A store down the road here has had them in their storage room for ages and the owner will be so glad to get rid of them you'll be able to get them for almost nothing. I will give you the guy's name and telephone number before I leave."

"I love it!" Kate was grinning. "The layout and color scheme looks so cozy. Intimate and welcoming."

"That's what I was aiming for," Abigail said, pleased Kate had liked her designs.

"Well, then I'd better get working. I still

have a lot of clean up to do before the construction crew get here and we can start ordering our furnishings."

"I thought they were coming today?"

"I put them off until Monday. I couldn't get enough done fast enough. I'm a little slow. I'm not as young as I used to be."

It didn't take Abigail but a moment to think about it and offer, "I'm going to help you."

"You don't have to do that. You're the decorator, the artist; I'm the cleaner and the baker. Besides," Kate's voice took on a thoughtful note, "I can't afford to pay you for clean-up. Just for decorating ideas and the paintings. The prices we agreed upon. That's all I have in my meager budget. But thanks anyway for offering."

"Nonsense. I know your mother Clementine, so you're already part of this town and we help each other out here. You'll see. And I have nothing else to do today."

"How do you know my mother is Clementine?"

"Myrtle Schmitt, our resident eccentric and an old friend of your mother's, told me."

"Oh, so you know Myrtle, huh?"

"I know Myrtle." The women traded a knowing glance. "She's a little on the eccentric side sometimes but she's my friend, as well. She's got a good heart."

"That she does."

"She can't wait until you open your bakery," Abigail added.

"I bet. She's a sweetheart all right, but she sure is a moocher. My mom says she's always showing up at her house begging for a meal or a snack. Mom doesn't mind, though. They're old friends as you said. Myrtle especially likes to mooch sweets."

"Don't I know it? She'll be visiting your business a lot then." They both laughed.

"Okay, so it's decided," Abigail affirmed. "I'm going to help. So hand me a broom and a dustpan, or some rags and cleaning fluids and I'll get to work. Because the sooner we get this cleaned out, the sooner the remodeling can start; I can get to the paintings and you can begin baking those delicious donuts of yours and open up."

Kate handed her a broom, a bucket and a bundle of rags.

The day passed quickly and by the time Abigail left the room was completely cleaned out and the real work could begin.

"Tomorrow I'll go have a look at those glass cases," Kate assured her right before she closed the door, "and I'll visit that carpet store you recommended. I think I know where I can purchase the perfect tables and chairs. It won't be long now before you can get in here to do your art. I'll call you or you can drop by anytime and see how it's coming."

"I'll do that. Drop by anytime. I'm in town often enough."

Abigail made her way to her car and at the last moment decided to stop by Stella's Diner to see if anyone she knew was there. The kids were at their friends' houses and a cup of Stella's coffee was just what she needed to perk her up after an afternoon of sweeping and scrubbing.

She was nearly to the diner, passing the Tattered Corner's display window full of bunnies and books when she glanced at her reflection. There behind her on the sidewalk mirrored in the glass, watching her, was a man. He might have been tall, but his body was slouched so she couldn't be sure. He was wearing dark clothes with a battered hat pulled low over his shadowed face. He looked homeless. Dirty. There was an air of sadness about him. Speeding up her steps, she swung around to look at him…but *no one was there*. The sidewalk around her was *empty*. *What the–!* Pivoting around to stare again into the glass she was even more shocked to see he was *still there* staring at her. His face, white and faded out like an old photograph, tilted up until the hat's brim was no longer hiding it and for a heartbeat she almost saw his features. It was his eyes that mesmerized her, though, and were all she could see. There was an intensity in his gaze directed at her as if he were trying to tell her something important. He lifted a stick of a finger, pointed at her and his lips curved up into a rictus grin. There was something familiar about him, yet her mind wouldn't or couldn't place him. With a gasp she once more turned around to look behind her. Again *there was no one there*.

That's it. I'm out of here!

Stella's door was flung wide as she yanked it open and raced through. She was still trembling when she dropped into a booth, dropping her purse and portfolio on the table. The anxiety the apparition had produced in her had nauseated her stomach and made her hands shake.

"Abigail, my, my girl, you look as if you just saw a ghost! You're all chalky looking and vibrating like an earthquake victim." Stella was at her side. "Are you okay? Can I get you a glass of water or something, sweetie?" The waitress held her order book and pencil in her hands, yet her expression was concerned.

"No, no water, thanks. I need coffee," Abigail muttered. "And I'm fine. I've just had a little shock, but I'll be okay in a minute."

Stella studied her. "Uh, huh. What kind of shock?"

Abigail asked herself later why she fibbed, but at the time, it seemed the thing to do. There was no way she was going to talk about disappearing shadow men to Stella. The woman didn't do the supernatural. "Nothing big. I, er, stumbled outside on the sidewalk on an uneven patch of concrete and though I didn't fall or anything, it gave me a fright. You know how it is?"

"Uh, huh. It must have been a hell of a fright. You should see your face, girl. White as mashed potatoes."

Abigail's trembling hand made a glib gesture. "It would have been a lot worse if I'd taken that tumble. I might have sprained or broken something. I don't need a trip to the emergency room. I consider myself lucky."

"You sure were. You need to be careful walking on those sidewalks. I keep telling the city council we need to fix them. Cracks and broken sections make for real safety violations. First time someone does take a fall and breaks something, sues the city, it'll be too late. Do you want anything else besides that coffee?"

Abigail avoided her eyes. "Just the coffee, please."

After Stella had bustled off to get it for her, she took a deep breath. What had happened and what did it mean? Was she seeing things now like Beatrice and Myrtle?

What had the thing wanted with her? All she was sure of was it had been an old man and he'd somehow looked familiar. She had an inkling he'd wanted something and that something was related to the case she and Frank were working on. Their case. What exactly was their case anyway? Was it teenage hoodlums making grief for the old ones, just pranks–or was there more to it?

There was more to it.

"Earth to Abigail. Earth to Abigail," a deep voice woke her from her reverie.

She looked up. "Frank. I was just thinking of you. What are you doing here?" Her lips smiled and her mind calmed.

"I'm flattered you were thinking of me, makes me believe you might truly care for me or something." He flashed her a quick mischievous smile. "I was at the IGA picking up some last minute things for supper and I saw you through the window. Since I needed to see you anyway, here I am."

He slipped into the booth and gave her a hasty hug and kiss. She thought they were too mature to be showing unbounded affection in public and though he didn't agree he respected the way she felt about it and kept it to a minimum. "But I recognize that uneasy expression of yours. What's happened?"

"If I tell you you'll think I've lost my mind."

"You mean you had one to begin with?" he teased and she jostled him good naturedly.

Still smiling she shook her head and told him about the man in the window glass, the way he'd made her feel and how he'd vanished.

He didn't make fun of her. He knew better. "You know it is strange that happened to you after what I learned from Beatrice. A couple hours after we left she called me. Again."

Stella had been hovering at another table and picked that moment to come in for a landing in front of them. "Hi there Frank. What can I get ya?"

"Coffee will do it, thanks Stella."

When she was gone, Abigail pressed, "So Beatrice called you *after* we'd been there this morning? So soon? Now what's happened?"

"Someone got into her basement and trashed it again."

"Again? But–wait a minute–when we were

there the basement was fine. It'd been cleaned up, twice, and everything." Beatrice had been friendly to them and had given them coffee in the kitchen. It wasn't bad. The old lady had been talkative, much more than the previous time they'd visited her. She'd taken a shine to Frank and never lost a chance to touch his arm or shoulder or smile at him, calling him *Sonny* whenever she addressed him. It was easy to see he'd become her substitute son because her own son wasn't around.

"Well, she said she took a short nap after we left, and then went down there when she heard the commotion and it was once more a disaster area. Windows shattered, the objects not smashed the last time now smashed; the whole shebang. Except this time there were words painted on the walls: *Get Out!* in red. She wasn't sure if it was paint or blood. It looked like blood to me, though. The lab will confirm or disprove that. The sheriff promised to send a sample and find out."

Abigail stared at him as Stella placed his cup of coffee on the table, he thanked the waitress, and she hurried off. "That's bizarre all right. And this occurred when she was upstairs sleeping?"

"Apparently. And she also spoke about other odd happenings she had forgotten to mention when we were there earlier. Her furnace and her gas stove keep turning themselves on. There are banging noises upstairs in the bedrooms when she's downstairs and noises downstairs when she's upstairs. She's really frightened now and talks about selling the house because it's so haunted."

"Does she still believe it's her dead husband?"

"At first she did. Now she's not so sure. He hasn't visited her again and she thinks the other more malevolent spirits have chased him away. She's afraid of them because they're extremely angry spirits, or so she says."

"What would they be angry about?"

"Now that's a good question." Frank put sugar and cream in his coffee, stirred it, and drank some. "Beatrice hasn't got a clue. There have been no recent deaths, murders or anything in the house that would trigger violent hauntings, so it's a mystery." His expression was grim. "But I'd predict it somehow might tie in with Alfred's problems."

"And, I'm afraid," Abigail paused, "it's not just Beatrice and Alfred's problems any longer. I saw Samantha this morning and she was going off to interview for a news story three other victims who have reported similar incidents in their homes lately. The same as what Beatrice and Alfred have experienced."

"You don't say? There's more? Do you have their names and where they live?"

"Sorry, no. Samantha had yet to talk to them. She was in a hurry. I was in a hurry. But she said I could call her later and she'd confess all."

"I'm going to save you that phone call,"

Frank said. "I'm going over to the newspaper as soon as I leave here. I have a hunch about all this and want to see if I'm right. Would you like to come along?"

"Sorry, I can't. The children will be getting home soon and they'll expect me to be there. You can call me or come by the house after you interrogate Samantha if you'd like. I'm also curious to find out what she's uncovered."

"I'll come by the house. It's on my way." Another mischievous smile. It wasn't on his way but he'd come by anyway.

They drank their coffee, paid Stella, and parted company. Frank drove to the newspaper office and Abigail drove home. The day had turned cloudy and chillier as early April could sometimes do on a whim. The winds blew spring blossoms off the trees and across the roads and had a sting to it. It looked like a storm was brewing.

On the way home she brooded over the unlucky things befalling the elderly in town. Were they really true hauntings? And, oh, how she wanted to know the answer because she couldn't get the man-in-the-window-glass out of her mind. Was his appearance a warning that something worse was about to happen? But just thinking like that made her shiver.

*****

The night rain was pummeling the outside walls of the house but the knock on the door was expected. It was late, though, after ten, and the kids were long asleep.

"It's storming like a hurricane out there," was the first thing Frank declared as she ushered him into the living room. "The Lemmons Creek is overflowing and flooding the roads on the east side of town and I had to backtrack more than once just to get here."

"Kind of late, isn't it?" She was in her nightgown and robe and had been about to go up to bed. Earlier she'd given up on Frank stopping by but here he was.

He wiped the wetness off his face and slipped out of his jacket. "What I have learned can't wait. Well, I thought of waiting until tomorrow morning or calling you, but I knew you'd want to know. And I wanted to see you." Frank settled on the sofa, pulled Abigail down beside him and gave her a kiss.

Snowball was asleep on one end of the couch and didn't wake when Frank came in. The cat was used to him coming and going. To her he was part of the family.

The living room was shadowed with faint light because she'd been busy at the kitchen table sketching ideas she'd had for a new painting. A section of evening woods filled with eerie looking trees and mist. She always had to be working on something. Besides doing commission work she sold her paintings in some of the local stores. They sold well so she always made sure she had a good supply of them out there.

After the kiss she prompted, "Okay, tell me."

"I cornered Samantha at the newspaper office and spoke to her about those other three victims around town. She gave me their names and addresses and I went to talk to each of them. All old folks…living in the vicinity of Beatrice and Alfred's houses; actually within a five, six mile radius. Just as I'd suspected."

"The same neighborhood?"

"The *same* neighborhood.

"They all had stories very similar to what we've already seen and heard. You might know them. Jeff Stricklin, Clementine Kitteridge and Dotty Cumming? Though Dotty is younger than the rest she only lives about five miles away from Beatrice."

"Now that's odd, isn't it?" she muttered. "Unless the trouble makers are targeting that exact area for some reason. I don't know Jeff Stricklin, but I know who Dotty Cumming is. I've seen her around town here and there and you're right, she's about fifty or so. I know Clementine Kitteridge, too, and she happens to be Kate Greenway's mother."

"Kate Greenway?"

"You know, the woman who's going to open the new bakery on Main Street? The commission I'm working on now?" Abigail's thoughts were contemplating what he'd just told her. "That's a coincidence."

"There are no–"

Abigail put her fingers to his lips. "I know, I know."

Her eyes went to the window as a flash of

lightning lit up the outside. The wind cried as if the lightning had hurt it. "What do you think is going on here, Frank? I mean, these vandalisms and all? What's behind them?"

"It sure as hell isn't ghosts, as Beatrice believes. That I'm sure of," Frank said, reclining against the couch.

"But why would anyone want to torment old people in their homes? I don't see any reason for it."

"I think I do," Frank replied softly. "After grilling those three people Samantha directed me to I have a theory."

"And that theory is?"

"Someone either has something against these people, they want to scare them or they want them to leave their homes. I know Alfred and Clementine said they'd never move but Jeff and Dotty are frightened enough to be considering it. They told me so. You should see the mess at Dotty's place. It's like a tornado went through her yard. Her flowers were yanked up by the roots and half her windows were broken or cracked. She's seen unexplained shapes flitting around her yard at night, making weird noises. She's afraid to let her dog, Spot, outside. And Jeff...someone burned his garage down two days ago."

"What does the sheriff's department say about all this?"

"Oh, what they always say. They're looking into it. No leads so far."

"What's new? And how was Clementine?"

Abigail had to ask.

"That was the hardest visit of all. She almost didn't answer the door, she was so afraid. She's close to ninety years old and obviously isn't well, physically or mentally." He lightly tapped his forehead. "She believes, as does Beatrice, that everything that's happening is supernatural. Poltergeists are behind everything. She hadn't even reported her troubles to the police; I had to do that. But then she doesn't know from minute to minute what day it is and forgets what she was going to say at any given moment. Half the stuff she told me made no sense. She might have dementia, Alzheimer's or an illness something like it."

"That's one of the reasons why Kate moved back here, to take care of her."

"From what I've seen, she'll have her hands full. I couldn't tell if Clementine's house was a pigpen or if someone had trashed it. And something else is bothering me. Because of the severity of the storm, after I left Clementine's place, and since I was so near, I decided to look in on Alfred. See how he was doing. He never answered the door. So now I'm worried."

"Maybe he didn't hear you? Or didn't want company?"

"That could be. But I can't imagine why he'd be rambling out in the bad weather, in the rain and wind. He's an old man. Old men huddle in their homes during a storm. I'll have to go back there again tomorrow or the next day and see if I can catch him home."

"That's a good idea."

Outside the thunder boomed and the water hit the roof hard. Frank didn't stay much longer. But before he left, they planned for their trip the following weekend with the children and Abigail showed him her new sketches.

Then he drove off into the rainstorm.

Chapter 4
Myrtle and Tina

It was the final night of the seven day cruise and they were floating back to where they'd begun and would be there by morning. It'd been a pretty nifty voyage, all things considered. Myrtle and her friend Tina had raked in the cash each night gambling with a group of rummy players so the voyage had turned out extremely profitable.

The cabin they shared on the top deck was a nice one. Sort of small, but they had a great view from the balcony of water...lots and lots of water. Not that it mattered. They didn't spend much time in the cabin because there were too many things to do–bingo, play cards, eat and watch live shows or movies–and people to watch, meet and talk to.

And then there were the glamorous port stops they made. Myrtle enjoyed roving the foreign streets and admiring the wares and souvenirs, but she rarely bought anything. Waste of money, she'd carp. She did the cruises for the gambling, the food and to get away. She and Tina would sample every stop but didn't stay out long. Besides, her legs were beginning to give her trouble and hiking around the livelong day off ship made her too exhausted to play cards all night. So she limited the physical activity.

The food on board had been lip-smacking; best she'd ever had. And she was determined to eat as much as she could before they docked. Shame she didn't have food pouches in her cheeks like chipmunks had. Boy, could she stuff a mouthful of food into those if she had them. Well, she did have an enormous purse, stuffed with plastic bags waiting to be filled, she'd been dragging around. That worked even better. Candy of any kind wasn't safe from her.

Myrtle sidled up for the third time to the dinner buffet, grabbed a clean piece of china, utensils and napkin, and began heaping food on the plate. All the shrimp, crab and fried chicken she could eat. Yummy. The desserts this time were spectacular. She'd eaten so much ice cream with all the toppings they could stick a cherry on her head and call her a sundae. A dollop of cocktail sauce slopped onto the front of her sunflower dress and she swiped it off with a napkin.

Oh, she adored these cruises, but she'd probably added five pounds since they'd left home port. What did she care? She was old. No one cared if she was fat or not. Her friend, Tina, didn't. But then Tina was a chubby dumpling herself.

Myrtle bobbed her head at her shipmate over

the buffet offerings, and they exchanged satisfied grins. Tina's plate was heaped higher than hers. Bet Tina had gained ten pounds so far. Tina could afford to because she was a good foot taller than her. Tina the giant. Tina had a bird's nest of curly dyed-strawberry hair and sparse fur on her chin; one of her hazel colored eyes sat lower than the other at half-mast. But they'd been friends since grade school and, of their entire decrepit crowd from that time, they were the last two left breathing. Sure Tina had her peculiarities but, by their ages, didn't they all? So she fell asleep at the oddest times, snored like a sick buffalo and had this quirk where she stuffed left over food into her pocketbook or pockets to devour later? And sometimes forgot it was in there…for days. Oh, well, no one was perfect.

On the plus side, Tina was an adventurous individual and was at all times open to going anywhere, anytime. She enjoyed gambling and could play a mean hand of pinochle or poker. Winning was her specialty. That's why Myrtle liked to take her along on cruises or to the gambling casinos. Of course Tina wasn't as well off as she was, her investments not chosen as wisely, so Myrtle had to often pay her way or help her out some. It didn't matter. The companionship was worth it.

She reckoned her time on earth was dwindling so she'd best grab all the excitement and gusto she could. Eat, travel and have all the adventures she could cram into the remaining years. Cruising was an adventure she'd come to later in life and she had catching up to do.

Years ago, thirty by her count now, when she'd been married, she'd never done much of anything. Her husband Oscar, sweet moose-of-a-man that he'd been, had been a home body of the worse sort. Looking back now, she supposed he probably had that sickness...the one where people couldn't or wouldn't leave their house. Agoraphobia she thought it was called. He'd never wanted to go nowhere but work and home, work and home. When their children, a son they'd named Silas and a daughter they'd called Alisha, had been young, her husband had forced himself to take them places. Doctor and dental appointments. The skating rink. Movie matinees. Sports events and school dances. Then, after they'd grown up and left home for distant shores, Oscar had permanently planted himself in his over-stuffed recliner, when he wasn't at work at the factory, and that had been that.

Myrtle frowned slightly as her memory replayed her life. When retirement finally arrived Oscar and his chair had been nigh inseparable and Myrtle, being the good wife, had stayed at home with him, except for visits to the store and bank. Until he got cancer and over a terrible four years slowly wasted away until there was nothing left. Myrtle had dearly loved her moose and had grieved for a long time. She'd been lonely. Sad. Then one day she'd said: *the heck with this!* and had grabbed

Alisha's old red wagon and started her roaming expeditions around Spookie looking for her treasures and new friends. Years after her husband had died she finally began to live.

Now she was virtually alone in the world, except for her friends, because she'd outlived Alisha and Silas, too. Silas had died twenty years before in an airplane crash. He'd grown up to be a shrewd investment broker with a national brokerage company, which is why and how she'd learned to so wisely invest. He'd set up her account, taught her how and what to invest in and how to grow it, and she'd been an excellent pupil. Silas never married. So Myrtle had no grandchildren. And her sweet daughter Alisha? Alisha with the curious brown eyes and long silky hair the hue of spun silk? She'd grown up to be a great artist living in New York, but one fateful, awful day she'd gotten on the subway and was never seen again. She evaporated into the city, the world, the ether. Forever. Childless also. That was a long ten years ago.

But life was for the living so Myrtle had gone on. What other choice was there?

She filled her plate and sat down at a table. Her eyes took in the wall of windows. A bird, possibly a seagull or a dodo bird, flew across behind the open expanse of glass to the right of her table, tipped its wings at her and winked.

They always got a table by the windows. Tina liked looking out at the ocean as it churned by. Myrtle didn't know why. The waves and water all looked the same to her with miles and miles of blue and green and every once and a while a monster fish or the Loch Ness Monster jumping out of the whitecaps. Oh well, that was in her mind. Truth was, the sea wasn't that exciting.

The water was boring, except during sea storms. They'd had a doozy of a tempest the third night they were out at sea. The ship bucked and rocked like one of those crazy machine bulls in a country bar. The sea had roiled with waves higher than the boat. The rain had come down in a solid sheet rippled with lightning.

Myrtle had perched by their cabin window in a chair and soaked it all in. Now that had been exciting. But Tina had cowered in her single bed behind her, moaning, praying that they'd live through the night; a throw-up bucket close by. Of course, the storm had eventually subsided, the seas calmed, and Tina had dragged herself from her bed. They'd dressed and went to breakfast. Tina hadn't eaten much, though, at that morning's spread. Myrtle hadn't minded. There had just been more for her.

The remainder of the cruise the weather and the seas were tranquil. They'd spent the nights in the lounges or the bars gambling with their new friends and eating. Myrtle wasn't much of a booze drinker. A person had to have a clear head to play cards so they could remember what they'd seen played and what was left to play. Tina never drank. She was a teetotaler from way back. She liked cherry Pepsi.

Tina loaded her plate at the buffet and joined her at the table.

"You need to try that roast beef, Tina. It's so tender you don't even need a knife."

Tina used her fork to point at the roast beef slice in between the lasagna and the mashed potatoes. She bobbed her head. Today Tina had chosen a lavender pants suit to wear that she'd had in her closet for years. It was way out of style and threadbare in places. There was an orange scarf tied loosely around her neck and in her hair she'd clasped a series of barrettes in the shapes of tiny animals. Myrtle thought she looked better than usual. At least her hair was combed.

"In my opinion, though, the lobster tastes undercooked." Myrtle kept yakking about the food and about the people laughing and munching down around them.

Her friend listened as she was eating and sometimes nodded her head, smiled or grimaced.

Tina didn't talk too much. Most likely that was why Myrtle got along with her. It meant she could rattle away as much as she wanted and was never interrupted. Worked for her.

After supper the women toddled down to the Kit Kat Lounge and met up with the gang. It consisted of three old codgers and three old hens. None as old as her and Tina, but Myrtle approximated they were in their sixties.

Two were a married couple. The rest were single and, like her, taking the cruise for excitement. One of the women still worked part-time as a beautician, getting money under the table. One of the single men was trying to write a book about real life crimes or something, but Myrtle didn't tell him she knew a mystery author. He'd be a pest then.

They were nice people on the whole. They had interesting life stories and liked to talk about them. They'd jokingly titled themselves the Gray-Haired Gang and they loved to play cards. Being all retired and living on budgets, they didn't often play for big stakes. Dimes and quarters mostly. The pots weren't allowed to be over ten dollars. That was good because Myrtle didn't like throwing money away. It was hard enough to lose, but if it was under twenty bucks a night she didn't feel too bad. She didn't have to gamble to get her money, her investments were doing just fine.

Tina won big that night. She collected twenty-four bucks and a handful of change. The woman was tickled. But around eleven o'clock she informed Myrtle she wasn't feeling so well, wanted to retire to the cabin and go to bed. She'd probably eaten too much at supper. Myrtle was having so much fun she told her friend to go on without her and she'd see her later in the cabin or in the morning.

It was their last night and Myrtle was resolved to squeeze every penny out of her cruise ticket she could get. Let Tina go to bed early. Not her. Besides one of the old men, a fellow called Wilfred, had been flirting with her most of the week and though it would end when the journey did, it felt good. Not that it could ever lead anywhere. At seventy-four, he was far too young for her and besides she was way past romantic involvements. She'd had the love of her life and no one could ever fill Oscar's old slippers.

The card game went on past two in the morning and then broke up. Everyone was sad to be saying goodbye and there were hugs all around. Promises to keep in touch…which no one would keep. They never did. That's the way it was on vacation trips. A person made temporary best new friends and left them behind when they went home.

Myrtle shuffled her way to her cabin, taking a minute at the railing to admire the sparkling night sea on her way, and let herself into the room. The cabin was empty. No Tina. No sign of Tina having been there. No clothes strewn in piles across the floor. Tina's bed hadn't been slept in. The covers were neat and flat over the mattress. There was no note. Very odd.

"Tina! Where are you? Tina?" Myrtle checked the bathroom. No Tina. Not on the balcony. No Tina bobbing around in the water below the balcony like an abandoned platypus. No Tina anywhere.

Myrtle telephoned for help and reported her friend missing.

And that's when the nightmare began.

*****

The next day Myrtle almost had to be

dragged off the boat. She'd stayed on board longer than she was supposed to; trying to find out where her friend had gone and what had happened to her. The captain and his minions believed Tina, drunk or not feeling well as she'd claimed, had accidently fallen overboard the night before and had drown.

"It happens more often than you think," protested Captain Milton, a middle-aged competent acting man with a mustache, who looked spiffy in his captain's uniform. "The sea was cold and Mrs. Thompson was not a young woman. She couldn't have fought the water for long. I'm sorry, but that's most likely what happened."

They didn't listen to Myrtle when she swore Tina didn't drink and wouldn't have gotten close enough to the rail to fall in in the first place, either.

"Not to Tina. She wouldn't have slipped overboard for no reason. She was as sure-footed as a boat goat. Something has happened to her! Have you searched the other places on the ship and the cabins?"

"We will as soon as the remainder of the passengers disembark. My crew has already searched every other possible location and any empty cabins. No sign of Mrs. Thompson. I'm sorry. We will keep looking of course. We want to know what happened to her as much as you and the port authorities do."

The captain tried to be as sympathetic as he could and comforted her. "I promise you there are boats out looking for Mrs. Thompson as we speak and they will keep searching until we decide there isn't any chance she has survived."

"How long will that be?" Myrtle had snapped at him.

"We look as long as we can.

"Mrs. Schmidt, please go on home and we'll let you know if we find her or learn anything else. We'll contact you. You can't be of any help here. Go home," the captain had dismissed her with a compassionate smile. Tina didn't have any surviving family. Myrtle was all she had.

After delaying her departure as long as she could, she finally disembarked and took a taxi home–where another shock awaited her.

Someone had burned up her trailer. As the taxi drove up in front of what had once been her home, there was only a blackened metal hulk sitting before her and mounds of smoldering rubbish around it that had once been her treasures.

She got out of the taxi and stood there frowning at the remnants of her life. "Holy moly!" she grumbled. "Not only is Tina fish food, it looks like I gotta get me a new home, too."

Then she climbed back in the vehicle and told the driver where else to go.

Chapter 5
Frank

Early Friday morning someone was banging on Frank's front door.

He'd gotten up before he usually did because he wanted to get in a whole day's writing so he'd have the weekend free to be with Abby, the kids, and to do a little housekeeping. He and Abby would spend the evening together at the family reunion and drive home later. It'd be a late night with the visiting and the trip back. Then he'd take Saturday, while Abby was working on the bakery renovations, to clean house and do his weekly shopping. Saturday evening he was having her over for a home cooked dinner. The weather was supposed to be warm, instead of chilly as it'd been all week, so he was planning on grilling steaks on the deck. Abby enjoyed barbequed T-bones.

It wasn't often they had a weekend alone so he was going to take full advantage of it. Before dinner they'd maybe go see a movie. Abby had been going on and on about this one film she wanted to see. It was a horror flick about vampires. It sounded acceptable, had had good reviews, so that was what they'd see, though he wasn't much for vampire films. Too bloody.

And Sunday before they had to pick up the children he thought a scenic drive out into the country to a nearby winery, with a picnic lunch, would be fun. He was looking forward to the weekend.

"Wait a minute, I'm coming!" he yelled as he made his way to the door. Whoever was on the other side was pounding on it like a mad person.

He opened the door and someone rushed in at him like a banshee. Myrtle.

"Frank! Someone killed my friend Tina. I need your help! Murder, it was murder!" The old woman was disheveled, her hair wildly disarrayed, her face agitated and she smelled like smoke. "She was there and then she wasn't! They say it was an accident, but I know better. Then I get home and someone's burned my house to the ground. It's nothing but black humps and ash. That's no coincidence I'm thinking. I–"

Frank took the woman by her shoulders and gently shook her. "Calm down, Myrtle. What are you talking about?" He guided her to the sofa and shoved her down to the cushions. "Start at the beginning."

And she did. She told him everything about the cruise and Tina's disappearance; her trailer's fate. She confessed what she believed had happened.

"I'm so sorry about your friend Tina," Frank said when she was done. "I'll call the cruise line, look into it and see what I can find out. I'll follow up on the situation."

"That's good of you. I'm devastated over what happened to her–if anything really has. If it has then it was *no accident*. Something's going on and I know you and Abigail can get to the bottom of it. My home being set fire to is part of it, too, I'd bet. It's a feeling I have."

"Have you called the police about your trailer yet?"

"No. I had no way to contact them. I don't carry those new-fangled cell phones around with me that everyone else has these days like some addictive talismans. Don't cotton to them and they cost too much. Lordy, they want a hundred dollars a month and you have to sign two year contracts. And in the end you end up talking more on them than you do to real people. No way to live if you ask me."

"Cell phones aren't new-fangled," he slipped in. "They've been around for a while."

"I know that." She sighed, rubbing her hands together. "I'm beat is what I am. I was up all night on that boat looking for my missing friend. I'm so upset and worried."

"About your trailer, could there have been bad wiring? Did you leave something on, like a space heater, when you left last week?"

"No. I'm always so careful. I turn everything off, even the lights and the heat. As you know it hasn't been that cold. But no matter," she shook her head miserably, "my house is *gone* but it can be replaced. I'll contact my insurance agent if you let me use your telephone and he'll take care of everything. I have copies of all my important papers with my lawyer. It's my life's keepsakes, love notes from my Oscar, photographs, and stuff like that, and my treasures I'm grieving over. It took so many years to gather them all. Now they're just grit and soot. Who would burn my place down?"

"We'll have to find that out." Frank had a thought who might have done it but kept it to himself.

"If I discover who did it, I'll burn *their* houses down. See how they like it. The creeps." Her face was flushed with indignation, her arms wrapped around her upper body. He'd seen that stance before. She was out for vengeance and blood and wouldn't rest until she got it.

He knew it was coming before she spoke, so he beat her to it. "Myrtle, you're welcome to stay here in one of my guest rooms until you get another place to live." She'd stayed with him, Abigail too, the year before during their last danger ridden exploit. His cabin was large and he liked having people in it. It wasn't a hard decision. She'd been an exemplary house guest, even if she'd eaten him out of house and home.

Her eyes went soft and she smiled for the first time since he'd let her in. "You're a saint, Frank Lester. A pure saint. My suitcases are outside on the porch. Good thing I had my best clothes and toiletries with me otherwise I'd have to run around naked."

"Yeah, a good thing." He tried not to think about Myrtle running around in her birthday suit. It was one image he didn't want bumping around in his head.

"I won't have to stay long, you'll see. I'll find another home quick as I can. I do have money, you know." This last was imparted with pride.

"Don't worry about it. You know you're welcome to bunk here as long as you need. My home is always open to you, Myrtle."

He handed her his cell phone and she made the call to her insurance agent. The conversation was brief. Myrtle didn't like talking on phones of any kind. When she was done she handed it back to him.

"I'm going to give the sheriff a call and report your house fire. He needs to know. Then I want to go over there to see the damage for myself."

"I'll come with you." Myrtle jumped to her feet. "Would you mind if we run by Tina's house first? Sometimes she does do cuckoo things and maybe, just maybe, she might have gotten off the boat without me seeing her and went on home? She was irritated with me because I wanted to stay in the lounge longer and she didn't. So I need to go to her place and see for myself."

Frank didn't hold much hope for the missing woman to be found at her house but he could understand how Myrtle needed that final confirmation.

"Okay. Let me bring your suitcases in and get them up to your room, the same one you occupied last time; call the sheriff and we'll go. If you need to use the restroom or anything, you know where it is."

Frank took her luggage to her room and while she was in the bathroom he telephoned Sheriff Mearl. For once the man was actually in his office and agreed to meet them at Myrtle's property in about an hour, which would give them time to go by Tina's first.

So much for writing that day, he thought. Yet he didn't mind. Real life always trumped the fictional life in his books. And tonight he was taking a road trip with Abigail. He could write tomorrow during the day. Of course living with Myrtle would be a distraction–she often was–but he could always retreat to his study in the basement and lock the door. It was soundproof.

Soon they were on the country road bouncing towards Tina's place in his truck. It wasn't far from Myrtle's. Frank wasn't surprised at that. He'd expected it, especially after what Samantha had told him at the newspaper on Saturday. The three old folks she'd interviewed about local vandalism also lived in the same area. Near Tina, Myrtle and the others. Frank wasn't absolutely sure what that meant yet, but he was now sure it was all linked in some way.

Tina's dwelling was a ranch style house

with dull siding, the shade of country blue that had been popular about twenty years before. It was a modest house, but it and its grounds were well tended and there were flowers sprouting everywhere because spring had at last arrived.

Myrtle knew where Tina kept her hidden key and after digging it out from under the flat frog rock, she unlocked the door and, not bothering to announce her entrance, barged in.

"Tina! You here? Tina!"

Inside, the house was silent and dark. It was a small structure with square rooms and sparse furnishings. There were large windows and brightly colored pictures on the wall. It was very tidy.

"Myrtle! Hold on a minute," Frank shouted after her. But the old lady was already gone, rooms ahead of him, yelling out for her friend Tina. He found her in a bedroom at the rear of the house, sitting on a bed covered in a gaudy quilt.

"She's not here." Myrtle's voice verged on despair. "I've been through the entire house and she's not anywhere; hasn't been here by the looks of it, either. No suitcases. Her purse isn't here and I know she wouldn't go anywhere without it. It was with her when she left the lounge last night." She looked like she was going to cry and he'd never seen the tough old bird cry.

Feeling awful for her, Frank put his arm around her birdlike shoulders. "I'm sorry, Myrtle. I know you were hoping she was here."

"I was praying," she whispered, gazing up at him, "and I'm not a praying woman." She rose from the bed and, after looking in the closet, hobbled into the living room where she collapsed on the couch. He sat down beside her.

"You know," she said looking around, "if you don't mind, Frank, I'd like to stay here instead of with you. Just for a short time. Just in case she comes home? That way I'll be here to greet her. You don't mind, do you?"

"No, no." He patted her hand understandingly. "You do what you want. Think about it first, though. We'll run back to my house and collect your suitcases before we meet the sheriff at your place and afterwards I'll drop you off here before I go home. But if you decide to stay here, I'd like you to keep in close touch with me. Call me if anything unusual happens or if you feel threatened in any way."

"Ah," her face lit up with comprehension, "because you don't think the fire at my house was an accident, do you? Or Tina's vanishing act?"

"I don't. Not with what's been going on around here the last few weeks."

"It's all part of the same story, ain't it?"

"It could be. And Tina's disappearance feeds right into my suspicions if you answer me the way I think you're going to answer me."

"About what?"

"Lately, did Tina mention anything about having any trouble here at the house? Were there any random acts of property defacement or strange incidents that had occurred? Anything that had frightened or unsettled her?"

Myrtle's face scrunched up in thought. "Now that you ask there was something. She said to me last week before we got on the boat she was happy to be leaving her house behind for a bit–something about hearing disturbances at night outside her windows and things going missing. She was afraid she was losing her mind and hoped the cruise would set her right again.

"Humph, she was dead wrong about that."

Frank took that moment to leave the couch. "Stay here, would you? I'm going to check out something. Be right back."

The basement. Frank found the door and descended into the lower level of the house, peered around, yet nothing seemed out of the ordinary. It was as neat as the upper floors, everything on shelves or in boxes. Everything in its place. No mess. He hadn't expected that, but after he thought about it more, it made sense. Tina had been taken care of in a different way, after all, hadn't she? Her house was untouched because she was no longer in it.

They got in his truck and drove back to his cabin where he got Myrtle's suitcases and then they went on to her place, or what was left of it. "How about you, Myrtle? Besides your trailer being burned has anything else out of the ordinary happened recently? Anything?"

"You mean my trailer being torched isn't out of the ordinary enough?" She was sitting in the seat next to him, her arms crossed over her chest and her eyes on the trees and fields speeding past them. Clearing her throat, she continued, "I've been thinking about that myself since you asked me the same thing about Tina."

She was silent for a moment.

"Well?" he probed further.

"Only thing I can think of is…well…I've had someone pestering me on the telephone a lot wanting to know if I'd sell my trailer and land. Sometimes it's a woman and sometimes it's a man. They've been persistent as hell. First time or two I listened and told them emphatically no…now when they call I just scream in the phone or hang up hard. I hate people bothering me on the phone like that." Her lips twitched up into a devilish grin. "They still keep trying, though. Usually when someone calls about buying my ten acres I only have to say no once and they leave me alone."

"You're a hard woman, Myrtle." To himself he thought the admission was right on point. "You get offers for your land often?"

"I have. Some over the years. I'll never sell. Not even now. It was the land my husband bought when we married and I plan to die on it, too. It has so many memories for me."

They'd pulled into Myrtle's driveway in front of her now scorched trailer. Wisps of smoke rose from the smoldering shell and the overpowering scent of burnt wood and metal was everywhere. There was also the strong stink of gasoline. Frank estimated the fire had been set sometime the day before. It was odd no one had reported it.

"Your trailer is gone. It's not livable at all. What are you going to do now?" Frank stared at what was left of it and then his eyes roamed the surrounding woods. Everything looked okay. No one lurking behind the trees spying on them. No one anywhere. The birds were in full voice among the leaves and they would have been squawking if there had been humans in the forest.

"I've been thinking on that. I'm going to go pick out one of those modular homes, buy it and have it hauled out here and put up. I'd like something larger, newer and prettier, than what I had before. I needed more space, and that trailer was too small anyway. Insurance should pay for most of it and I'll cough up the rest."

"Sounds like you know what you want."

"I do. I want to stay living here."

Myrtle got out of the truck and limped over to the trailer's steps that were still attached to the porch. Frank caught up to her and, putting out an arm to block her, had to keep her from going inside. "It's too dangerous in there Myrtle. You just have to accept whatever was in there–your furniture, clothes and personal items–aren't worth salvaging. I'm sorry."

"So am I. But don't feel bad for me, friend, I always bounce back. A trailer is just a trailer. Material possessions are just things and I still have my memories. Right now I'm more distressed by Beatrice's problems and Tina's disappearance. People are more important that things."

"That they are, Myrtle." He was anxious to pay a visit to the ship, after he talked to someone at the cruise line to obtain permission, poke around some and interrogate the captain. The boat wouldn't pull out of port again for a day or two while cleanup was going on, and until the next passengers boarded, so he had time.

They sat in his truck and waited until the sheriff's squad car drove up. They didn't have to wait long.

As usual Sheriff Mearl was courteous but unhelpful. So an old lady's beat up trailer had accidently burned down? In his mind there was nothing criminal about that. It wasn't worth much. The whole town thought of it as an eyesore anyway. Good riddance. "Probably bad wiring or you left something on. You were gone a whole damn week, Myrtle," the officer reminded her. "You have insurance?"

"Yeah." The old woman was glaring at the cop. They had history. She didn't like him much and never had and he felt the same way about her. He thought she was a public nuisance, thought she was half a sandwich shy of a picnic. It didn't help that Myrtle let him keep believing it by some of her bizarre actions. She enjoyed tormenting him.

"Then you're covered. No harm, no foul. It was falling apart anyway. Now your insurance will give you a brand shiny new one. And all the trash you had around it? It just saved you a lot of work and the trouble of getting a monster-sized dumpster."

Myrtle stomped off without answering him.

Frank made it a point to draw the sheriff aside and inform him about the other local disturbances and that he believed they were all connected in some way.

"You need to bulk up the patrols out here, sheriff. Possibly do nighttime stakeouts to catch whoever is terrorizing these old people."

"Now Frank, you and I both know it's probably only a bunch of bored teenagers doing their mischief at the old one's expense. It happens all the time."

"You believe it's only mischief? It's a lot more than that, Mearl. Property has been destroyed and elderly citizens have been terrorized and I don't think it's going to stop there. Mark my words."

"That's your take on this situation, Frank, but this is police business, not yours. Not anymore anyway. You're retired, remember? I advise you to stay out of it and let us handle it." The sheriff's glance was stern. Frank was tired of the man reminding him he was retired. Frank knew that. He couldn't help it he was always being sucked into the mysteries of the town and it was in his nature to solve them.

Frank could have argued with the man, but the two, like him and Myrtle, had never seen eye to eye much, either, so he let it go. No matter what he said the cop would go his own clueless way, like a blind cow in the middle of a highway. He always did.

When the cop left Frank drove Myrtle to Tina's. "You sure you want to stay here? It might be better if you were someplace safer. Like my house."

"Sure, I'm staying. I'm waiting for Tina. And, hey, my home was already burned up, what else can they do to me? Besides, the ghosts are everywhere. I can't escape them. Could be they set the fire. I wouldn't put it past them. Some of them are spiteful little creatures. So one place is as good as another. I ain't afraid of no ghosts!"

Frank almost laughed at Myrtle's eternal spunkiness. "If you have any problems, any at all, telephone me, you hear? And I'll be right over."

"I know that Frank. You go on home now and get ready for your night with Abigail and the kids. Go. Shoo."

And Frank went.

*****

At three o'clock Frank picked up Abigail, Laura and Nick and drove them to Sheila's house for the reunion. All the brothers and sisters had made it. The evening was fun, the food everyone had prepared was wonderful, and it was heart-warming to see the children together. Frank knew these gatherings helped assuage the guilt Abigail had over not being able to take all six under-aged Brooks children when their parents died. The other four children had been split up between the extended family, while Giles, the oldest at nineteen, had joined the army the year before.

At Shelia's Frank watched Laura and Nick interacting with their siblings, laughing and catching up on each other's lives. It was a lovely evening. It always was when the children were together. Because they lived apart, they rarely fought among themselves, had few of the usual sibling rivalries and were happy to see each other.

Later on in the evening he and Abigail stole some time alone, sitting on Shelia's covered deck as a spring rain drizzled in the darkness. Behind them they could hear the adults' voices conversing and the kids' giggling.

Frank caught her up on Myrtle's troubles, about her trailer burning down and Tina's vanishing act.

"You waited until now to tell me all this?" she exclaimed, her eyes on him. The deck was surrounded in solar lights, casting a soft glow. Shelia had a nice house. It was small but comfortable, and filled with love.

"I didn't want to discuss it in front of the kids and didn't want to disrupt the evening. There wasn't anything you could have done anyway."

"Poor Myrtle. I'll have to go over and see her tomorrow. I only wish she would have stayed with you instead of camping out at Tina's. She must be so distraught after everything and with her friend missing."

"You know Myrtle, she pretends nothing

fazes her, but we both know better. I also feel sorry for her. Losing her home, her collection of treasures stockpiled around it, and her friend at the same time, must be hard."

"Someone also set fire to her *treasures*?"

"Uh, huh."

"That's low. She's spent years gathering those things and the loss of them must hurt her," Abigail said. "Have you called the cruise line or spoken to the ship's captain yet?"

"I called earlier today and got the runaround. About what I expected. I'm going down to the ship tomorrow and have a look for myself before it leaves port the day after."

"You're searching for any overlooked clues to Tina's disappearance, huh?"

"I'm going to try. All these random things happening to our people in town scare me."

"Why?"

"All the people who have been affected are elderly and all are within a ten mile radius of each other."

"That's interesting, but where it ties into these incidents, I can't see."

"Yet, but you will. It's a pattern and I have one or two suspicions to what might be going on. Only time will tell if I'm right. I have a hunch the last pieces of the puzzle won't be long falling into place, either. Events seem to be escalating." Frank sighed, rose from his chair and strode to the edge of the deck to study the night. An owl was hooting somewhere and, far in the distance, dogs were barking. The evening, with the rain, was cool but not chilly as it'd been the last few nights.

That's when his cell phone rang. He unhooked it from his belt and answered it. "Myrtle?" A pause. "Slow down. What's wrong?" Another longer pause. "All right. Abby and I are still at Sheila's but we can be back there within three hours if we leave now. Okay." He flipped his phone shut, reattached it to his belt and turned around.

"I heard. Myrtle, huh? What's wrong now?"

"She says now Beatrice is missing. She went over to see how her friend was doing and found no one in the house. After losing one friend already, she's freaking out."

"I take it we're leaving?" Abigail rose from her chair.

"As fast as we can get out of here. I'm sorry. I know you wanted to visit with everyone."

"It's fine, Frank. Myrtle and Beatrice come first. I can visit more when we pick the kids up on Sunday evening. Let's say our goodbyes and get on the road."

Ten minutes later they were going out the door.

*****

"Where is Myrtle now?" Abigail queried when they were on their way.

"She's waiting for us at Beatrice's."

"Has she looked everywhere in the house for her?" Abigail sat beside him looking out as the night world went past them. With the warmer weather people had begun to emerge from their homes and businesses after dark, going places, seeing friends or strolling around. But tonight the rain had decreased their numbers and there weren't many out. And if they were they huddled under umbrellas or were wearing raincoats or water-proof jackets as they hurried down the streets and sidewalks.

"Everywhere but the basement...she refuses to go down there."

"That doesn't sound like Myrtle. She's usually so fearless."

"Except when it comes to ghosts. She said she heard mysterious noises below her and swears it's the ghosts. Arthur's ghost, to be precise."

"Oh," Abigail muttered, stretching out her legs beneath the dash. "The ghosts again. Those sneaky critters."

The rain had suddenly morphed into a curtain around them. Frank drove as fast as he could under the conditions because he was anxious to get to Beatrice's. Myrtle had sounded hysterical. Of course, if truth be told, she often sounded that way.

*****

The closer they got to Spookie the heavier the rain fell, and as they drove into the town's limits the fog snuggled up against the truck, curling around the tires. Ah, spring in Spookie. Fog central.

Beatrice's house was lit up like a shopping center.

"Well, looks like Myrtle has made herself at

home," Abigail said after they'd gotten out of the vehicle and were walking up to the door. The rain was drenching them so they dashed up to the entrance. "Should we knock?"

As an answer Frank grabbed the door knob, opened it and shoved through. "Myrtle, we're here!" he yelled and closed the door. No answer.

He and Abigail forged deeper into the house, dripping water as they went. Empty doll eyes stared at them from different surfaces, sitting on every piece of furniture as before, and didn't blink. Everything appeared as creepy as the last time they'd been there, except no Beatrice. The only occupants of the house seemed to be the dolls. Perhaps they'd killed their mistress?

"Myrtle, where are you!"

Myrtle appeared behind them. "Stop shouting, Frank. There's nothing wrong with my hearing, for heaven's sake. I heard ya."

"Sorry. Have you found Beatrice?" He wanted to also ask if Tina had shown up but already knew that answer. Myrtle would have told them already if she had.

"No, not hide nor hair of her. It's a mystery for sure. And after my house burning, the boat fiasco with Tina going missing, I've had my stomach full of them," she complained and slid around them into the living room.

"I'm sorry about Tina." Abigail laid a hand on Myrtle's shoulder. "And now Beatrice."

"Yeah," Myrtle replied, "I'm losing friends like ducks in a shooting gallery. It isn't natural."

"If you two ladies will excuse me," Frank

interrupted, "I'm going to have a look around. See if I can find anything that would help us locate the missing owner."

He left the women, Abby consoling her friend, and checked the upstairs first; every place he could think of where a batty old woman could be hiding. Beatrice hadn't struck him as completely irrational since he'd met her, close but not totally, but one never knew. She could have just wandered off somewhere.

Myrtle had been right, though. No Beatrice anywhere in the house. No notes. Nothing. Beatrice didn't drive any longer and she didn't have a car. So she couldn't have driven somewhere. Returning downstairs Frank strode through the living room towards the basement door. "Nothing or no one on the main floor or upstairs so last place is the basement. I'll be right back," he informed the women.

The basement was still a disaster area. Broken windows, glass and objects were strewn all over the place…and after a bit of searching he found a lifeless Beatrice sitting up against a wall in a darkened corner; partially covered in trash and old clothes. A life size dead doll. Her face was serene, almost happy. In her arms was the same Raggedy Ann doll she'd carried around when they'd been there last.

Frank's first thought was that the woman had come down there looking for her dead husband's ghost again and had had a heart attack or something, plopped down on the cement floor and died. Then he spotted the blood on the sides of her neck. He carefully reached his fingers behind her head and they came away covered in blood from a wound. Well, she could have fallen and hit her head. But he didn't think so. Someone had covered her in trash. His cop instincts were whispering *murder*.

And suddenly all the harassment, vandalism, so-called haunting occurrences and Tina's vanishing didn't seem so innocent any longer. It was as he'd suspected: something deadlier was going on.

He hated telling Abigail and Myrtle what he'd discovered beneath them but he did. Myrtle wanted to see her friend's body so, fortified with the two of them on either side of her, they descended into the basement.

"Someone killed her you know that, don't you?" was the first thing Myrtle said as she gawked at the corpse. "I talked to her before Tina and I went on our voyage and she was positive her dead husband Arthur was appearing to her for a reason. Sort of like a warning or something. She just didn't know what he was trying to warn her about, but she was really scared. Perhaps he was trying to tell her something, I don't know. But this, this isn't Arthur's doing. He loved her. He would have waited on the other side for her forever while she lived out the rest of her mortal life. He was never the kind of man who'd want harm to come to her.

"Someone alive did this to her." Myrtle's

eyes were glittering with unshed tears. She was attempting to be brave.

But Frank wouldn't have blamed her if she had burst out weeping and wailing. Losing two old friends in twenty-four hours couldn't be easy.

Abigail put her arms around her. "It's okay to cry, Myrtle. Go ahead. We won't think less of you, will we, Frank?"

"We won't."

As Abigail sat with Myrtle, Frank put in a call to the sheriff's department and reported the death. Soon police cars and an ambulance pulled up in the dark rain and the house was full of strangers and officers. Sheriff Mearl hadn't come out on the call. He'd gone out of town on a retreat for police officers, but he'd sent his second-in-command, Deputy Caruthers, a middle-aged man who'd been on the force for a decade and knew the town and its people well. He was an adequate cop and a fairly nice man, but not the smartest marble in the bag. They were questioned by him after the body was taken away. He didn't believe Beatrice had been murdered.

"She was an old lady," Caruthers reminded them. "She most likely fell and hit her head against the wall or tripped on all this junk and it fell down around and on her. I mean, look at this place." His disapproving eyes traveled the basement. "And she was a big time bona fide hoarder. Look at all this crap piled to the rafters. She wasn't right in the head. This was an accident and you have to see that, Frank. Hoarding killed her."

Frank didn't see it that way, but the deputy was adamant it wasn't murder, though Frank advised him of the other unexplainable happenings around town and Tina's cruise ship misfortune.

"It doesn't mean any of these things are connected, Frank," Caruthers drawled condescendingly. "Just coincidences, I'd say. Bad luck all around. Sorry."

But when the body was taken away and the officers abandoned the scene, without leaving crime tape anywhere, and allowing them to remain, Frank felt frustration at how cavalierly the death had been treated. Just because Beatrice was elderly didn't mean her fate should be less important than anyone else's. It made him angry.

"You should call Beatrice's son now," Abigail told him when the ambulance and the cops were gone. "He should know his mother is dead."

"Ha, like he would care." Myrtle's expression was doleful. "That boy hasn't been to visit Beatrice in years and she suffered from it. He was too busy with his family or his fancy high-paying job...making and spending money, is what. She used to wake up in the middle of the night, she confessed to me often enough, and lay in bed fretting over what she'd done so wrong raising him; why he didn't love, care about or see her. She adored that boy and his neglect broke her heart. She never stopped believing one day he'd see the error of his ways and become a good son to her. But it never happened and now it's too late.

"I wouldn't be surprised if he finds he can't squeeze in her funeral. He's too busy. He'll send a check and a bouquet of flowers and let the funeral home take care of everything. That's the sort of son he is."

Frank understood Myrtle was grieving over losing two friends so he didn't begrudge her her anger. Instead he found Beatrice's private telephone book and keyed her son's number into his cell.

He was taken by surprise after he told the son his mother was dead and the man broke out into genuine sobs on the other end of the phone. Who would have known? The son might have loved his mother, just not enough to show it to her when she was alive. Maybe now he'd feel the pain she'd been feeling all these years without him. It was just another one of the many sad stories of life.

Chapter 6
Abigail

Abigail stood at the kitchen window, cradling a steaming mug of coffee in her hands. It was nice, in a way, having the house to herself for the weekend. It was quiet. Though she missed the kids she knew they'd be home tomorrow so she cherished the time alone.

Snowball was trolling around her feet like a fur shark, begging to be noticed, food or both; purring loudly. The cat began meowing and Abigail set the cup down on the counter and scooped her up in her arms to snuggle her fluffy head. "I know, I know, sweetie pie, I've been ignoring you. I've been gone a lot and now I have to go meet Kate at the donut shop. Sorry. I promise I'll give you more attention when I return." She put the cat down on the floor and the animal nipped her on the ankle and, tail indignantly straight up which was the cat's way of showing displeasure, ran off.

Abigail couldn't resist one last look out the window. The spring day, the first truly warm one so far that year, with a slight breeze, was so beautiful. The trees and flowers were blooming and their perfume came in through the window and filled the house. Oh, she loved spring.

It was early Saturday morning and she was dressed and ready to go. Yet the events of the night before were still haunting her. She couldn't get Myrtle's stricken face or Beatrice's dead body propped up against a dirty basement wall out of her mind. It seemed unnatural on such a pretty day her mind would be so full of dark thoughts.

Everything that was happening made her uneasy. For over a year things had been calm in Spookie and she'd gotten used to a normal existence, loving Frank, raising the children and expanding her free-lance art career. Now her life was shadowed by all the horrible misfortunes befalling the town's old people.

What was really going on? She had her theories and so did Frank. And she was sure he was working on solving that puzzle. But she still had a job to do. Kate would be waiting for her. So it was time to go.

She left the house and because the morning was so nice, she walked into town. Passing Stella's Diner she spied her friend Martha at one of the front tables waving furiously at her through the window. *Come in. Come in.*

Abigail looked at her wristwatch. There was time to spare before she was supposed to be at the donut shop so she veered off the sidewalk and through the diner's doors. When she got near Martha's table she saw her friend wasn't alone. Samantha was there, too. They were eating waffles loaded with cherries and whipped cream on top. Waffles must be the morning's breakfast special.

"Good morning Abigail," Martha spoke up. Samantha echoed the greeting. They all smiled at each other. It was good to have friends.

"I can't stay long, girls," Abigail said right off as she lowered herself into a chair across from them. "Kate's expecting me at the donut shop in, oh, about twenty minutes. We have workmen to supervise, furniture arranging and color coordinating to do. I also have some sketches to show her for the wall artwork."

"Is Kate still expecting to open by June?" Samantha poured more syrup on her waffles. Her cup was empty and the reporter gestured at Stella for more coffee and smiled at the waitress when she refilled the cup. "Thanks Stella."

"You're welcome, Sam." Then Stella was on to the next table.

"As far as I know, she does. Take or give a week or so. I talked to her on the phone this morning before I came into town and she says everything's on schedule. She's excited the shop is coming along so well."

Stella had automatically brought another cup, placed it in front of Abigail and filled it. Abigail didn't have a chance to tell her she wasn't staying before the woman had scurried off again. "Thank you Stella!"

The coffee smelled so good, Abigail couldn't resist so she added milk, sugar and drank it. She had time to squander and it seemed as if Martha had something to tell her. One look at her friend's face and she knew that was true. Martha always got flushed when she had gossip to spread. Eventually, Martha would tell her what was on her mind.

"I can't wait until her shop opens," Samantha had gone on to say. "It'll be great to have a choice when it comes to baked goods. Actually, I welcome any new small businesses to our village. As a town we need to keep growing on some level or we'll just wither away; become a ghost town someday."

Abigail nearly choked on her coffee at the mention of ghosts, seeing that so many people were claiming to being haunted by them these days.

"Here, here," Martha agreed, flashing Abigail a sharp look. "I also think the town needs to keep expanding. We need to stay up with the times."

"Spookie?" Again Abigail nearly choked on her coffee.

"Yes, even Spookie. Hey, we're not doing too badly," Samantha interjected. "We have a new IGA and a couple of new residents. Now another new business. We're moving right along, if you ask me."

Yeah, moving right along at a snail's pace. Spookie still reminded her of the quaint English town she'd tagged it as the first time she'd seen it and she liked it that way. But as long as the businesses remained small and individually owned, she was for expansion, too.

"Not to change the subject," Abigail spoke to Samantha, "because I love the thought of the town growing and donuts as much as anyone, but I have some information for you; for the newspaper. It's bad news I'm afraid. Beatrice Utley is dead and Tina Thompson went on a cruise with Myrtle a couple days ago and is now officially missing. She disappeared right off the ship the last night out. Nothing has been seen or heard of her since. Myrtle's devastated."

"Oh, my!" Samantha's fingers went to her lips and her eyes widened. "It's getting worse then."

"What is?" Martha, expression startled, demanded to know.

"There have been a lot of unfortunate *incidents* occurring against our old folks here in town," Martha answered and then caught Martha up on them. "But I can't believe Beatrice and Tina are dead."

"Only Beatrice is dead. Tina is just possibly dead," Abigail amended. "The cruise line is still looking and hoping to find her, but it's been days since she went missing from the ship."

"Abigail, what happened?" Martha had put her fork down, had stopped eating.

Abigail repeated the story she'd heard from Frank and Myrtle about everything, keeping it as simple as she could. She hadn't yet processed it herself and Frank was still investigating, so she was careful what she revealed. It was all too fresh.

When Abigail had finished, Martha's face

was troubled, but there was a spark of comprehension in her eyes. "I'd already heard about the home harassment situation from my other realtor friends who'd been approached to sell some of the old one's houses. Quite a few are thinking of moving it's gotten so bad. What's going on? Who'd do these sort of things to old people and why?"

"We don't know, but Frank thinks he's uncovered a common denominator between the old people involved."

"And what would that be?" Samantha voiced, in reporter mode, as she leaned in to hear what Abigail had to say. She was probably taking notes in her head for the next edition.

"All of them live fairly close together within about a ten mile radius in an area out past Myrtle's trailer–which by the way, I almost forgot to tell you, was also set fire to while she was on the cruise with Tina."

"Oh, no! That's awful about Myrtle's trailer. A friend dead, one missing and now her wreck of a trailer is gone. A lot of bad luck for Myrtle," Martha contributed in a flat tone. "On the other hand, all the rest of what you're saying is kind of interesting." She lowered her eyes as her fork tore off another chunk of waffle.

Abigail knew Martha well enough to know she'd stumbled onto something. "How so?"

"Well, I've been hearing rumors for months now from some of my realtor friends there's some mysterious corporation wanting to construct something big on the outskirts of our

town. It's all hush-hush right now to what it will
be or where it will be and what it would mean to
Spookie. Some of us believe it's all smoke and
mirrors, rumors like always, but there are some
who see it as a possibility. Of course, that's the
last thing the town council wants. We like
Spookie the way it is. Small, eccentric and
charming. An IGA and a new donut shop are
fine, but I, for one and a lot more of our citizens,
don't want some huge mall or blocks of cookie-
cutter apartment buildings to ruin that. But the
rumors persist."

"Now that is interesting," Abigail repeated
thoughtfully. "Because both Beatrice, Alfred
and Myrtle had mentioned they'd been
approached recently by people pressuring them
to sell their land. Of course they all said an
emphatic no."

Martha looked up and met her eyes. "Hmm,
did you know Tina Thompson not only had a
house out in that vicinity but it sits on fifty
prime acres? The land's worth a small fortune."

"No, I didn't know that." But the revelation
was another small shock.

*Someone was terrorizing and possibly
killing the old people who lived out in a certain
area–and some mysterious corporation wanted
their land.* Wait until she told Frank what she'd
found out.

"I'd love to stick around, you two, and chat
more," Abigail concluded, coming to her feet,
"but I have to run. Got to get to work." In a
voice loud enough for the waitress to hear, she

called out, "Stella, can I please get two large cups of your great coffee to go? And the check?"

Stella acknowledged the order with a wave of her hand and bustled off to get it.

Then Samantha asked, "Abigail, can I stop by later, either at Kate's shop or your house and get more information on Tina's disappearance and Myrtle's trailer burning down? Anything else you might know about all this? I can include it in the article coming out this week."

"Sure, just call me. But I'll catch you up with things after I get done at the donut shop but before I head home. Frank and I have plans for the evening." She smiled. "Tell you what, I can just drop by the newspaper on my way out of town about three or so. Would that be okay?"

"Sure, I can be at the paper around three. After I leave here I think I'll go out and see Myrtle's crispy trailer and maybe have a chat with her in person. Ask about the cruise and Tina, too. Get some direct quotes."

"All right. She's staying at Tina's house for now. You know, in case Tina shows up? If you can't find her there, go to Frank's. He'd invited her to stay at his cabin until her lodging problem was solved, but she opted to stay at Tina's. But you know Myrtle, she likes Frank's cooking."

"Okay, I'll check Tina's house first and then Frank's. Thanks."

Stella sashayed over and placed two large paper cups on the table. "Four twenty-three is what you owe, sweetie."

Abigail thanked the waitress, paid for the coffee and headed to the door saying, "Bye Martha. Bye Sam. Catch you later," on the way out.

She was anxious to see Kate and what the shop looked like now.

*****

Kate was in the middle of a room filled with shiny new tables and chairs, positioning them, probably trying to decide where each one would go. The shop had been thoroughly cleaned up, the glass display cases for the donuts were in, new flooring had been put down; lighting fixtures had been put in. Everything gleamed. It didn't seem like the same place Abigail had been in the week before. It was beginning to look like a real business. All it needed now was the walls painted, pastries under glass, customers at the tables and buying things at the cash register.

"This looks great, Kate. It's so colorful, but cozy. I like it. This is going to be the hot spot to gather, slurp coffee and munch donuts."

"You should like it. It's your layout, the furniture and color choices you picked out." Smiling, Kate came over to her and Abigail handed her one of the coffees.

"That was sweet of you," Kate said. "Let me pay you for it."

"No, it's my treat. Next time it'll be yours." Abigail returned the smile and began helping the other woman move the table and chairs into the right configurations.

143

"Thank you. And it won't be long before I have freshly made coffee here. The machines and such are being delivered later today. So I'll be able to brew java myself. Thank goodness. I can't wait. I'm a coffee addict and not having it here to guzzle down every day has been hard. Not to mention the money I've spent getting it from Stella's every morning." Kate laughed softly but she looked tired. There were shadows around her eyes and she moved slower than the last time Abigail had seen her. The woman must have been working her behind off all week or perhaps her childhood injuries were acting up. But the shop did look good.

"Tell you what." Abigail sat down in one of the chairs and took a sip from her cup. "Let's take a minute and drink our coffee. You look like you're ready to drop. Besides, I have sketches to show you." She'd placed her portfolio on the table and now opened it. A flutter of nervousness coming like it always did when she first showed her sketches to a client; hoping they liked them.

Kate didn't argue but claimed a chair with a grateful sigh. "You're right. I do need a break. I've been at this non-stop for weeks and I am exhausted." She drank her coffee and instantly looked better. Then her head tilted down and her left hand began to rub her neck. "But, to tell the truth, my exhaustion isn't merely because of this shop and the work I've been doing to get it ready. It's my mom."

Abigail caught the frustration in the

woman's voice. "Your mom? That's Clementine Kitteridge, isn't it?"

"How did you know that?"

"Small town. Myrtle Schmitt, a dear friend of mine, told me. She saw me last week coming in to meet you and told me who your mother was."

"Oh, Myrtle. Yes, she's a very old dear friend of my mother's, too. I've always thought she was a little strange, with her quirks and her entourage of ghosts," here she smiled, "but she's good to my mom and mom loves her dearly."

"As we all do. I know Myrtle's a little odd but she's a good friend to have and smarter than most people think." She could have told Kate about Myrtle's recent troubles but decided not to. The woman seemed troubled enough. She'd tell her about it later. "What about your mom?"

Abigail waited for Kate to go on, yet the woman seemed hesitant to do so.

"Come on, you can tell me. If we're going to be friends you can trust me. Maybe I can help?"

Kate appeared to come to a decision. She straightened up in her chair and inhaled deeply. "You know, my mom's getting up there in years and she needs a lot of help. She can't live alone any longer. That's half the reason I moved back here. I've been gone for far too long and I have so much catching up in that respect to do. For years I've unintentionally neglected her and now I have to make that right. I'm going to take care of her. I go over there after I get done here and make her supper, help her with her bills, make sure she's taken her daily pills, watch television with her, and keep her company for the evening. I come back here," she glanced upwards at her loft apartment, "really late at night because she doesn't want me to leave. Thing is, my mom's scared. Someone's been playing cruel pranks on her. She's been hearing odd noises at night in her basement and there have been petty vandalisms at her house. Some of her windows have been broken and various things, furniture and her knick-knacks, have been moved around during the night. Some items have disappeared." Another deeper sigh.

"My mom thinks she's being haunted. Haunted...by *ghosts*." She shook her head.

"Ghosts?" Abigail's skin prickled. Not another one. "Why does she think it's ghosts?"

Kate dropped her face into her hands. It was an honest gesture of defeat. "Suffice it to say, it's a long story. But I can see Myrtle's hand in it. She probably told my mother it was ghosts and there you go. I don't want to muddle into it now, but I believe it's all in my mother's imagination. She's being haunted by the past, that's what. There are no such things as ghosts."

"Now you sound like my boyfriend, Frank. He doesn't believe in ghosts, either."

"Do you?"

She didn't answer right off, but looked away and then back. "Let's just say I'm ninety-nine percent sure they don't exist and leave it at that."

Kate nodded. "Well, I'm at one hundred percent.

"Anyway, spectral beings aside, the situation with my mother is wearing me out. Sometimes mom calls me in the middle of the night, terrified the ghosts are going to get her or she thinks someone is outside her kitchen window peering in at her. Once she called me at two in the morning and swore she was seeing green neon lights pulsating over her house. Says they're aliens. Sometimes she forgets and thinks my dead father and my dead siblings were taken by them. She's insists we go look for them and gets highly aggravated if we don't. Of course, we don't. It's one thing after another."

"You know," Abigail confessed gently, "Myrtle told me about your tragic family history. About your father and your siblings and the accident. I'm sorry for your loss."

"Don't be. It was ages ago. Ancient history. I just hate it that some weirdo is tormenting my mom like this. Why? She's a sweet lady and at her age and with her delicate state of mind doesn't deserve to be scared out of her skin every night. It makes me so *mad*." But when Kate raised her eyes to meet Abigail's they were tinged with worry.

That's when Abigail asked, "Out of curiosity, where exactly does your mother live?"

Kate's reply was what she'd been afraid it would be. Her mother lived in the same neighborhood as the others being bothered.

She knew she had to tell Kate what was

going on in her mother's neighborhood.

So she spent the next few minutes enlightening her and concluded with, "I know my retired cop boyfriend Frank will want to talk to you. He's looking into these incidents and he wants answers. He thinks they are all related. Don't be surprised if he shows up here tomorrow if not sooner to ask questions."

"Thank you for telling me this. It's such a relief to know my mother isn't totally off her rocker and making these things up. If this has been happening to other people, then it isn't just her. But on the other hand if it is happening to others it's a bigger problem. If someone is scaring, hurting or killing these people, I think I'd better move in with her to protect her. For a while anyway. I have a gun, I know how to use it and I will if I have to. No one is going to hurt my mother. You will let me know if Frank finds out something else on this, won't you?"

"I will." Abigail didn't say anything to Kate about the gun, but it made her look at the woman differently. The donut maker wasn't as helpless as she had at first thought.

Kate's coffee was gone, their break was over and the woman finally smiled. "Okay, now let me see those sketches you've brought. The painters are coming in Monday so the walls should be ready for your artwork by, oh, I'd say, Wednesday or Thursday at the latest."

"That'll work for me. I could have another commission by the end of next week sometime. An acquaintance of my realtor friend, Martha, wants me to paint a humongous picture of her house complete with the family members and their pets lounging outside it. She's got a husband, three kids and two dogs."

"Sounds like a big job."

"It will be. But her house is in town and it's old-fashioned, elegant, and gorgeously landscaped. There are weeping cherry trees on both sides. It's lovely. I'm looking forward to painting it. It'll make a stunning painting."

By then Kate was studying the sketches, her fingers sliding across the paper, the smile still on her lips. "Wow, these are great, perfect, and the colors are subtle but enticing. It was as if you read my mind. The donuts look so real. Good enough to eat."

"That's what I was aiming for."

Abigail spent the morning helping Kate do other tasks around the shop and then she went home. She was supposed to be at Frank's at four to make a five o'clock movie matinee but after the events of the last few days she wasn't sure they would be going to any movie. She didn't feel like it. They'd probably just stay in.

*****

Frank and Abigail sat on Frank's front porch in the twilight, their hands clasped between chairs. There was a splendid sunset and they were enjoying it. It was a warm evening, as warm as the day had been. No rain in sight. They hadn't gone to the movies. Neither one had been in the mood to, not with everything that had been going on.

Frank had spent the earlier part of the day on Myrtle's cruise ship, gently interrogating the captain and crew and going over Tina's last known movements on the boat.

The two were discussing her disappearance and what may have happened as the remaining rays of the sun lingered around them.

"The captain was cooperative but couldn't add anything else helpful to my inquiries," Frank disclosed as shadows partially hid his face. "No one saw or heard anything and Tina hasn't been seen since she left the lounge night before last. It was as if–poof–she basically vanished off the boat. If I had to make a judgment on what happened, I'd concur with the captain. Tina somehow fell overboard and drowned."

"Or was pushed." She felt a shiver up her spine even though it wasn't cold outside.

"Or was pushed."

Before she arrived Abigail had clued him in on the phone about what she'd learned from Kate. That Kate's mother was being persecuted, too.

"After you called me today and after I left the boat I also dropped by Clementine's," Frank had said over the supper he'd made them, "and attempted to speak to her about what she's gone through. But I'm afraid I didn't get much from her and even less of what I did made sense. She ranted on and on about roaming phantoms, men in suits coming to her door in the middle of the night, and couldn't remember what I'd asked her seconds after I'd asked. I'm no doctor but she definitely has late-stage dementia or something. She kept asking me where Kate was and who I was. I told her her daughter would be there soon and I didn't stay long. I'm not sure if anything she told me was true or not, not with her state of mind or lack thereof."

"Kate probably was there soon after. When I left the donut shop she was getting ready to go over to her mother's house. After she spoke with me she was eager to see her and make sure she was okay.

"You know if you'd like I could go with you tomorrow morning and talk to Clementine. I had a great-aunt with dementia when I was younger and I always found a way to get her to talk to me and make sense of what she said. I can listen to what she says and see what I come up with?"

"That's a good idea. I had the feeling the woman knew more than she was telling but was afraid. And I was almost a stranger to her. We'd met on the streets and at the town's functions before over the years but she didn't seem to remember me. And at first she was frightened of me. Before I left, though, I did check out the house and grounds and didn't see any damage of any sort anywhere. If someone wants her to move they aren't subjecting her to the same treatment as the others. Probably because her mind isn't there. Terrorizing her wouldn't do much good. Her mind is confused enough."

"Then tomorrow we'll visit her. I'll bring a coffee cake or something. Be a good neighbor.

That might put her at ease. I'll call Kate when I get home tonight and tell her what we're doing because I'm sure she'll be at her mother's house in the morning–if she isn't at the shop. If Kate's there perhaps Clementine will really open up."

"Another good idea. All right," Frank squeezed her hand, "operation friendly visit tomorrow morning. But I've provide the refreshments. The town bakery makes the best cheese cake. I'll pick one up on the way there."

"Oh, I know that cheese cake you speak of and it is heavenly. If anything can melt an old woman's heart and clear her cloudy mind, it should."

A breeze danced and sang around them as the light ebbed away. The dogs were barking in the backyard. They wanted out to roam free and be with Frank. But he had other ideas for the rest of the evening and the dogs would have to stay where they were.

After Frank gave her a kiss, she asked, "You said you had your own theories on what may be going on with the old people? Are you going to explain it to me now? Have you solved the puzzle yet?"

"I might have. As I've pointed out before: all the victims live in a ten mile radius, some are thinking of selling and moving, some stubbornly are not. The ones that don't want to sell are the ones being besieged. It's the properties. Someone wants their land and they want to scare the owners into selling and, in some instances, it's working."

"That simple?" She was shocked. The same solution had occurred to her but, for the life of her, she couldn't imagine any land or house being worth killing for. Some of the houses were not much more than shacks or run-down mansions which had seen better days. And Beatrice was dead. Tina could be as well. "You mean the awful things that have been done to the old people were calculated and coordinated?"

"Oh, it's not all that simple. Take Beatrice and Tina…they would never sell their homes or the land they're on. I know that for a fact. Probably that's why they're dead. The true mystery is why someone wants their land enough to torment and kill for it. I'm still working on that angle."

"Hmm, you know Martha said something to me the other day that might or might not play into that."

"What?" He'd moved their chairs closer together and his arm had slid around her.

"She said there have been insidious rumors going around in her real estate office for months that a private corporation wants to build a massive complex somewhere around here. It's been all hush hush, though. That coincidence seems suspect to me."

"It does to me, too."

"The thing is, there's available land everywhere, so why would they have to have our old people's land and why this particular section of land on the outskirts of Spookie?"

"There's not as much available land as you think, especially around here, away from big cities and prying eyes." Frank exhaled and rose from his chair. "But those are important questions I'd also like to get answers to. And I'll let you know when I do. I have a friend in the Naval Intelligence Service, NIS–Charlie Bledsoe–who is really good at uncovering those sorts of answers. I'll give him a call first thing tomorrow morning before we visit Clementine and see if he'll look into it."

Abigail laughed. "You *always* have a *friend* you can call."

"It's true." His tone was playful. "I have many friends. Isn't that what life's about? Friends, family and...lovers?"

This time when he kissed her there was no need for further words. They went inside and closed the door. Having a weekend, having two nights, to themselves was a gift they never squandered. On those occasions she often spent the night with him. After two years their love affair had matured into a committed relationship. And she knew her dead husband Joel was smiling down on her, pleased she'd finally found love. That was the kind of man he had been. He'd want her to be happy.

Abigail wondered what she'd do when Frank asked her to marry him because she supposed it'd be soon. It was her woman's intuition. She had the children, but Frank loved them and they loved him, so no obstacle there. They could be a family. One day.

*****

"I've never seen the fog so thick this late into the morning." Abigail was gazing out Frank's kitchen window the next day. It was ten o'clock and they were eating the breakfast she and Frank had made together; both still in their pajamas. He'd fried the bacon and eggs and Abigail had made the toast and squeezed the fresh orange juice.

"It is unusually thick, isn't it?"

"It's like pudding. I can't see past your deck. There are only muted orbs of light bouncing around out there in the yard. It's spooky, but sort of pretty."

"Here in the woods it's often like this. The fog closes around my cabin like night. It feels as if I'm all alone in the world." Frank took her hand, the one she wasn't using to eat with, and brought it to his lips, lightly kissing it.

Abigail smiled at him. The night they'd spent together had been perfect and in some ways she didn't want it to end. But it was Sunday and they had places to be, people to see. Then that evening they had to go pick up the kids and it'd be life back to normal.

They were done with breakfast when Abigail's cell phone, on the table beside her, rang.

It was Myrtle. "Abigail, I'm at Clementine's house—just dropped by to check in on her because now after Tina going missing and Beatrice coming up dead I'm worried sick about all my friends—and she's not here. She's not anywhere. I've looked. Upstairs, downstairs. Well, everywhere but the basement. I won't go down there, no way. Clementine told me often enough that's where the spooks congregate so I stay out of there. But I yelled all over for her and no answer. Oops, another one missing!"

"*Oh no.*" Abigail gave Frank a horrified look. "Myrtle, is her daughter Kate there?"

"No. No one's here but me." The old woman hesitated and then jumped back in. "I ran into a glob of phantoms in the fog on the way over here. There's more than usual and you know what that always means? Trouble. They were hiding behind the trees observing me with their sly ghostie eyes. They're up to something I'd bet my next social security check on it. And I might have seen Clementine with them. I'm not sure, though, because I couldn't get close enough to her. Or it. You gotta come over pronto. Something's not right here. We got to look for Clementine."

Frank stopped eating and murmured, "What's happened?"

She moved the phone away from her mouth and whispered, "Now Clementine is missing." She brought the phone back to her ear.

"I'm at Frank's. We'll be right over, Myrtle. Don't go anywhere, you hear?" But Myrtle had already hung up.

"Well, this running over to help a distressed Myrtle is becoming quite a habit, huh?" Abigail said to Frank as they got up from the table.

"It is, and I don't like it one bit. There's too

many missing and dead people for my liking. We better go, though."

"Yes, we better."

They dressed and drove over to Clementine's. Frank had looked her address up in the local telephone book and found it was, of course, in the same area as the others. Later she would peer out of one of Beatrice's rear windows and see Clementine's tan roof across the field. That close. The house was a box style with a second story stacked on top and it was surrounded by stately maple trees. Its green paint was flaking and some of the wood beneath was rotted and cracked. It had a long porch spanning the front and worn-looking shutters on the windows. It could have used some work. A lot of work.

As they were coming into the driveway Kate drove up as well. The three of them met at the front door, which was standing wide open.

"What's going on?" Kate stared first at the open door and then at Abigail. "What are you doing here?"

"Hi Kate," Abigail spoke first. "We just got a call from Myrtle from here. She said your mother was missing and she's not anywhere in the house. So we came right over."

"We?" Kate's eyes were on Frank.

"Kate, this is my boyfriend, Frank Lester. He lives in Spookie, he's an ex-cop, and since we've been looking into a rash of older people in this area being hassled, he came with me." Abigail didn't mention the murders.

Kate acknowledged him with a bob of her head and shoved through the doorway into the house. "Mom! Mom!" she shouted as she made her way through the rooms. "Where are you? It's all right, if you're hiding somewhere, but please come out now. These are my friends and they won't hurt you."

No response. The house and the ghosts were silent. Kate ran upstairs and as the Abigail and Frank waited in the kitchen, she searched the top floor. Her frantic footsteps could be heard above them.

Abigail swung around and there stood Myrtle. "Where did you come from?"

"I was outside the back door there in the yard," she jerked a thumb in the direction behind her, "searching for Clementine. But the darn fog is so thick I couldn't see a thing. And there's no way I'm going into the woods around the house hunting for her when there's so many ghosts out there lurking, ready to pounce on me.

"I'll leave that part of the deal up to you young ones. Just be careful of the spooks…they're on the warpath today for some reason." The old woman's head bobbed on her skinny neck. Her hair, on top of her head, was a riddled with bobby pins and her polka dotted dress had smears of dirt down the front of it. She'd been rambling around outside all right. She hobbled to a chair and dropped into it with a weary sigh. "I'm taking a rest for a minute."

Abigail asked her about Tina and the doomed cruise while the three waited for Kate to return. Grief glimmered in the old lady's eyes as she talked about her missing friend and there was desperation in her voice when she spoke of Clementine. "What's going on in this town with the old people anyway?" she inquired petulantly. "They're being haunted, tormented or they're disappearing like chocolate eggs at Easter. Someone or something is doing this. We have to stop it!" She glared at Frank and Abigail and slammed her small fist on the table. The salt and pepper shakers jumped.

"We're trying," Frank assured her.

"You got any leads?" Myrtle demanded.

"Not exactly. But I do have a couple of possibilities I'm looking into."

"Just be sure to keep me updated if you find out anything for sure." The fierceness in her eyes was finally the old Myrtle again. "Right now we need to find Clementine, right?"

"Right," Frank said.

Kate's footsteps were heard coming downstairs and she stumbled into the kitchen. Shaking her head, the expression in her eyes were one of growing alarm. "Mom's not up there and her bed hasn't been slept in. As befuddled as she's become, she still religiously makes her bed every day." She collapsed into a chair. "We should start looking around outside, huh?"

"We should." Abigail scooted her chair closer to Kate's and touched her shoulder lightly. "Don't worry, we'll find her."

"Hi Myrtle," Kate murmured, her eyes

barely flicking across the old woman.

"Hi there, Kate. Like Abby said, don't you worry. We're going to find your mother. These two," she cocked her head at her and Frank, "have a real knack for finding missing persons, criminals and murderers. I have faith in them and you should too."

"Criminals and murderers?" Kate repeated, eying Myrtle as if she'd uttered something bizarre.

"I'm not saying your mother's been murdered or nothing. She's just up and disappeared like Tina. But Frank and Abigail here will get to the bottom of it, you'll see. They're the best."

"Where's the basement?" Frank interrupted, and Kate pointed to a door on the opposite wall. He walked over, opened it, and descended into the darkness.

Kate's anxious eyes fell on Abigail. "I knew I should have spent the night, after what you'd told me, that is. But I worked overtime at the shop, was exhausted, and called her really late. She seemed fine. Even clear headed for once. So I thought it was all right. I thought me moving in this morning would be soon enough. My car out there in the driveway is packed with my clothes and things. Now I feel terrible. If anything has happened to her…." Her voice had become frantic. "*Where is she?*"

Abigail thought of Tina and the cruise ship and didn't want to give the woman false hope. "We're going to search high and low for her.

160

We'll try to find her." That is if she was anywhere to be found.

Frank returned from the basement. "No one's down there. It's a normal a basement as I ever saw. Your mother liked things in order."

"That she did," Kate agreed, a faint smile on her lips. "Or she used to. Lately, the disease has changed her. Some days she's herself and some days she's not."

"Unlike the other old people's houses nothing has been disturbed down there," he reported to Abigail. "Or anywhere else apparently. This isn't like the others. It's different. Now we have to figure out why.

"Let's look outside before we call the police, though."

"Good idea," Abigail concurred.

"After you all poke around out there in the pea soup," Myrtle came out with, "you think we could get some kind of lunch or something? I'm starving."

"I'll fix you something after we get done wadding through the pea soup," Kate bantered back at her with a restrained smile.

"Nah, don't bother, child. I know this house well. Your mom and I go way back. I know where she keeps the sandwich stuff so if it's okay with you I'll just make me a sandwich while you all are gone."

"It's okay. You're welcome to whatever you find."

The three exited the house, leaving Myrtle to forage in the refrigerator, and searched in different directions, shouting out Clementine's name as they went. The smoky haze clung to the ground, trees and bushes and made it difficult to see ten feet ahead or around them, so they kept in constant touch with each other with their cell phones.

"Damn, how are we going to find anyone in this mist," she grumbled to Frank on her cell after they'd been hunting for a while out in the woods. Days before Easter, spring was leisurely slipping into summer, and the days had become warmer. She was sweaty and tired of traipsing around in the woods, tripping over dead branches she couldn't see, attracting cockleburs, early season bugs and scratching up her exposed skin. Yet she was desperate to be sure Clementine wasn't lost out there so she pushed herself and kept looking. They all did.

They didn't find Clementine.

An hour or so later they were in the kitchen and Frank was calling the sheriff's department. Again. "Oh, Mearl's going to just love this. Another missing old one. Another unsolved crime. It means he might actually have to do his job."

"Or we will," Abigail voiced, meeting Frank's gaze.

"Or we will," he whispered back.

Kate sat at the table, looking lost. She didn't cry but Abigail could see she was on the verge. She kept getting up and going to the windows or pacing the kitchen like a trapped animal.

Myrtle had made a plate of bologna and

cheese sandwiches and a pitcher of iced tea for them. She urged Kate to eat something and hovered over her as if she were her own child. Abigail thought she was being really sweet. For Myrtle.

"I don't know if this means anything," Myrtle mouthed around a sandwich as she sat next to Kate, "but Clementine telephoned me, oh, about twelve-thirty last night–I'd called her from Tina's earlier, gave her the number, and let her know about Tina's vanishing–and she was a scared wreck. She was babbling all manner of nonsense. She declared there were scary noises outside her house and men in black, or some such thing, roaming around shouting out her name. She said her husband and children's ghosts were speaking to her from the basement. She asked me to come over. Of course I couldn't that late. The forest phantoms were out, the fog was already rolling in and who could see a foot before their own eyes? Ha! I couldn't.

"Anyway, I told her to stay inside and not– for anything–go out. Those crafty eyeless wraiths would get her for sure. She seemed to listen, said all right and hung up. I called her again around four a.m. or so but got no answer. I scurried over here as soon as the sun came up. Too late, though. I *told* her to stay inside, I did. But I suppose she didn't listen. Sorry, Kate." Myrtle dropped her head in shame for a second, then she popped up from her chair and began rummaging through cabinets looking for goodies, as she called them. "I got to have chocolate. It reduces my stress, you know, and right now I have a ton of it."

"Spooky noises…men in black," Abigail echoed. "I wonder what Clementine meant by that?"

"If she meant anything at all." Frank stood up and went to answer the door. Sheriff Mearl and one of his deputies had arrived. It occurred to Frank the sheriff was supposed to be on a retreat of some kind. Either he'd come back early because of the escalating situation, he'd never gone in the first place or Frank had been fibbed to the other day when the dispatcher had said the sheriff wasn't reachable.

After they conferred with the officers the search began in earnest. The sheriff called in all available deputies and, even with the fog, dispatched them to comb the woods around Clementine's house and the surrounding neighborhood. They also checked unlocked outbuildings and garages, knocked on doors and asked if the residents had seen or heard anything. Frank, Kate and Abigail, until she had to go pick up the kids, helped.

The day dragged on but by the end of it Clementine was still missing.

And worse, later, Frank called her cell phone with an update, and told her that during the neighborhood search he also discovered Alfred still wasn't home. He knocked and knocked and, again, Alfred didn't answer.

"Where could he have gone in this fog and in his bad health?" Abigail had quizzed Frank, cradling her cell phone against her ear as she spoke with him. She was on the road returning with the kids who, exhausted from their weekend, were dozing in the front and back seat. She was glad they weren't overhearing what her and Frank were discussing. They didn't need to be bothered with it. It'd only upset them, especially since the ordeal with their missing father the year before, who ended up dead at the hands of a killer, was still too fresh in their minds.

"I don't know," Frank had replied. "But, as the other night during the storm when I checked up on him, I can't see him out stumbling around in the forest when he could barely walk the last time we saw him. So it's a possibility Alfred, too, is missing and has been since the night of that storm."

Neither one of them said anything to that. There wasn't anything really to say.

That's just great, Abigail fretted after she'd hung up. She had to watch the road. She was coming into the city limits and the fog, true to form, was thickening around her. *Just great. More missing old people. Now she had more of them to worry over.*

Where were they?

Chapter 7
Frank

Frank aided in the search for the rest of the day until it grew dark. But Abby needed to leave early to pick up the children from their cousin's house because they had school the next day and the round trip took time.

He was uneasy about Alfred's absence. He'd been the one to knock on the old vet's door and after a long time without an answer he'd gone in anyway. A detail he hadn't told Abby or Sheriff Mearl about because he'd had no right to waltz into another's person's house without permission, but he couldn't help himself. The house was unlocked and, after exploring every room, he found the place empty. There was a half-eaten meal on the table and the television had been on as if the man had only stepped out for a moment. It had been strange.

Alfred rarely went anywhere and never that close to dark. He'd told Frank that himself. His nineteen-seventy-six truck was an unreliable heap parked in the middle of his yard and Alfred tried not to use it unless he had to. He walked or hitch-hiked a ride with a friend most destinations, or had until recently before his health and his legs had begun to fail. A monthly foray into town to bring back supplies was usually the most he used his truck. When Frank visited, the rusted red jalopy was parked in the yard among the other junk, but Alfred was nowhere to be seen. Oh, where was the old coot? Only time would tell. But as with Tina, that answer didn't satisfy Frank.

As he'd told Abby, now they might be looking for two missing people.

The night fell and the search for both old people went on. As frail as both Clementine and Alfred were, time couldn't be wasted. But when the following morning dawned the missing were still missing.

Frank dragged himself home when he couldn't keep his eyes open and his body moving any longer. Abby had called him late the night before for an update on her way home and he'd hated telling her the bad news.

"Should I come back and help?" she'd asked.

"No, we have plenty of people beating the bushes for them. You should stay there with the kids. Get some rest. If Clementine isn't found, though, you might give Kate a visit tomorrow morning. She's going to need a friend and you seem to fill the bill lately since she's still so new in town."

"I'll do that. I felt so bad for her today. She's already lost so much and now this."

Frank knew she was referring to Kate's dead

family. Having grown up in Spookie, he was well aware of her childhood tragedy.

After he'd spoken to Abby he had rejoined the search party and the night had gone on. Then he'd driven home as the new day had begun.

Outside the cabin the sun was shimmering, predicting a balmy day. The fog, which had persisted for most of the night, was finally evaporating. He was tired and, at the least, needed a nap. He wasn't as young as he'd once been so all-night activities didn't come as easily or their aftereffects leave as quickly.

Before he went to bed he put in a second call to his naval friend Charlie but was only allowed to leave another message. He was still attempting to get a hold of the man, but Charlie could be occupied with a case or out on a mission. The intelligence service kept him busy. It was frustrating. He would have liked the man's input, his help, or both. There was a reason for what was happening and Frank would have liked Charlie's take on it. The man was good with conspiracy situations, plus he had contacts that might shed some light on the corporation behind it all. Well, he'd just have to wait, be patient. Charlie, if he was available in any capacity, would get back to him when he could. He wasn't the sort of man to ignore a friend's request for help.

Frank had always been able to get by without much sleep, so he rested for four hours and then was out again with the others hunting for the lost old lady and absent veteran. One of the sheriff's deputies, because Frank had asked him to, had also gone out to Alfred's house. The old man still hadn't come home.

The search for both of them continued.

In the middle of the third day they found Clementine, or her body. It appeared she'd tumbled into a steep, rock lined ravine and the fall had killed her. It *appeared*, but Frank didn't believe it for a second.

"Yep, looks like she left her house and went wandering–as a lot of elderly with Alzheimer's do–got lost in the fog and tripped over something," Sheriff Mearl pronounced complacently. "No crime here. Just another accident. The fall killed her. It looks like her neck is broken."

Frank wasn't as sure. It felt too easy after the others' misfortunes. Too convenient.

"Are you going to have the ME do an autopsy?" Frank got the sheriff aside and inquired.

"Why? It's easy to see what happened. No reason to put her daughter through all that. I'm not requesting one. As far as I'm concerned this was an accident. Case closed."

And nothing else Frank said about the matter could sway the sheriff. It was frustrating to Frank not to be able to force the issue, but he didn't have the authority. So as desperately as he wanted an autopsy on Clementine, he knew he wasn't going to get it. He could ask Kate to request one, but he had the feeling she wouldn't agree to it. She'd want her mother, considering her age and her illness, to go to her grave as she'd lived her life: her corpse not desecrated.

After the ambulance collected the body and was on its way to the morgue, Frank walked back to Clementine's house to deliver the bad news.

Abby was there with Kate and had been all morning.

It was difficult telling Kate her mother had been found lifeless at the bottom of a ditch but he did it. He didn't tell her everything, though. He didn't tell her he believed foul play had been involved, no matter what the sheriff was telling her. He couldn't do that to her in the same moment she'd found out her mother was dead; time enough for that later after he investigated it further. She cried and Abby was there for her. They both tried to be. True grief is something that can't be shared and Frank felt dreadful for the woman. She'd returned home to be with her mother and now her mother was dead.

"I guess I have a funeral to plan," Kate monotoned, sitting in her mother's kitchen, staring at the cheery curtains fluttering in the open window's breeze. She looked awful. There were circles under her eyes and her face was puffy from weeping. "Oh, I knew one was coming, just not this soon. My mother has been sick for a long time. Before her mind got too muddled she was considerate and farseeing enough to purchase one of those pre-arranged burials. All the details have been taken care of so I won't have much to attend to. As if she'd had a premonition of her own death, she showed me where the paperwork was last week. All I have to do is hand it over to the funeral home director."

"I'll go with you," Abby offered. She'd been at the table drinking coffee with her friend and waiting for news.

"And I'd be grateful if you did."

"If you two have that in hand, I'll go home now." Frank was leaning against the sink where he'd been since he'd come in. "Because I can't keep my eyes open."

"Go home," Abby had told him. "We can handle this from here." Her eyes on him were sad. "Maybe we'll need you later for something or other and we will need you rested."

He nodded. "Just call me."

Before he left he faced Kate. She was crying but trying hard to keep it all together. There were things to do now and she had to do them…for her mother. "I'm so sorry for your loss, Kate. I didn't know your mother well, but she was respected and liked in town by many people. Spookie is a good place to live and you can count on us and the town standing behind you through all of this. You're not alone."

Kate wiped her eyes again and gave him a brave smile. "Thank you, Frank. That means so much to me. You and Abigail being here for me means a lot, too. Thank you both."

He kissed Abigail goodbye and murmured in her ear. "How about after I get some sleep you meet me for supper at Stella's about six or six-thirty? My treat. Ham and beans today and I try not to miss that. Do you think the kids can be trusted to be left on their own for an hour or two?"

"I believe Laura can handle Nick for that long. She's old enough. And I have left-over stew in the fridge they can have for supper. Okay, I'll meet you around six at Stella's. If Kate and I are done, that is."

He glanced at Kate and directed his next words to her as well. "And of course, Kate, you're also invited for supper at Stella's. My treat. If you haven't eaten there yet, you'll be glad you did."

"I don't know." Kate's eyes misted up again. "I have so much to do–"

"No matter how much you have to do, you have to eat. Come on, let me do something nice for you. Now that you're going to be one of our neighbors and a town business owner to boot let me welcome you officially to our town. This is the time you need friends. You shouldn't be alone."

"All right. Supper it is. That way I can stop by my bakery later to check up on some things. No matter what is going on in my private life, how devastated I am by my mother's unexpected death, I still have to make a living and pay bills. The bakery needs to open on schedule or I'll lose everything. All my life's savings."

Grief clouded her eyes, she did a slow inhale of breath as if pulling herself together and forged on, "I need to go to the funeral home first. As to her wishes, she wanted to be cremated. She wanted a simple funeral. A one day viewing and an informal get-together at the house here afterwards for her friends who are still living. I'll be honoring her requests, though I'm not sure how many people will show up at the funeral home or here. Mom has outlived her family and most of her friends, except Myrtle and a handful of others; most of them are now housebound. I'm all that remains of her immediate family."

"I'll see you both at Stella's." Then Frank left and went home to sleep. His head hadn't hit the pillow before he was out. It'd been a hard few days and he had the suspicion there'd be more ahead. Because instead of Clementine's death being the end he had the uneasy feeling it was just the beginning.

*****

When he woke it was after five o'clock. He showered, shaved, and drove into town. But Abigail and Kate weren't at Stella's. They were probably still at the funeral home. Things must be taking longer than they'd thought. He almost called Abby but decided against it. If she wasn't there meeting him for supper she had a good reason. He'd find out later what it was. In the meantime he could get some coffee and catch up on any other gossip there was going around because Stella's was the place to do it.

He ordered the special of the day. Stella's grandson, the cook in the back, made the best ham and beans he'd ever had and much better than his own. One day that boy would have to give him the recipe, but the kid guarded it like a pit bull guards a bone.

Frank saw the boy, baseball cap slammed down on his unruly blond hair and his body almost too big to fit the space he was in, peek out from behind the partition behind the counter and he waved at him. The kid waved back. He'd graduated from high school the year before and had officially become the full time cook for his grandmother. Frank hoped he'd never leave. Stella's distinctive cuisine wouldn't be the same without him.

The diner was filled with his friends and neighbors so he didn't feel lonely. Some of them stopped by his table as he was eating and they shot the breeze. He spread the sad news that Clementine was dead, but didn't go into the details. No one needed to know that the woman's death was suspicious. It was enough that she was dead. He knew the word would soon spread like wildfire. It always did in Spookie.

Sitting there chatting with his friends he once more felt grateful he'd moved back to his hometown when he'd retired from the Chicago Police department. He was comfortable in Spookie, respected and accepted. He lived in a beautiful cabin in the woods, had a good life, and a woman he loved. Five years ago, alone and still grieving over his dead wife, he never would have imagined it. He was a lucky man and he knew it.

If only people would stop ending up missing or dead around him. Though he was no longer a homicide detective, it seemed that particular curse had followed him into retirement.

When Stella cleared away his plates and poured his final cup of coffee he spied Martha sweeping into the restaurant. She was dressed in a blue power suit and was wearing heels. A flashy and expensive looking leather handbag hung on her arm. Her brunette hair was upswept into a bun with one of those large sparkly barrettes holding it in place. Her face had been made-up to impress with eyeliner and a shade of flame-colored lipstick she usually favored. She was dressed for success and must have been showing someone a house or would be. To this day the woman amazed him; she was a dynamo and had more energy than any other person he'd ever known, but she was also an old and true friend to both him and Abby. He gestured at her and she made a beeline for him like a dart to a board.

"Well, Frank, on your own today, huh? Where's Abigail?" She smiled as she lowered herself down across from him. She plunked her purse down on the table and it took over half the surface. Good thing Stella had cleared it off. As he had so many times before, he wondered what Martha had in her purse that made it so big and fat. One day he'd have to ask her.

"She's probably still with Kate Greenway at Dashner's Funeral Home."

Instantly Martha's face reflected compassion. "No! What's happened? Who died?"

Frank told her. He divulged Alfred was most likely missing as well and confided to her some of his suspicions.

"Oh, no, that's so sad. It's a shame, about Clementine and all, especially with Kate recently moving back here to take care of her. I'll have to be sure to visit the funeral home tomorrow and pay my respects. Clementine was a grand old lady, last of her kind, if you ask me. When she was younger she used to read a book a week, sometimes two, I recall, and she could debate any man into the floor on current events and social issues. She was so smart.

"She had a tragic life, though, with her family dying and then with the dementia taking away that brilliant mind of hers. Such a brave woman." Martha cocked her head, her coffee-brown eyes overflowing with sympathy. "Poor Kate. Poor Clementine. Poor Alfred, if he's truly missing, too.

"Though you do know he's famous for his nomadic tendencies? They say he sometimes disappears for days, you know? He's like one of those nature men who love to be out in the wild communing with the squirrels and the birds. He's been like that ever since he returned from Viet Nam decades ago. The trauma of the war made him crave the peaceful tranquility of the countryside. So he may not be missing at all, merely hiding from people."

"You don't say?"

"Uh huh. So I wouldn't take it too seriously he wasn't home the last few days. He'll show up eventually, mark my words. He used to come into town quite often and ramble about. I've seen him, lurking in the alleyways and peering into store windows. He especially likes to do that around holidays. Alfred's like a child, drawn to the whimsical decorations in the shop windows. Don't worry about him. He'll show up."

"But when I saw him last he said he wasn't getting around all that well lately, leg problems, and he said he was ill. He looked ill."

She fluttered her hand at him. "Ah, he always complains about one ailment or another, believe me, he still gets around just fine. I saw him in town only a week or two ago, aimlessly meandering down the sidewalks."

What she said calmed his anxieties some. Could be Alfred wasn't missing, but wandering around somewhere, as she said.

"Since you're here, Martha, let me ask you something."

"What?" She was signaling Stella to come over and when the waitress did she ordered a meatloaf sandwich and potato salad. Frank waited to ask her what he wanted to ask until Stella bustled away after collecting the order.

"Abby said you mentioned something to her last week about rumors you've been hearing of some secretive company or corporation buying up a huge plot of land somewhere around our town. Heard any fresh stories lately in that vein?"

"Funny you should ask. Ryan was saying last night some private company has been buying up land right on the town's limits. Land with or without homes on it. They're paying outrageously high prices, too. He's in heaven over the commissions he's been earning."

That snagged Frank's attention. "You don't say?"

"I do say. But Ryan thinks it's strange because the land is basically useless because it's scrub, hills or soil eroded gullies. There is shifting sand beneath the dirt so the soil's unstable. It's not good for growing, building on or much or anything. But it's his job so he's making the sales and chortling all the way to the bank."

"Any of this land been purchased from elderly people?"

"I don't know that. I only know what Ryan told me and it's what I just said. I, myself, haven't been part of the bonanza. It's Ryan's baby, although I'm jealous as all get out. I wish my commissions were as large as his have been lately with these sales. Lucky stiff." She pursed her rosy lips and openly sulked. Martha was extremely competitive when it came to her job.

"Could you show me on a map where this plot of land is located? The one being bought up?"

"Sure. On the map in my office I can point it out easily enough. Let me eat my sandwich first.

I've been showing houses all day and haven't had a chance to get in a meal. My hungry stomach won't leave me alone until I fill it."

Frank could wait.

Stella had delivered her supper and Martha was forking potato salad into her mouth. "Best potato salad in the county," she muttered approvingly between bites.

As Martha ate, Frank had another cup of coffee and the two friends talked about the worsening situation with the old people. A lot of it surprised her.

"You better be careful investigating this Frank. As you do, I have the gut feeling something isn't kosher. Everything you've told me sounds real suspicious."

"I'm always careful, nonetheless I promise to be extra cautious. I'm keeping my investigation discreet and not many people know about it. Me, Myrtle, and Abby, is all so far; a naval intelligence friend named Charlie. Since we found Clementine's body this morning I don't think we have much time before the next corpse shows up."

Martha finished her meal. Frank ordered two meatloaf sandwiches and potato salads to go for Abigail and Kate because they'd be easier to eat than a bowl of ham and beans. Abigail had called him as he sat with Martha. She and Kate had been delayed at the funeral home and, in the end, Kate couldn't bring herself to go out in public.

They were at her bakery, supposedly

working, but Kate couldn't stop crying and Frank assumed not much work was being done. He thought taking them supper would be a considerate thing to do.

At the real estate office Martha showed him on the town's wall map where the area being sold off was. It was exactly where he thought it would be.

*****

Frank left Martha's office and walked towards the bakery a couple of block away.

A giant furry Easter bunny strode past him and waved a furry paw at him. It had a pink body and a white stomach, long floppy ears, two human eyes and a huge beribboned Easter basket full of candy. Its gait was an energetic bounce.

"Hi there John Cranston!" Frank bellowed and gave the rabbit a salute.

The hare halted in its tracks. "Hi Frank. How did you know it was me beneath this disguise?"

"Because every year around this time you don that same costume and entertain the kids at the library when the librarian reads Peter Cottontail and other Easter stories. I'd know that pair of long ears and cotton tail anywhere."

The rabbit laughed. "And that's exactly where I'm going now...to the library. It's storytelling day and the children are expecting me—and the goodies in this basket. See you later." Its big furry paw dipped into the basket and handed Frank a paw full of jelly beans.

"Happy Easter, neighbor." And the fake bunny hopped away from him.

"Thanks," Frank's voice chased the bunny. He dropped a few of the jelly beans into his mouth and kept walking.

He was looking in the windows of the book store, eating the jelly beans, admiring the Easter display and thinking about how much fun Easter would be the following weekend with Abigail, Laura and Nick. They'd made baskets for both of the children.

Laura claimed she was too old for a basket but Abigail was going to give her one anyway because she and Nick hadn't had many baskets as kids. Their family had been too poor. Yet the baskets wouldn't only be filled with candy. Nick's would have miniature toys and puzzles in it and Laura's basket would hold a golden bracelet and necklace among the Easter candy and the biggest chocolate bunnies they could find. On Sunday Abigail was baking a ham and he was making the side dishes. It was going to be a great Easter.

Standing there looking at the books through the window and thinking that in about six months another one of his murder mysteries would be prominently displayed among them, he was taken by surprise. He could have sworn he'd seen someone mirrored in the window's glass.

It looked like Alfred.

So Alfred was here in town and doing one of his lurking around excursions. He wasn't missing at all.

Frank experienced a sense of relief until he spun around...and no one was there. The space behind him was empty, yet he could have sworn he'd seen someone. It'd been a man in drab clothes similar to what Alfred had been wearing when he'd seen him last. But there was no one there.

Frank was moving away when he caught the image again out of the corner of his eye. He examined the murky figure, but this time didn't take his eyes off the refection in the glass.

"Alfred?" Frank whispered.

The reflection wavered and spoke, "*You're looking in the wrong place, Frank. It's the land they want. The land. More are going to disappear, to die, before they get all they want. Warn them before it's too late. Warn them!*"

"Warn who?"

"*The others.*"

"What others? Warn them of what?"

"*No is not enough.*"

"Not enough of what? What others? Alfred, what are you trying to tell me–" Frank swung around to face him but, once more, the space behind and around him was vacant. That Alfred and his games. Popping up and popping out like that. Frank didn't find them funny at all, not after the missing persons and deaths they'd already had.

"Alfred? Was that you? Alfred? This isn't funny. Come back! Show yourself. Who am I supposed to warn and about what?"

No one answered and no one reappeared to him as he glared into the glass.

Had that even been Alfred? He wasn't sure. It had looked like the old man, but then it could have been anyone it'd been so blurry. Perhaps it'd only been his imagination or wishful thinking. He'd really liked the old derelict when he'd met him at his house, felt an instant bond with the veteran as if he'd known him better than he had, and he wanted to believe he was somewhere. Somewhere alive and not dead like Beatrice, Clementine and, most likely, Tina. Was it lack of sleep? Had he imagined it? That was it. Not enough sleep.

Perplexed and shaking his head, his hand clutching the bag with the food, he continued his journey to the donut shop. He couldn't wait to see Abigail and tell her what he'd learned from Martha and what he had thought he'd just seen in the window. Could be she'd have an explanation for it because he sure didn't. Unless he was finally losing the last of his sanity and seeing apparitions like Myrtle? No, he was simply tired and worried, that's all. Just tired and worried.

*****

"This place is coming along beautifully." Frank had entered The Delicious Circle bakery, hugged Abigail, and looked around. "It's going to be a perfect place to savor coffee, devour donuts and coffee klatch."

"Coffee klatch? I haven't heard that term in ages." Kate had been weeping. Her face was puffy and her smile forced. "Hopefully you're right, though. It'd be good if this was a place people could come to socialize as well as buy my donuts. My mother was so proud I was opening a business here in town. She loved Spookie and its quaint shops, or she did when she was well enough to come into town." The tears escaped and trickled down her face before she could say another word.

Abigail laid a hand comfortingly on the woman's shoulder. "There, there, let it out. You'll feel better." The look she gave Frank said it all. It'd been a tough day.

"Hey, you two, since you didn't make it to our supper date, I brought the supper to you. Stella's famous meatloaf and potato salad. And I brought coffee." Frank laid the white boxes on the counter. He really felt sorry for Kate. It was heart-wrenching to lose a parent and the heart grieved for each one in its own way; nothing anyone could say could ease the pain. Time was all that helped, and often even time wasn't enough.

"That was sweet of you. You and Abigail have been so kind to me, I don't know what to say." Kate smiled at them. "But I have plenty of coffee." She nodded her head to the brand new coffee machine on the shiny new counter. "I had the machines put in yesterday. I couldn't go one more day without coffee here." Another tentative smile.

"Well, sit down and eat," Frank urged the women, "while the meatloaf is still warm."

"I'll get us some napkins." Kate went off to get them.

"Abby," Frank confessed, "I just had something weird happen to me. I thought I saw Alfred out there on the street, saw his reflection in a shop window, but when I turned around there was no one there. It was sort of...unnerving. The figure spoke to me before it disappeared."

"Now that is weird, Frank. I saw something like that, too, the other day. I glimpsed a reflection, in a window, that wasn't there when I looked behind me. And it was a man as well, I think. But the features were hard to make out it was so indistinct. I couldn't tell who it was."

"Did it speak to you?"

"No it didn't. It appeared, I saw it, and it simply vanished. I thought I'd been working too hard or something and had imagined it."

"Same here. I chalked it up to worry and exhaustion."

"Well, what did it say to you?"

He told her.

"*Warn the others, huh? No isn't enough*," she let the phrases roll slowly off her tongue. "Hmm...that's cryptic all right."

"What do you think those words meant?"

"I'm not sure. You're the writer. Words are your thing, right? What do you think they meant?"

"I'm not sure, either, but I'm thinking about it."

"I know," Abigail spoke hesitantly and he

could almost hear her mind working as she mulled the ambiguities over. "Perhaps you're supposed to *warn* the other home owners in the area where our victims lived…and the part about *the land* and *no isn't enough*? That could mean the people who don't want to sell their homes or land, their saying no to selling isn't enough and it could put them in danger? Something like that?"

Frank's head nodded. "I think you might be right. The man in the glass, and I still think it was Alfred playing tricks on me and he's in town somewhere chuckling it up over it, was telling me to warn the home owners in Beatrice and Clementine's neighborhood that they might be in *danger* if they *don't* sell and to be careful. That could be it. So what are we going to do about it?"

"Warn them," Abigail supplied for him.

Their eyes met and Frank sighed. "That'll be fun, won't it? Sell your house, you old ones, because some man in a window glass said you'll be in danger if you don't. They'll all think we are bonkers."

"Maybe we are. We did both see him. And if it was Alfred, why would he be playing games with both of us like that? Appearing and disappearing like a demented magician, unless he, as Clementine, isn't in his right mind. Maybe he has a touch of Alzheimer's, too?"

"You know that's entirely possible, but I don't think so. He was a little unbalanced, all right, but not totally unbalanced." Frank fell silent for a moment, thinking. "Oh, I didn't tell you I ran into Martha at Stella's and she revealed something else of interest. Some shadowy entity, a company with very deep pockets, wants to buy up the land for some unknown reason our old people live on. Martha and her realtor friends don't know why but there is a lot of speculation on it."

"Ah, perhaps there is our connection—and the mystery deepens," Abigail imparted as Kate returned with the napkins.

The three talked of other subjects less distressing as the women ate their food. Kate was distraught enough over her mother's death and they were careful of what they spoke of. They tried to keep the topics on happier things, like when the bakery was going to open and how nice it already looked. They wanted to cheer her up, not make her feel worse.

Making jovial chitchat wasn't easy because Frank had other things on his mind.

After lunch he drove Abby home. The women had been in Kate's car and Kate had decided to sleep over at the bakery. She had more work she had to do. Frank thought she was afraid to step through the door of her mother's house that night after all that had happened. He didn't blame her.

On the way to Abby's he had the feeling more than once that someone was following them, which in his experience wasn't a good sign. Not a good sign at all. So he speeded up.

Chapter 8
Kate

It was odd being in her mother's house without her mother. Kate lingered in the open doorway, hand on the knob, and surveyed the yard. The grass needed cutting because it was tall and full of weeds and dandelions. It'd be the first cut of the year. She'd have to haul the mower out, get it running, and cut it. If she waited much longer the mower wouldn't stand a chance. The rusty blades would choke on the thick grass. But it had begun to rain...so she'd cut the grass tomorrow. Yes, tomorrow.

It was Easter morning and a light rain moved around on a gentle wind. It was warm, though; not chilly like the last two days had been. In her mother's house she hadn't needed the furnace on for the first time. At night the small gas fireplace in the living room, flames down low, had been enough.

Her eyes gathered in the wet world outside. The yard, the bushes and trees just beginning to bloom and the gray sky dampened her spirits even more. Oh, how she wished the sun would come out and shine away her misery. Sunlight always cheered her up and she needed cheering up something awful. She was so damn sad and she wondered how long she'd feel this way. Possibly she'd never be happy again.

Her mother was two days in her grave and Kate was relieved the funeral was over and behind her but, oh, how she missed her. With one last deep breathe of the spring air, she shut the door and went back inside. She looked around at the stacks of dusty books, grimy ceramic and glass collectibles, nicked furniture, dirty floors and curtains. She'd have to buckle down and give everything in the house a good scrubbing. Her mother had let it fall into disrepair and filth the last couple years. It wasn't her mother's fault because she'd been ill. But now, now she had to take better care of it. Now it was her home.

Yet for today she'd only do a basic cleaning, the real work would have to wait until The Delicious Circle was finished and bringing in customers. She still had to open at the end of May. Now without her mother's social security check every month the house's expenses were also on her shoulders, and extras for the funeral had taken more of her savings. She'd had to buy funeral flowers and food for the guests. More people, mostly townies, than she had planned on had showed up at the house afterwards to show their respect for a dead neighbor. Of course Frank, Myrtle, Abigail and the kids had been there. It had touched Kate, their caring. And they'd brought so much food. Silly her. She hadn't even needed the food she'd provided. At least now her freezer and refrigerator were full. She wouldn't have to go grocery shopping for a month.

She'd moved into the house after the funeral. Someone had to live in it and protect it. It had to be her. She'd made the decision, too, that the loft above her bakery could be better used for baking supplies instead of her living quarters or eventually she could expand it into another section of the shop. It'd hold four or five tables. More space for her business couldn't be bad.

She spent the day cleaning and arranging the house to be more her home. She cried often when some item or memory triggered her mother's presence. To her, in every corner of the house, there were ghosts. She saw her mother everywhere. The way she'd looked when she was young, with her long crimson hair and flashing jade eyes, and when she was older with her slumped shoulders and wrinkled face. Her enigmatic smile. And from many years past she sometimes glimpsed her brother, Jason, or her sisters, Irene and Jessica, and their father, hiding in the shadows of the rooms; or heard their faint voices and laughter. They were all as young as when they'd died. Their paler ghosts roamed the rooms as much as her mother's. Kate was the last one left. She felt so alone. A ghost among ghosts.

Around five o'clock she had a call from Abigail.

"Kate. Happy Easter! I just wanted to see how you were doing."

"I'm doing okay. Cleaning house, settling in and trying not to cry every second. But I'll be back at the donut shop first thing tomorrow morning. Are you still coming around nine to begin the wall paintings?"

"I am. I have your approved sketches, paint, brushes and everything. I want to at least get started. I'll bring us McDonald's sausage biscuits for breakfast," Abigail added. "I know you like them, too. You supply the coffee."

"No problem."

"Have you had supper yet, Kate?"

"No. I've been too busy. I'll scrounge up something here later. There are plenty of leftovers in the fridge."

"Ech, leftovers. I have a better idea. I made the best Easter ham ever and all the side dishes and we're about to sit down and eat. Frank, Myrtle, Samantha, Martha and Ryan are here, too. It's a real party. We're going to play cards or Dominos after. Come over and join us for supper? We have more than enough. I have a chocolate Easter bunny here with your name on it."

Kate, as Abigail, was a chocoholic. "You do know how to tempt me." She wasn't going to go over there. She didn't want to intrude on their holiday, not with all her tears. Then Abigail said the final thing, along with the chocolate enticement, that could change her mind.

"These are people who will become your

neighbors, your friends, visit your shop–Martha and Myrtle, I can guarantee, will be there most mornings wanting their donut fix. They'll be your best customers and promoters. Besides, my kids want you to come. They can't bear the thought of you, or anyone, being alone on Easter. Please come over."

So she did. She'd wanted to see Abigail's house. People had told her it was so lovely inside. She washed her face and hands, brushed her hair, put on clean clothes and drove the short distance to the home Abigail had rehabbed. It wasn't hard to find because Abigail had given her detailed directions.

And she'd spent the evening with her new friends. She'd eaten a grand meal, laughed a little and played Dominos until late that night. She went home with a chocolate Easter bunny. She had the best evening she'd had in a long time and was glad she'd gone.

There was a churning fog creeping over the town and its roads around her mother's house, hiding the driveway and the trees. She'd been warned about the fog but this was the first time since she'd moved home she'd actually encountered it. Living in town it hadn't been as bad and for the life of her she couldn't recall it ever being this dense when she'd been a child. It scared her but inching her car along she made it home.

The minute she unlocked the door and entered the house she knew something wasn't right. It was a shiver that rippled up her spine and she was suddenly cold. Someone had been in her home. Everything she'd already cleared out and reorganized, everything she'd straightened up, was now trashed. There was rubbish littering the table and the kitchen floor. The table had been moved. The chairs were piled up in a corner. The refrigerator was wide open. Someone had taken the food out and scattered it everywhere.

She moved from room to room and, shocked at what she was seeing, took in the blatant destruction. Who would do such a thing and so soon after her mother's death? Who would be so heartless?

Who would be so vicious?

She didn't know what else to do so she telephoned Abigail. "I hate to bother you so late...but is Frank still there? I need to talk to him." As quickly as she could she let Abigail know what had happened and then Frank got on the phone. The two of them were at her house ten minutes later.

"I was afraid this was going to happen." Frank studied the chaos. "It follows the pattern."

"What pattern?" she pried. "You mean the destructive poltergeists?"

Frank sent her a stern glance. "There is no such thing as poltergeists. This was deliberate vandalism made by live people for a human reason. Whoever did this wants you to be scared so you'll sell this house. Someone wants the land around here. They've been buying it up and when the home owners won't sell then these sort of attacks, or worse, start. In the scheme of things, Kate, this isn't too bad. Windows or possessions haven't been broken beyond repair; nothing burned. Your basement wasn't touched, either. I'd guess you came home before they completed the damage."

"Funny you should say that about someone wanting to buy this house...because before she died my mother kept going on and on about ghosts and men in suits who wanted her to sell. She said they were bothering her day and night. I thought she was making things up, part of her illness, but now I'm beginning to think not."

Frank and Abigail didn't stay long. Kate was advised to call the police in the morning, because Frank doubted if anyone on the sheriff's department would come out on Easter night, and make a report so it'd be on file.

"Do you have a gun?" Frank asked.

"A gun? No. I won't have one in my home. I don't believe in guns. Guns kill people."

"Guns don't kill people," the ex-cop said with a frown, "other people kill people."

"If you won't have a gun in the house," Abigail gave her an alternative, "then get yourself a big stick and always lock your doors."

"Do you actually believe whoever did this will return and do it again?" Kate had been at the door showing them out.

"From what I've seen I wouldn't be surprised," Frank said. "But let me know if anyone comes out to talk to you about buying the house. Call me right away. Anytime. I want to come over and talk to them myself. Just call me." Frank had given her his cellphone number.

"I will do that," she'd promised. And Frank and Abigail had gone home.

She was too weary and disgusted to tackle the cleanup that night so she went to bed. She kept a baseball bat next to her on the dresser, in case, because she didn't feel safe and Abigail had warned her to.

*****

She and Abigail arrived at the shop later the next morning than they'd planned. They had agreed on a later time the night before after the house break-in. Kate had to report the crime, wait for the sheriff to come out and inspect the premises, and then clean it up some before she could go into town.

For days she was uneasy, living in her mother's house and waiting for something else to happen. During the daylight hours she was in her shop preparing for the grand opening, Abigail painting the donuts portraits on the walls that were turning out wonderfully. Kate's business was almost ready to open. All the furniture and glass cases had been brought in and installed. The tile and carpeting had been laid; the ovens and frying vats brought in.

At night she reluctantly traveled back to her mother's house because she couldn't leave it empty after what had happened. Someone had to watch over it. It was more than just a house, it was her inheritance, her ties to the mother and family she'd lost.

She breathed easier every day when nothing else happened.

Then the impeccably dressed man and woman in suits knocked on the door and, glancing out the window, she grabbed her cell phone and called Frank.

"Keep them there as long as you can. I'm coming right over." He hung up.

She waited in the open doorway behind the screen door, her hand on the locked latch. "Can I help you?"

"Good evening Mrs. Greenway," the man in the dark suit with the fancy white shirt opened with. A tall, thin fellow, he was wearing a blood red tie. "I'm Scott Lethgrow and this is my associate Maria Smith. We're with Lansing Corporation." He had a business card held out towards her in his hand. She didn't open the door to take it.

"Lansing Corporation?" Kate repeated. "I've never heard of it. Is it a realtor?"

"Not exactly."

"What kind of company is it then?"

The man evaded her question. "It's privately owned, but it is interested in purchasing your house and land here." The man's middle-aged face attempted to reflect compassion when he spoke his next words. "We're sorry for your loss, Mrs. Greenway. We heard your mother passed away."

"She did. Over a week ago. And I don't want to sell this house or my land. So you're wasting your time." Kate's inner alarm had gone off. She could read people fairly well and these two in front of her weren't what they presented themselves to be. They wore fake smiles on their fake faces. Their eyes held a tinge of slyness. They made her nervous.

"Are you sure, Mrs. Greenway? We've already purchased quite a few parcels around here and the company is gun-ho on obtaining the rest. There are only two holdouts and a few other homeowners we need to see until they have what they need. We were told your mother's property is run down. The structure itself is shifting on its foundation and needs extensive repair work. We heard your mother left it in disarray, a real pigsty. We know you're opening a business in town and never expected to live so far out here with all its problems. We could take it off your hands and for a very fair price. Top dollar, in fact."

How do they know all that? "Then why would you want it?" She wished Frank would get there. He'd know how to handle these vultures.

The man seemed to be studying her, assessing her resolve. His gaze avoided hers. It wasn't a good sign. "Could we come in and talk about this?"

Her inner voice whispered: *Don't let them in.* "I don't think so. We have nothing to talk about. As I told you the house is not for sale, nor the land. I'm staying here. End of discussion."

For the first time the woman, a short brunette with long hair swirled up into a tight bun at the base of her slender neck spoke up. "Surely you have heard about the unfortunate incidences that have been occurring around here to your neighbors? It doesn't seem to me this community is very safe. You know," the woman's eyes were boring into her through the screen mesh, "anything can happen to a woman alone these days. If I was you I'd consider selling and getting out, moving into town where it's safe. As my associate here said, we are authorized to offer you an excellent price. Are you sure we couldn't just come in for a minute and discuss it?" The woman had her hand on the doorknob.

Now Kate was angry, yet underneath it she was growing more and more uneasy. Why wouldn't these two take no for an answer and just go away?

"I said *no*. No to you coming in and no to me selling this house. Ever. I am not interested. Don't you understand English?" She made sure her voice was firm. "I'd like it if you both would go. Now. Get off my property or I'll call the police."

The man shifted on his feet and a forceful expression slid over his features. "We don't like taking no for an answer. Is there anything, anything at all we can do to persuade you to sell?"

"Nothing. Just leave please."

The woman was about to say something else

but Kate beat her to it. She couldn't help herself. They were frightening her. "I'd advise you to leave now before my friend gets here. I've called him and he's on his way. He's a retired homicide detective who used to work for the city of Chicago. He's been following, investigating actually, these recent unfortunate incidences in the neighborhood and I'm sure he'd like to talk to you—"

The change in their demeanor was instant. They apologized for disturbing her and the man shoved out the words, "I'll just tuck our card here in your screen door in case you change your mind. Call us anytime. Nice speaking to you." And they hurried off to their shiny ebony sedan with the tinted windows and raced away as if the police were after them. It almost made Kate laugh, seeing who they were essentially running from. But in reality she was sorry they'd left before Frank got there. He'd really wanted to speak to them.

Five minutes later he was at the door and she let him in.

"Sorry Frank, you just missed them. They've gone. They were getting really pushy— even more than that I felt *threatened*–and I asked them to leave. They weren't going to until I said you were on your way. Then they were out of here like spooked birds."

"Why would they run off because I was coming over?"

She hated to admit her mistake, but she thought it might mean something if she did.

"Well I might have mentioned you were an ex-cop. Sorry. But they were creeping me out and it popped out."

"They didn't want to talk to me. That's kind of telling."

"They left their business card." She handed the scrap of paper to him.

"Lansing Corporation," Frank read the name in a black block font off the card. "And there's a telephone number. That's all. No address or anything. Now in my book that's suspicious."

"It is unusual. Are you going to call them?"

"Darn right I'm going to call them *and* Google them on the Internet. But I don't think I'll get much satisfaction either way...unless...I actually set them up in person, but somehow don't reveal my true identity. I know for a fact they want Tina's house and she's gone...so perhaps I can set a trap for them."

"Set a trap for them?"

"Pretend to be a relative of Tina's who expects to inherit her house."

"Oh, I get it. Pretend to be her heir and have them come out to discuss you wanting to sell everything, huh?"

Frank nodded. "Why not? They don't know what I look like or my name."

He shot her a questioning look. "You didn't tell them my name, did you?"

"No."

"Good. I'll take on a false identity and act gullible. Possibly I'll get more information than a telephone number and I'll be able to track them down and find out who they're working for. "

He was sitting at the kitchen table, staring around at the destruction. "This really is still a mess, isn't it?"

Her eyes scanned the room. "It is. I've cleaned it up a lot since it happened, as I hope you can tell, but I have so much more to do. I still can't believe someone trashed my house."

"Take my word for it, there are some really bad people out there, Kate. I've seen worse things than what's happening here in Spookie back in Chicago. Much worse.

"You know I've been thinking, as much as you believe you should stand guard here over your mother's home, it might be best if you stay above the donut shop for a couple of days and away from here. After what happened Easter and especially those visitors of yours today and what you said to them–telling them you definitely aren't selling–I don't think you're safe here alone. Just a feeling I have."

He was scaring her, but she knew he was trying to protect her. "All right, I'll go back to town for a while.

"I'm curious, you've never found that missing man, Alfred, then have you?" She'd heard him and Abigail talking about the old man's disappearance a few days before.

"Not yet. If he doesn't show up by tomorrow I'll be putting in a missing person's report at the police station. I go by his house every day, but it's still empty. No one appears to have been there for a while."

"I'm sorry. Abigail said he was a feisty old gentleman and you had taken a liking to him."

"That's true. I keep having this strange feeling that I know him better than I had thought. I'd probably seen him around town when I was young or something. I don't know."

Frank came to his feet. "All right. I think it's time to leave. Night's coming and Abigail expects me over at her house. I don't want you to be here alone so I'll wait around until you pack some things and I and my truck will escort you in your car until you hit the highway into town. I don't trust those two jackals not to come back and give you some kind of grief."

"If you insist. It won't take but a jiffy for me to pack. I have most of what I need already above the shop, seeing Abigail and I are still working there. All I have to do is replenish a few of the basics: clean towels, toiletry refills and stuff." She met his eyes and she felt tears in hers. "Thanks Frank. You and Abigail, everyone, have been so good to me. I really appreciate it."

"Think nothing of it. We are neighbors. You're one of us. Remember I told you we take care of our own in Spookie. That's what we do."

Smiling at him, she left the room. He was right. She didn't want to be alone in the house when night fell. Something about those two who'd just dropped in on her suddenly made her want to flee the house. There'd been something menacing about them; something wrong in their eyes. And it was best to be safe instead of sorry. Her mother always used to say that and her mother, in her healthier days, had been a very smart woman.

Chapter 9
Frank

The following morning Frank got up, fed the dogs and released them into the backyard for exercise. It was going to be another warm day. The sun rose above him in all its glory but it didn't lighten Frank's mood. The situation with the missing and dead old folks worried him. He had to find out what was going on and deal with it before someone else got hurt. Sheriff Mearl maintained he was on the case, tracing leads and doing his job, but the police officer wasn't that dedicated so, as usual, Frank didn't have much faith for a swift resolution. The people who had disappeared and were threatened were his neighbors, his friends, and he had to do something.

He had the nagging suspicion Lansing Corporation was at the center of the mystery and it was vital he made contact and infiltrate them somehow. He'd already searched on the Internet for them but, surprise, surprise, there was no Lansing Corporation. How had they managed to hide from the Web he had no idea, but they had. How was he going to find them? He was mulling over his options while cooking up breakfast when a loud pounding exploded on his front door.

Frank opened it and there stood Myrtle. Her dress was yellow which made her look like a giant walking flower and her hair was a nimbus of rat's nests surrounding a pale face. She grinned at him with her cherry-pink lips. For some reason, and there was rarely a sensible one when it came to Myrtle, she had a ratty umbrella in her one hand, but there wasn't a cloud in the sky. He recognized that look on her face, though. Oh, oh, more trouble.

"Myrtle, how nice to see you. Isn't it a tad early, though?"

"Not too early to go after the criminals who tossed my friend Tina out into the damn ocean and incinerated my trailer down to a pile of ashes. I only wanted to see if you've learned anything more about either. And has Alfred showed up yet?"

"No to all you've asked. Sorry, old friend. But I am working on it. Come on in. I was just about to have breakfast. Scrambled eggs with bacon. You may join me if you'd like."

The old woman's face drooped at his words then was transformed by a rapid smile when food was mentioned. For Myrtle life was simple. She got through every day to become a day older and if it was with a roof over her head and a full belly she was grateful.

She trailed him to the kitchen and dropped herself in a chair. Frank scooped out a hefty spoonful of scrambled eggs from the pan, put them on a plate and set it before her. With a mouth full, she asked, "So you didn't find out anything else about Tina's disappearance from the ship, either?"

"Nothing else of importance. No one saw or heard anything just as you'd uncovered. I've kept in touch with the captain and there's no further news. We might never know what happened to Tina, but I'm afraid she's gone. Truly gone. I'm so sorry. Alfred is still missing as well. No one's seen him in over a week." Frank shoved away the haunting image of the man in the window's glass. Just because it'd looked like Alfred didn't mean it had been Alfred. He was beginning to believe Alfred was as gone as Tina, Beatrice and Clementine. They were, most likely, all dead. His gut told him that.

"Oh I figured Alfred was most likely dead, too. Then I saw his ghost out in the woods with the others–Beatrice and Clementine–this morning on my way over here. That clinched it. Alfred's a goner. Funny thing is I haven't seen Tina yet. And I've been looking. Possibly coming back from the ocean takes a while longer or something. Maybe she's lost her way and is on some other continent or something because she never was good with directions and finding places. I don't know."

Frank settled in a chair beside Myrtle and began to eat. "You saw Beatrice's, Clementine's and Alfred's ghost in the woods?"

"Sure did. I had a bloody mob of them surrounding me this morning. Yakking, poking at me and grabbing at my clothes. Wanting to tell me things or just gawk at me. Like I said before, they're really riled up these days. Anyone could see something is going on. But what pests! Then I yelled at them to go where they belonged and they slid back into the dirt and grass.

"You know the ghosts live deep in the ground beneath us, don't you?" She pointed a finger downwards. "They're everywhere but they hide and sleep in the earth. They're always trying to reach us. Tell us their sad stories. Murder victims are the absolute worst. They're the strongest ones, for a time anyway, because they are often so angry or they want justice for what happened to them. Then after some years they're as ineffective as the other lost souls."

"Do these ghosts ever show themselves in mirrors or as reflections in windows?"

Myrtle thought about that, scratching the side of her face. "Never heard of that myself or seen it. But who knows? Like I said those ghosts are everywhere. Some can see them, like me; some can't."

He knew she was waiting for him to say more, but he didn't.

"Why, Frank? Have you been seeing ghosts?"

He laughed as if the very notion was a joke. "Everywhere."

She didn't laugh but the look she gave him

said it all. He couldn't fool her.

Avoiding any other further interrogation, he went on, "You know Kate had some people in suits who stopped by and wanted to buy her mother's house? I tried to waylay them but they slipped away before I got there."

"Describe them."

From Kate's description he did.

"They sound like the two numbskulls who came to my trailer some time back and tried to pressure me into selling. The same two, I reckon. The man was sickly nice and the woman was way too prissy and pushy. I sent them packing. Now look, my trailer's a hunk of melted metal and I'm living in a dead woman's house."

"Talking about Tina's house...I wanted to pass something by you. Kate was given a telephone number for Lansing Corporation. That's the company that wants to buy all the land. I now believe they're somehow involved in all our problems and I was thinking about calling that number and pretending to be Tina's nephew. I want to meet those two in person and ask them a couple questions."

"Tina doesn't have a nephew."

"You and I know that but they don't. I'll only pretend to be her nephew and now sole owner of her house and land who wants to quickly unload it. I'll invite them to Tina's house to discuss price. Then perhaps I'll get some answers and if not, I'll tail them after they leave. See where they go. Hopefully they'll lead me back to their lair."

"Sounds like a dandy plan to me, detective. Here's the house keys." She pulled them from a pocket in her dress and threw them at him. He caught them. "When you going to do this?"

"Soon as we get done with breakfast I'll drive over, let myself into the house, and make the call. See if I can get them flushed out."

"Well, that's better than nothing, I suppose. At least we're finally doing something to get to the bottom of things." Done with her breakfast, Myrtle jumped up from her chair and headed for the door. "While you sit in my friend's house and play act at being someone you're not," she presented him with a devious smile, "I'm going to go watch the big machines clear away what's left of my trailer and then go visit the Modular Home Center to let them know they can now deliver my new home."

"I bet you can't wait for that new trailer, huh?" Frank walked her to the door and let her out.

"It's not a trailer, it's a *modular home*."

"Sorry. Modular home."

"You want the truth? I can't wait to be back on my own land and out of Tina's spook house." Myrtle stood on the porch and her rheumy eyes watched back at him from under the shade of it. "Her place is infested with the critters. It's as if since she went into the sea the ghosts have gone wild and have overrun her place. It's so crowded there I spent the night on Abigail's couch. She said I can stay as long as I want.

"She baked me chocolate chip cookies last night. Sweet girl. She's a great cook, too, you know?" The old woman gave him a knowing grin, always trying to be a match maker.

"I know. But, don't forget, Myrtle I have a whole spare room upstairs you're welcome to use anytime. You don't have to sleep on anyone's couch."

"I know that." She waved her hand at him in an affectionate gesture and patted his arm. "But as I see it my new home will be up and ready to move into within days. The Modular Home Center promised me that. Nothing like a big fat bonus to get things done in a timely fashion. They just bring in the two halves by truck, drop them on my land, stick them together and connect all my electricity, plumbing and Internet and I'm good to go.

"Though I will keep your generously kind offer of a room and a bed in mind if that sofa gets too hard to sleep on."

And Frank was sure she would.

"Meals included with that offer?" she tacked on at the last second.

"Of course."

"Might take you up on that then, Mr. Big Shot Author, next meal time." She chuckled and pivoted around to go down the steps.

She hobbled off across his front yard towards the road, her umbrella swinging beside her. She wasn't going near the woods today, she'd informed him, because of the aggressive wraiths. He'd offered to drive her to her old homestead but she insisted on walking. She'd declared it was a beautiful day and she liked walking.

Frank did the dishes then walked out the door, got in his truck and drove to Tina's house. He let himself in with the key. The place did have an eerie ambience about it. It was gloomy, musty inside. All the windows were closed; shades drawn. The shadows that congregated in the corners and crevices of the rooms seemed to have a life of their own. Myrtle was right, the place was sort of creepy. It could just be his fancy because he was nearly one hundred percent positive its owner was no longer on this earth. Murdered, in all likelihood. As Myrtle had said, he was in a dead woman's house.

He raised the shades and opened some windows. Rummaged around until he found the ingredients for coffee and made a cup. He wanted to look at home when his guests arrived.

He took the card from his pocket and dialed the telephone number on it. It didn't surprise him that when the man on the other end of the line found out who he was pretending to be and what he wanted he made an immediate appointment to meet him at Tina's house. Frank had expected nothing less.

Thirty-five minutes later, he shepherded a man and a woman into the living room and then into the kitchen. By their looks they were undoubtedly the same two who had visited Kate the day before. They arrived in their shiny car, expensive suits, phony smiles, and set off his detective's inner alarm for falseness the minute they began jabbering. He'd bet his retired badge their hidden agenda, whatever it was, had nefarious roots and he'd uncover it one way or another.

"Come in, come in." Frank plastered on his own phony smile and a mindless expression. He subtly became someone else because when he wanted he could be a good actor. Years as a homicide detective had honed his skills. Today he was playing a good-natured but dumb country boy in dire need of cash hoping to hastily unload his dead aunt's property. He'd dressed for the part in frayed jeans and a T-Shirt with holes in it; had left his hair uncombed and hadn't shaved that morning to make himself look scruffier than usual. Now all he had to do was create a believable performance.

The man, as he entered, was examining Frank closely. The woman, dressed in a steel gray suit with a pastel silk blouse and heels, was studying him as well, but more secretly from under half-masted eyelashes. He pegged her as the brains right off; the man, the brawn. She was the one he had to convince.

"Good morning Mr. Stanus." The man shook Frank's hand. Stanus was the fictitious name Frank had given them on the phone. The man, as Kate had described him, was taller than Frank and thin. His hair was short and a striking shade of silver. Yet he wasn't old. Frank pegged him at being about forty. He had cold blue eyes that reminded Frank of blue glass. "I'm Scott

Lethgrow and this is my colleague Maria Smith. We represent the Lansing Corporation." He shoved a business card at Frank, the same one Kate had been given, and shook his hand.

The woman smiled condescendingly at Frank as a greeting. She didn't shake his hand. She most likely thought he was the country bumpkin he was playing and his hands would be dirty.

Frank led them into the kitchen and with a welcoming hand gesture offered them seats at the table. The woman sat down but the man remained standing. Frank plopped down on a turned around chair, slouching. He had a toothpick and picked at his teeth with it. He didn't offer either of his guests coffee or anything he normally would have done. It wouldn't have gone with his act.

"So you're Tina Thompson's nephew?" Lethgrow confirmed. "And her heir?"

"I am. She didn't have any children," he lied, "that I know of and only the one sibling, my ma. Ma always told me that when my Aunt Tina passed, I'd inherit all this." Frank swept his hand around and allowed a manifestation of greed to spread across his features. "Sweet, huh? It's probably worth a bundle, wouldn't you say?"

"You're not interested in living here then?" the woman queried, not answering his question.

"Nope. I live in the city. I hate living out in the country like this. Too damn many bugs and no fast food. Have you looked at the one road town here? They have nothing. It's like being out in the backwoods with the hillbillies. Nope, I don't want this old ruin of a house or to live here. I'm just interested in what I can get for it and then I'll hustle back to the city."

"So you want to sell this?" Lethgrow was smiling like a shark now.

"Sure as hell I do. Faster the better." Frank gave him a shark's grin back.

"But from what we've heard, your aunt's body hasn't been recovered yet, Mr. Stanus. She was on a cruise, wasn't she, and fell overboard? My condolences, by the way." Lethgrow feigned sympathy as he hovered behind the sitting woman, but there was a self-satisfied glint in his eyes. Frank had seen that glint often enough when a person was lying or hiding something sinister. In that moment Frank knew this man was the man who probably pushed Tina off the boat and to her death in the cold sea. He *knew* it. "Do you have the right to sell this property under those circumstances?"

"I would think so. Everyone believes the old lady is dead so I don't think it'll take long for me to get this house and whatever else she had. I'm meeting with her lawyer later today so I bet I'll find out more. Gee, could be she'll have a pile of money in her bank account." Frank greedily rubbed his hands together. "I'll get that, too."

"Did you know your aunt very well?" The woman was trying so hard to behave as if she really cared, yet her voice was abnormally flat.

214

"I met her once or twice when I was a kid. My ma and her didn't get along too well. You know how that is? Family," he huffed, throwing in a scowl to make it look good. "What a circus. I'm only here for the money."

Both his visitors stared at him. Frank would have loved to know what they were thinking behind their snake eyes. He trusted his performance had fooled them.

No one was saying anything. This was his opportunity to get the information he was performing for.

"Lansing Corporation, huh?" Frank restarted the conversation, glancing at the business card. "Never heard of it. What kind of company is it? There's no address."

The woman answered, "It's a private agency owned by a consortium of highly respected and wealthy business men. They live all over the world and buy land for government facilities across the country. We're authorized to offer and buy for them."

"Where's their home office?"

"New York," the woman replied a little too quickly and didn't elaborate. "But you don't have to worry about that, Mr. Stanus. The check will cash, I assure you."

"Hmm. In town they were talking about how you've been buying up all the land around here. Your company must really want it for something important, huh?"

"We're not privy to what they want it for. We just work for them." The man was lying,

215

Frank could tell, and had suddenly decided to sit. He settled in the chair next to his partner.

"This private company," Frank went on, not giving up, "why do they want this particular hunk of land? They're not going to build some top secret hidden fortress where the government does weird experiments on people or animals or something like that, are they?"

"No, nothing like that. As I said I don't know what they're going to build. We represent them and acquire what they tell us to acquire. We're just the messengers."

Frank listened to the lies and bobbed his head. "You two heard about all the bizarre incidents and accidents that have occurred in this neighborhood lately? Pretty strange. Some say there's a widespread haunting going on. Some say there's a murderer loose. Wild, huh?"

"Ridiculous. Ghosts don't exist and they don't kill." But once more Lethgrow's tiny smile tipped Frank off. The salesman knew a hell of a lot more than he was letting on; his associate, too.

"The people are so provincial around here," the woman remarked with a barely contained smirk. "So gullible."

That's when Frank was absolutely sure the two were part of what was going on. It was in the way they avoided his looks, the way their shoulders straightened and the dismissive tone of their responses.

"We don't know anything about any of that Mr. Stanus," mouthed Lethgrow, glaring at him suspiciously. "We're here to buy this house and land if you want to sell it to us. We'll give you top price. What do you say?"

Frank also knew when he'd gone too far so he returned to his act. "How much?"

Lethgrow was back on track now. "Based on the house and the land here and the neighboring houses and what they've gone for, we've been authorized to offer you two hundred."

"Two hundred dollars?" Frank blurted out the erroneous amount on purpose. "You've got to be ******* kidding. It's worth a hell of a lot more—"

"No, Mr. Stanus, two hundred *thousand* dollars," the woman corrected.

The price astounded Frank. "Whoa! That's a hell of a lot of money. This place ain't worth it, no way." Then he smiled. "But if you're offering it, I'll take it. I'm no fool."

Now both his guests gave him back big satisfied shark smiles.

"Then we have a deal?" Lethgrow lifted himself from his chair, so excited he nearly knocked it over and thrust out his hand to be shook. "We have the paperwork with us—"

Frank had learned what he could from the two, or all they were going to tell him; which hadn't been much. Now for the second part of his plan. "Uh, wait a minute. Like I said before, I have to talk to the lawyer later today and see when I can take possession of all this. But I'll call you right away when I know it's mine to sell, you can count on it." He handed them a scrap of paper with the telephone number of the throw away cell phone he'd bought just for that reason.

They weren't happy but they were also smart enough to know he couldn't sell what wasn't his until it legally was.

"We will stay in touch then, Mr. Stanus. Nice meeting you." The woman was already halfway towards the door and her companion was a step behind her.

Frank watched them leave and waited until their car was at the end of the driveway before he sprinted out the rear door, slid into the truck he'd parked behind the house so they wouldn't see it, and fell in behind them at a safe distance. Almost losing sight of their car after it'd turned onto the highway, he caught a glimpse of it up the road. He made sure he pursued far enough behind so he wouldn't tip them off.

Though he strained to see the license plate, which would have made everything so much easier, he couldn't make it out. They'd covered it in mud.

It was a long trip through small towns and past larger ones. At times he wondered where they were going. He'd expected them to drive to a five star hotel where they had rooms. He'd planned on sweet-talking or intimidating a naive desk clerk into letting him into those rooms once the two left to go eat or something, and look around some. He'd also try to get the phone records of any outgoing or incoming calls which might help him trace them back to their company. Apparently they were returning to a satellite or headquarters and not a hotel. He'd lucked out. If he was led to where they worked he'd stealthily break in any way he could–best do it in the middle of the night–and find out what he needed to know. If the company wasn't legitimate he'd find out.

The sun was dazzling on the road before him. The dark sedan ahead glinted in its light. Sometimes he let the car surge far ahead and sometimes, when tighter packed traffic allowed it, he would move in closer. He was very careful because he didn't want to lose them.

It didn't do him any good. About an hour away from Spookie he noticed the sedan was increasing its speed. Could be they'd realized they had a tail or else they were in a hurry to get wherever they were going. Either way, he got caught behind some cars and an eighteen wheeler and couldn't get by them. When he finally drove around, the sedan was nowhere to be seen. He'd lost it or they'd lost him.

"Damn!" He slapped his hand on the wheel and slowed the truck down. "Where could they have gone? They were just ahead of me."

He backtracked a ways and checked the side streets, driveways and the motels' and hotels' parking lots. No black sedan. No suits. Finally he gave up, swerved the truck around and drove home to Spookie.

This time he was the one peering into the rearview mirror and hoping he wasn't being the one tailed. He couldn't afford to have his cover blown. He'd be meeting those two again and he didn't want them to be suspicious of him.

An hour later he was in town parking in front of Kate's donut shop. He'd called Abigail and learned she was there finishing up the last of her wall paintings. So he decided to meet her. He had things he wanted to talk to her about.

Chapter 10

Abigail

"So you never found out where their headquarters was located?" Abigail put down the brush on the table's edge and wiped her hands. She'd put the final touches on the last wall picture in the shop and was proud of what she'd done. Now Kate could open her business on schedule tomorrow as planned.

The images of the giant donuts, of all the varieties requested, lined the freshly painted walls and looked good enough to eat–and if that didn't get people hungry for the pastries, nothing would, Kate had claimed. And the shop was done. Everything was in its place, the furnishings and all the baking equipment, the ovens and fryers, in the rear rooms were ready to do their jobs. Kate had already done a dry run and everything had worked perfectly. Even Abigail had to admit, the place looked amazing.

Frank, sitting nearby at a shiny new table, answered, "No, I never found where they were going. I lost them somewhere past the JB Bridge. To be truthful, I'm afraid they might have made me early on and led me on a wild goose chase. Maybe it gave them a thrill or they were under orders never to let anyone discover where their home base was. Who knows? But it was odd how they suddenly skedaddled off the road. One second there and the next gone. Darn, and I really wanted to find out where that mysterious company of theirs was located."

"Where exactly were you when you lost them?" Abigail was putting her paint stuff away in her artist's supply bag. Kate was behind the counter doing last minute preparations before the grand opening. Abigail noticed the woman was listening to their conversation.

"Going into St. Louis."

"Then their headquarters is in the city somewhere."

"That's what I think too."

"You know," Kate broke in. "I got another one of those calls from the Lansing Corporation last night. They really are hot to buy my mother's house and land. They've doubled their previous offer. The amount is ridiculous. Who'd pay that much for my mother's wreck of a house? They were quite pushy on the phone. I said no for the tenth time and I don't think they cared much for it. I finally had to hang up on them because they wouldn't take no for an answer." She shook her head. "I don't see why they want my house so badly."

They want the land. Everyone's land. "Who did you speak with...a man or a woman?" Abigail had taken a chair beside Frank.

"A woman, and she was persistent, I will say

that."

"So you hung up on her?"

"I had to. She wouldn't stop trying to convince me. Coerce me is more like it. Said the house was falling apart. Said there'd been criminal acts all around lately in my neighborhood and I was a woman alone...and so on."

Frank threw Abigail a look she could read easily enough. He believed the Lansing Corporation was behind the troubles, no doubt about it. He didn't say anything but stared out the windows onto Main Street and her gaze followed. Midday, the sun was high in the sky and there were no shadows along Main Street. Every shop was awash in sunlight. Nothing could hide.

They were supposed to go out for lunch after she was done at the shop. It was Friday afternoon and the sidewalks were full. Townspeople were bustling here and there going about their daily affairs. Everything was normal to them. It was business as usual in the world and the town. Abigail always found it sad that life went on as other people went through their individual miseries, losses and dangers. People disappeared or died. The world didn't care.

Many of the people passing by stole looks through the windows, smiled, waved or gave them a thumbs up. They knew that weekend was the grand opening and they were trying to be encouraging. Kate would be beginning the actual donut making very early in the morning so the pastries would be ready when she opened the shop at seven a.m. That evening she'd be going upstairs to the loft to get the sleep she'd need while Abigail would be going home to cook supper for her children.

Abigail exchanged smiles with Kate. They were becoming friends. Not just artist and patron, but real friends, and Abigail could always use another friend. "Well, Kate, it's all done and ready for the crowds tomorrow morning."

"Crowds? That would be great. Or all those donuts I'm going to make tonight will go to waste." Kate's smile had become uncertain. She'd done her share of crying over her mother's death and was ready to begin her new business and her new life. A person could only be sad for so long.

"They won't go to waste," Frank piped up. "Abby, the kids and I will be here first thing in the morning to sample them. My mouth is already watering. I can't wait."

Kate's smile grew. "Thanks Frank. I know I can depend on you guys if no one else."

"Don't worry, my friend," Abigail said. "You're going to be mobbed tomorrow morning, you'll see. The people here love The Bakery but to have some new and different choices, will bring them all to your doorstep this weekend. Take my word for it. Your shop is going to be a rip-roaring success. And Samantha's newspaper article today was a good one. Pictures and everything. Everyone in town gets that paper and they've read about your bakery. It'll bring in a lot of people tomorrow, you'll see.

"By the way, have you found that part-time helper you wanted to hire?"

"Oh, I forgot to tell you, I sure did." Guilt faintly shaded Kate's face. "It's Laura."

"My Laura? She's only fifteen." It took Abigail by surprise, but she was also impressed that her daughter would be so resourceful as to find a job in the first place. The girl had been talking about getting a part-time one for months and Abigail hadn't completely objected. She'd had a part-time job herself when she'd been sixteen working at an A&W Root Beer stand and working at that age had taught her valuable life lessons.

"Your Laura. She offered to help me out for a while on the weekends and an afternoon or two a week until I find someone full-time. The shop closes at five each day so it'll only be a few hours after school on Wednesday, Thursday and Friday. Half days on Saturday and Sunday. I'll close early on Sundays. She said she had a work permit and will be sixteen next month; wanted to make some extra money so she could help you pay the bills. I said okay because I haven't found anyone else yet–been too busy with my mother's illness, her death, the funeral and all–so I agreed. She told me she'd spoken to you about it. Is it all right?"

"No, she didn't speak to me. Not yet anyway. She probably thought she'd spring it on me tonight and because you're opening tomorrow I wouldn't be able to tell her no. But I imagine if she went through the trouble of getting a work permit and the job she should at least have a try at it." Laura wanted to make money, Abigail thought; trying to grow up faster so she could help. That touched her. "It's okay, Kate. I'd be the first to admit Laura is mature for her age and if she thinks she can do this, she can. As long as she keeps her grades up it might be good for her.

"And don't worry about anyone else you need to hire right away. I'll help you out in the beginning, too. Anything you need until you find your other workers. I always wanted to work in a donut shop."

"Thanks Abigail. I'll be posting a help wanted ad online and in the newspaper before Monday. Maybe I'll get some responses."

"Maybe you will. Just let me know when you need my assistance, I'll be here, and I'll be here tomorrow morning early to help you kick off the place." Abigail slung her bag over her shoulder and nodded at Frank. "You ready to get some lunch?"

"I am."

After goodbyes to Kate, she and Frank went out the door, down the street and into Stella's Diner.

*****

The cheeseburger and onion rings she had ordered hit the spot. After a morning of painting she was more than hungry and ate them with gusto. Yet as Frank rambled on about his adventure that morning the uneasy feeling she'd had the whole day continued to grow until it was a silent scream in her head. Since Clementine's body had been found there'd been no more incidents of any kind. No hauntings, disappearances, vandalisms or attacks. It was far too calm.

After lunch, at home again, she did laundry and prepared supper. When Laura and Nick came in the door from school she listened to Laura's reasons for taking the job at The Delicious Circle and, as she knew she would, gave her permission for her daughter to try it on condition it didn't interfere with school. Laura was excited.

*****

Frank had said he'd see her at Kate's shop around nine, though she would already be there helping Kate from seven on. Laura would be riding her bicycle into town before seven to help Kate put out the donuts in their cases and open up. She couldn't wait to see how her daughter would do in her first job.

When Abigail got up Laura was already gone. Nick was sleeping and she roused him. "Good morning kiddo. It's time to get up," she called from the doorway, "if you want to come with me to Kate's grand opening you need to get up now. Free donuts. As many as you want." She'd already taken a shower and was dressed.

Nick, drowsy but with a grin on his face, crawled from bed and slipped past her headed for the bathroom. "For donuts I'll forego my usual amount of weekend sleep and will be ready in a couple minutes. Don't leave without me."

"I won't."

Abigail waited in the kitchen, drinking coffee and thinking about the day ahead. She tried not to dwell on the missing and dead elderly that had been plaguing them; the mystery of Lansing Corporation, conspiracies, and where it would all end. Today was a day to celebrate. Kate's lifelong dream, owning and running her own business, was becoming a reality and after all Kate had gone through in her life and now with her mother's passing, the woman deserved something to celebrate.

When she and Nick drove through town and parked a block away from the shop because of the number of cars and people flocking to the fledgling business, she knew Kate's enterprise was going to be a success. Kate must be ecstatic.

They entered the shop and in Abigail's eyes it appeared transformed. Bursting with talking and laughing people milling around ordering donuts and coffee it had finally achieved its full potential. The glass cases were overflowing with trays of donuts: Chocolate and Iced Cake, Peanut Covered, Long Johns, Cinnamon Raisin, Cinnamon Buns, French Crullers, Custard, Raspberry Jelly, Crème Filled Long Johns, Twists, Lemon, Cherry Cheese and Cheese Tarts, Fritters, Crème Horns, Donut Holes,

Sugar Rounds. It was amazing that one woman had produced all those scrumptious creations in a couple of hours but Abigail had seen the modern kitchen and the efficient, time-saving baking equipment. Kate knew what she was doing and how to get the most out of them.

Nick spied one of his friends from school and went off with him. It was nice to see how social the once reclusive boy had become and how these days he was happy more than not. He'd also changed in other ways. He was going to be tall as his father had been; he had the same calm temperament and generous heart the man, a victim of the Mud People Killer two years before, had had. Abigail smiled as Kate handed Nick a Danish and chocolate milk and the boy found a table with his friend to enjoy them. No way was he going to sit with his mother. Abigail didn't mind. She remembered what it was like to be a teenager and no teenage boy ever let anyone know he needed his mother.

The place was packed. She could hardly move through the crowd. It looked as if the entire town had gotten up early to taste Kate's donuts and see what she'd done to the place. The aroma of the donuts was heavenly. Kate had outdone herself. She'd even made Abigail's favorite Crème Horns as a thank you for everything she'd done for her.

The mouthwatering smells sent Abigail back to her childhood when her grandmother would take her to church on Sundays and after mass they'd stop at the local bakery. Strolling through the doors she could almost close her eyes and see her grandmother's sweet smile and taste those Crème Horns. Today it wouldn't just be a memory. The first thing she wanted with her cup of coffee was one of those Crème Horns and they were as good as the ones of her youth, no, even better. Kate put chocolate sprinkles on the ends of them.

Kate didn't seem to need her help yet, so she took a table by the window and observed Kate at the counter selling and Laura scurrying around waiting on or serving people. The girl looked pleased with herself. Her face was animated and so was her smile. Over blue jeans and a blouse, she had on a crisp white apron with The Delicious Circle's logo on its lower pocket. She carried donuts and coffee to a couple at the adjoining table and then scooted over to Abigail's.

"Hi Mom. Isn't this great? Look at all the people who are here." Her hand on her hip, the girl's gaze swept around the room and came to rest on Abigail. She looked so grown up it made her catch her breath. The girl was becoming a young woman in front of her eyes.

But for a moment in Abigail's mind she once again saw the skinny, sad-eyed waif Laura had been when they'd first met in the library. The girl who'd ravenously desired the donuts she'd had in the bag and who had desperately dreamed of someday becoming an artist like Abigail. The lost child and her brother. It seemed so long ago, so much had changed, but it had only been about a year ago. Now Abigail couldn't imagine her life without them. They were hers as much as if she'd had them all their lives. They were her family.

"It's been like this since we opened the door at seven," Laura bragged. "There were people waiting to get in out on the sidewalk even. Myrtle was in here about eight for her free donuts and Kate ended up sending her off with a bag of them." She laughed. "That Myrtle, she sure doesn't miss a trick, does she?"

"She sure doesn't, although she's known Kate and her mother Clementine for years. She and Clementine were childhood friends, so Myrtle thinks of Kate as one of her own children."

"I know that.

"But really," Laura chattered on, "everyone *loves* Kate's donuts. Most of them order one or two and end up either asking for more or taking a bag of them home. It's been fantastic!" The girl grinned at her and refilled her coffee cup. She bent down and whispered to her, "And I've eaten so many of them I feel like a donut myself. I know you've already had a crème horn, but be sure to try her glazed, they'll melt in your mouth. Really."

"I will," Abigail promised. "How about bringing me one?"

"Sure Mom. Coming up. I'll be back in a flash." And she was.

"Where's Frank?" her daughter asked.

"He should be here any time. Should have

been here already." Abigail wondered what was keeping him but wasn't worried. Frank would get there when he got there. If he was late, there was a reason for it and she'd bet a dollar to a donut it had something to do with the Lansing Corporation enigma. Frank was like a hound dog on the hunt when he was trying to solve a case. Retired or not, he would always be a cop. He couldn't help himself.

As Abigail bit into the sweet confection and drank the coffee she observed the customers around her doing the same thing. Everyone seemed to be having a good time, enjoying the food. *Yes,* she thought, *this shop is going to be a big hit. Everyone will come here for their donuts.*

At some point she began eavesdropping on the conversations around her. An older couple behind her, a gray-haired man with a cane and a woman who was eating a blueberry Danish, were talking. "Oh, I'm still not sure we should have sold the house, Jeanette," the man was saying, his head bent. "But after the weird goings on around us and Bernard's house fire I didn't see as we had any other option. All that racket every night was giving me headaches. And when we came home that night to the windows and doors wide open; blood splattered over the table and floor…that was the last straw. I don't know what's happened to our neighborhood, but whatever it is, it isn't good. You know, I hear on the news how these drug crazed perverts are breaking into old peoples' homes, stealing everything in sight, and still torturing and beating them to death. That isn't going to be us. We're getting out of there."

"But," the woman said as she stuffed the last of the pastry into her mouth, "you know, as soon as we signed those sale papers all of that crazy stuff stopped. Ah, I guess it doesn't matter now. We're moving." She looked around. "I think living here in town will be really much better for us, honey. We'll be so close we can walk here or to anywhere else we want to in town. Be kinda nice."

He smiled. "That is a compensation. We'll be near to everything. But I still hate leaving our home. We lived all our lives and raised our kids there. We're leaving a lot of memories."

The woman took his age-spotted hand and held it. "It will be okay, dear. You'll see. We will make more."

That's when Abigail became aware of the two men whispering on her right. They both had bakery bags in their hands and were going towards the door. They walked past her but she heard a snippet of their conversation.

"No, the police haven't found my Aunt Violet or her husband yet. It's been a week now."

"I'm sorry, Leroy. But that's strange, when you think about it, because the other day I heard Deputy Jacob Stevens talking about another missing person in town. Another old person. I asked him about it but he clammed up real quick."

"What the heck is going on around here lately?"

"I don't know, but something is."

It had always amused Abigail, knowing that if you wanted to find out anything that was going on in Spookie all you had to do was have a meal at Stella's and keep your eyes and ears open. The discussions around you would give you every morsel of news happening around town. Now it looked as if Kate's place was going to be the same, another gossip central.

The men headed out the door and Martha wandered in. She saw Abigail and as she sailed by her she muttered, "Hi Abigail! Fancy meeting you here. I'm going to get something to nibble on and I'll be right back. Save me a seat."

"I sure will." Abigail glanced at the three empty chairs around her table and chuckled. Every other table was taken. People had been eying her and her table for some time, trying to send silent messages, most likely coveting her unoccupied chairs. She stared out the window and again wondered where Frank was.

Soon Martha was in the chair next to her with coffee and glazed donuts. "Lord, these donuts are wonderful. The flavor and consistency are exquisite. I can see where I'll be spending most mornings. I'll have to ration myself, though, or I'll be popping out of all my summer clothes.

"It looks like this establishment is going to be in big demand. It's lovely inside. Kate and you did an incredible job with the decorations and color schemes. It's cozy and welcoming. Your donut paintings are whimsical but accurate. They look so real it's as if you could reach out and pick one off the wall and eat it." She laughed. "You are a great artist, my friend. I'll say that for you. Who would have thought donut images could be so enticing?"

"I did my best."

"And your best is always the best." Then Martha's expression became serious. "I was hoping Frank would be here so I could tell you both what I've just learned."

"Me, too. But I'm sure he'll be along soon. What have you learned?"

"Well," Martha had devoured the first donut, was working on the second, and leaned in towards Abigail so what she said wouldn't be broadcast across the shop, "Ryan told me last night that the corporation you and Frank are investigating, Lansing, has gobbled up practically every house in Myrtle's neighborhood. They've purchased Beatrice's house from her son; bought Jeff Stricklin's and Dotty Cumming's house, too. Many others. So far in total they'd acquired fifteen houses and the land that goes with them. They're still feverishly trying to get Alfred's, Tina's and Clementine's homes, though. Ryan says everyone in his office is curious about what they want it for and about the shady dealings they've used to acquire some of the properties."

"How many houses in total were they wanting to buy?"

"Counting Tina's, Clementine's and Myrtle's? Nineteen or twenty, I'd say."

"What in the world do they want all that land for? What would be important enough for them to strong-arm, torment and conceivably dispose of the homeowners if they won't sell? I've been racking my brain but not much that makes sense comes to me. It's just land. Lansing Corporation can buy land anywhere with the money they seem to have at their disposal. Why this town? This land?"

"Ah, not that's the big mystery, right? Scuttlebutt is there's government funding involved so perhaps the corporation wants to build a top secret lab of some sort there and for some unfathomable reason has to have that exact plot of land. There's so much speculation. Some speculate they're going to build a toxic biological warfare facility or something to do with our national defense or another high-security prison for foreign terrorists–and who in their right mind would want that anywhere near their town? Not me. But who really knows why they want the land? I've heard so many bizarre theories, but none of them makes a lot of sense."

As Martha was speaking Abigail saw Frank outside making his way along the sidewalk towards the door. A minute later he was lowering himself into the chair beside her and giving her a kiss on the cheek. "Hi Abby. Wow, is this place packed. What a turnout. Kate must be doing a happy dance. Sorry I'm late, but I see you've started without me."

"I couldn't help myself. You know me and baked goods."

"I do. You're as bad as Myrtle." He was wise enough not to laugh, but she sent him a dirty look anyway.

Turning to the other person at the table, Frank said, "Hello Martha."

"Hi Frank. Nice you could join us."

"I would have been here sooner but something came up."

His sideway glance at Abigail had an air of secrecy about it. "I'll tell you about it later, Abby," he whispered. Then loud enough for Martha to hear, he added, "Right now I'd kill for a cup of Kate's coffee and some of those delicious donuts I could smell a block away coming here. I'll be back in a second." He got up and wove through the throng to the counter. When he returned to the table he had a stack of chocolate covered Long Johns cradled in a napkin and a cup of coffee.

"Aaah." He sighed sipping the coffee. "This is hits the spot. Good coffee, as good as Stella's, but don't anyone ever tell her I said that or next time I go in there she'll refuse to serve me any." He bit into a donut and a smile came over his face. "Kate sure can make these things. They're absolutely delicious. I feel sorry for The Bakery. Once the townies taste Kate's donuts I don't think they'll ever go back. Well, except for the cakes, pies and cheesecakes."

"There's enough business to go around," Abigail told him. "Be sure to get some donuts to take home with you."

"Don't worry, I will."

Frank centered his attention on Martha. "So I saw you and Abby, heads down, conspiring together as I came in. Knowing you two, I bet it had something to do with what's going on with the old people in town? Am I correct? Any new developments I should know about?"

Abigail caught him up on what Martha had told her. As she finished, Samantha came into the shop and made a beeline toward their table.

"Sad news," Samantha exhaled, joining them. "Alfred Loring's body was found late yesterday afternoon in the creek on the edge of his property by some neighborhood kids. I was listening to the police scanner when the call came over and I followed up the story this morning. I dropped by the police station and demanded information about it. He's dead all right. Police say he drowned."

"Oh no," Abigail exclaimed.

"In four feet of water!" The shock was clear in Frank's tone.

"How do you know," Abigail pressed him, "that the water was only four feet deep?"

"That's how deep the creek on his land is and no deeper except during the rainy season and there hasn't been much precipitation so far this month. It'd be a real trick to drown in that shallow of water no matter how old and decrepit Alfred was."

Sorrow had settled on Frank's face and wasn't seeping away. He wasn't a stranger to loss but Abigail realized he'd developed a fondness for the old war veteran. She could see the death was hitting him hard.

No one at the table had to say anything else. The words *murder* and *another one* floated around them in the air like ectoplasm but weren't spoken out loud.

Frank slowly drank the rest of his coffee and ate the remaining half of his last donut into his mouth, but he seemed to be thinking about something. "Samantha, did the sheriff say anything else at all about the death?"

"Our illustrious sheriff? No. He shrugged it off like the other deaths as another old person accident. So sad, too bad. He actually made me mad saying who'd care anyway? That Alfred was just some aging bum living in a shack on a piece of worthless land and no one would miss him. But that's the sheriff. He's got as much compassion as a turnip.

"He did tell me Alfred seems to have been dead for days by the condition of the body and there are no relatives to attend to the funeral arrangements. The man was broke so the city would have to spring for the bill. I asked him where the body had been found and he said it was at the place in the creek lined with the large boulders. You know where that is?"

"In fact I do," Frank replied, catching Abigail's gaze.

So Abigail knew where they were going after they left Kate's shop.

"It's too bad Alfred is dead." Martha had

come to her feet, ready to run off. She'd already mentioned a dental appointment at twelve and had to go. "But perhaps it *was* simply an accident? And he was as old as the hills. Old people fall and hurt or kill themselves all the time. Why, I had a great aunt who fell down her basement steps one winter and broke her neck. We didn't find her for two weeks." Martha made a disgusting face. "And it was an accident."

Abigail shook her head. "Alfred's death was an accident like his neighbor Tina's disappearance from the cruise ship, Beatrice's and Clementine's deaths and all the other weird things that have been happening to the other homeowners in the same vicinity? Myrtle's trailer burning down? Kate's house being ransacked? *All* accidents? We don't think so."

"Well, I can't deny your logic there, Abigail. And I bet you and Frank will keep digging at it until you find the answers you want. You won't let this go, will you?"

"No way," Frank informed Martha. "There is something really wrong here and someone or something is behind it, causing it. We aim to find out who and stop it."

Martha threw him a sharp look but there was worry beneath it. "If you're going to keep investigating this, you two, just be careful. I remember what happened the last time."

The serial killer had almost kidnapped her and nearly killed Frank.

"So do I." Frank's hand was gently holding

hers now. "We'll be careful, Martha. Aren't we always careful?"

Martha rolled her eyes. "Yeah, your lips are moving but I don't believe you. Both of you have an uncanny knack for finding and getting into trouble. I know you two."

Now Frank smiled. "It finds us. And I have guns. No one is going to mess with me."

Martha just shook her head and, grabbing her purse from the table, left the building, looking back once with a stern expression on her face meant for Frank. *Be careful.*

Samantha exited soon after, a bag of donuts clutched in her hands. "Enough goofing off. I have stories to edit for next week, and a car that sorely needs a tune-up. Bye!"

Abigail was finally alone with Frank. That is if you didn't count the horde around them. "I bet you want to go out to Alfred's place and snoop around the creek, huh?"

"As soon as I have one last cup of coffee and another one of Kate's donuts I do. You want to come with me?"

"You better believe I do, but I have Nick." She nodded to where the boy was a couple of tables away.

"We can either drop him off at your house or leave him here in town with his friends. He looks content enough here."

Which was true. Nick was surrounded by a gang of his school buddies and they were laughing and cutting up, whispering among themselves like teenagers liked to do. Abigail went to Nick's table. "Frank and I are going home now. You want a ride or would you like to stay here longer?"

"I'll stay here, Abby. I can walk home later." Nick's friends, two guys and a girl were busy eating pastries and drinking chocolate milk. Abigail caught the soft look Nick slid over at the girl and the look she sent back at him. The girl had somber blue eyes and blond hair the color of wheat. She wasn't what anyone would call a beauty but when she smiled, she was.

She could tell Nick was sweet on the girl and it made her smile. Ah, young love. She remembered it well and was glad, for herself, it was long ago. The flip side of young love was always heartache.

"Okay, Nick. See you back at the house later. Supper at six. Don't be late."

Her son bobbed his head, his lovesick eyes still on the girl with the blue eyes.

She said her goodbyes to Kate and Laura, letting Kate know how great her opening day was going and letting Laura know how well she was doing on the first day of her first job. Then she left the shop with Frank.

Kate gave her a box of donuts to take home and Abigail wished her luck for the rest of the day.

"I have my car here," she told Frank as they went out the door.

"I'll follow you to your house and we can drive over in my truck."

Fifteen minutes later they were driving up to

Alfred's house. They'd make that their starting point.

*****

It was a short hike to the creek on the border of Alfred's property. Abigail straggled behind Frank as they trudged through tall grass and weeds until they came to it, the boulders and the water. What there was of it anyway. Frank was right about the stream not being very wide or deep. It wasn't either.

The sun, high above them, illuminated every section of the creek and the water sparling in it. The boulders were above her head in height and lined the flowing water for a short distance. They were riddled with quartz and glittered in the sunlight like prisms. The effect was kind of pretty. Overall it was an appealing spot with the water, the trees and the rocks. Too bad someone had died there.

She'd never been to this part of the creek, though it meandered through Alfred's land and others and encircled most of the town in one way or another. In its largest incarnation it rushed behind Frank's cabin and then babbled along parallel to and behind Main Street. She didn't know if it had a name but perhaps it might have had one at some time or another. Samantha would know and she'd have to ask her next time she saw her. That woman knew every scrap of minutia about Spookie's history.

"What exactly are we searching for here?" Abigail probed as she watched Frank scramble down to the creek's edge and stomp around in the mud, head and eyes downward. She remained on higher ground and swatted at the tiny flying creatures pestering her. No way was she going to get creek mud on her shoes.

"Anything…anything at all that might give us clues to how and why Alfred actually died. I can't buy that claptrap put out by the sheriff's department that his death was another mishap."

Abigail waited until he was done doing whatever he was doing and he was back up on the bank with her. "Did you see anything of interest down there?"

"I might have. I don't know exactly where the body was found but now I have an idea. Because the sheriff didn't think a crime was involved, again, there's no crime scene tape to show us, but there's a patch of mud down there by the rocks where there appears to have been a scuffle. A violent one. There are signs of a struggle and drag marks. Shoe prints in the mud and from what I can tell, from more than one shoe size or one pair of shoes. I'm going to get a deputy out here to do some impressions of these shoe prints for evidence. Eventually, we're going to need them."

"You think someone attacked him, dragged him to the water and pushed his head under or something?"

"I believe so."

"So he *was* murdered?"

"That'd be my professional guess." Frank squinted up at the trees shading them and Abigail felt sorry for him. He'd known the old people who had died and some he'd known well. After all he'd grown up in Spookie and she hadn't. He'd confided in her the night before he had suddenly remembered when he'd been a child and Alfred had been a much younger man freshly returned from the war. Frank now recalled seeing him around town in his uniform; hearing talk about him and meeting him.

"I don't know why I didn't remember this when we went out to see him at his house, but I did know him years ago. He used to talk to me when I was a boy. For a short while he was my friend when I needed one, when my dad was sick. My dad had heart problems most of my young childhood. It's what he eventually died from when I was fourteen.

"My memories of that time are faded now but there was this one winter night around Christmas, many years ago, I recall clearer than the rest for I was really sad. Dad had lost his job because he was too ill to continue working, and Alfred, I think it was Alfred, saw me in town and took me sledding on the courthouse's hill and for hot chocolate afterwards. He was just one of those men who cared about other people. He saw I was upset and he took some time to find out what was wrong and then cheer me up. That's why I didn't make the connection with the present day cantankerous Alfred in comparison to the caring and kind man he used to be. Not at first anyway."

She put her arm around him. "I'm sorry, Frank, that Alfred's dead."

He let her hug him. "I know you are. I need to solve these deaths. Not only for Alfred and the others but because I think it isn't over yet and they're tied to something bigger. I'm afraid more could die.

"Also, I'm going to see to it that Alfred has a decent veteran's burial with all the ceremony it entails. Even if I have to pay for it myself. He proudly served our country once so he deserves it."

Abigail smiled at him. "I think he deserves it, as well."

They were walking to the truck, hand in hand, when she thought of something else. "Did you ever hear back from your NIS friend–Charlie was his name right?–about what the Lansing Corporation is and their supposed involvement in all this?"

"Oh, I meant to tell you. I did hear from him. Last night. It's pretty much what I thought. Lansing is a front for a group of powerful and surreptitious government facilities. It's actually part of a massive world-wide conglomerate. They've been buying up the land out around Myrtle's place now for months. This, by the way, is about the time the strange happenings in her neighborhood began. Charlie isn't sure what the government facility's purpose is but he suspects it will be building something like a psychological, chemical or biological research center; extremely top classified stuff and, as all high-level government business, shrouded in deep secrecy. Charlie's going to try to get more information and will let me know what he discovers as he does."

"All right, I'll ask what you've probably already asked yourself. What research facility could be so important they'd kill people to get land for it?"

"I don't know. Charlie didn't know the answer to that, either. Yet. He did say whoever was behind this appears ruthless and he's informed his superiors of what's going on. There's going to be an investigation."

"Thank goodness. I feel better knowing someone with the right government authority is also looking into it. With Alfred's death I'm really concerned. Myrtle still lives out here. Kate will eventually be living full time out here. I hate to think they could still be in danger."

"I feel the same way. And I'm worried about what is going to be constructed on this land and for what intention. Why all this secrecy? We need to find out."

"Yes, we do." She got into the passenger's side of the truck and Frank drove her home, both of them silent with their glum thoughts.

Abigail wondered what would come next. She prayed someone else didn't mysteriously come up missing or die. Things had been going so well in Spookie before this, it'd been so peaceful, and that's the way she liked it. Apparently fate didn't.

But stealing a glance at Frank, she also had the impression he was enjoying it. Just a little.

*****

A night later, the children already asleep, Abigail sat in the living room and tried to watch television. She'd recorded a marathon of The Game of Thrones the weekend before when her cable service had offered three free days of the HBO channel. Tonight she was going to watch some of them. If she could stay awake, that is.

The last week had been difficult. The weekend with the grand opening, Alfred's death and traipsing around in the woods had worn her out, and...the bad feeling hadn't left her. It'd grown.

The show was fascinating, exciting, and for a while she was lost in the stories and stayed up past two o'clock in the morning. Which was way too late. But tomorrow was Monday and she didn't have any early plans, no place she had to be. She had a lead or two on more free-lance jobs and would follow up on them later in the day. So she could go back to sleep after she sent the children off to school. She always made them breakfast, even if it was only cold cereal, and saw them off.

Finally her exhaustion won out. She shut off the television, the lights, and checking the front door to be sure it was locked, she was moving away when she caught something in the glass panel on the other side of the door. The something moved.

There was someone outside on the porch staring in at her.

Through the glass her eyes met the shadowy shape's eyes or she thought they did. Its eyes were empty sockets in a misty silhouette. The features of its face settled into one that became familiar. The man outside her door looked like Alfred.

But Alfred was dead. They'd found his body days before. No it couldn't be Alfred, could it?

She wrenched open the door and was about to ask the person, whoever it was, to come in but when she did it dematerialized before her eyes. There was no one there. It was so unexpected she cried out.

Rushing onto the porch she looked around in the dark. If someone had been there they no longer were. No one was. What the hell?

Then at the end of the yard where it was the gloomiest she spotted the figure again. It was floating there, just watching her. Then its eerily haunting voice came drifting across the grass. *"Warn my friend Myrtle she's next. Warn her not to stay out at her house. Warn her…"*

"Alfred, is that you? Alfred? What are you trying to tell me? Why is Myrtle next? Next what?" She walked towards him across the yard, the light from inside the house spilling out behind her. But with each step she took the man in the shadows seemed to move farther away until she lost him among the trees at the fringe of her property. He'd merged into the night woods. There was no way she was going to follow him there. That's where the ghosts all lived, Myrtle always said.

Warn my friend Myrtle she's next.

Slowly she turned around and reentered the

house. It was late but she'd call Frank and tell him what she'd seen, middle of the night or not, if she'd even seen what she thought she had; heard what she thought she'd heard and what it might have meant. She wasn't sure where Myrtle was right now. The old lady, gypsy that she was, was camped out on her land somewhere waiting for her new home to be delivered and set up. It was scheduled for Monday, she'd said when Abigail had spoken to her last. That was tomorrow. So she was probably out there now. Alone. No telephone. There was no way to get a hold of her except to go out there and find her.

Warn my friend Myrtle she's next. The message had sounded urgent.

She telephoned Frank, waking him up, of course, and explained why she was calling.

"I know you don't believe in manifestations and such, Frank, but the visitation was a warning. I'm sure of it. We need to find Myrtle."

"Now? In the middle of the night? It'd be hard in the dark to find her. I know she spent a night or two on your couch and in between she was staying at Tina's house. But she called me the other night saying Tina's ghost had finally showed up and wouldn't leave her alone; that she had to get out." Abigail could hear the skepticism in his words, but it wasn't as strong as usual and she wondered why. She'd have to ask him when she saw him next.

"Then she said something about going to

protect her land because her modular was due to arrive soon. Protect what? They hauled the burned trailer away days ago. It's a parcel of flattened dirt right now."

"She told me she was going to camp out," Abigail offered what she knew. "She'd gotten some of Tina's old camping things from Tina's basement, a bedroll and a tent, and she was determined to spend the night there."

"I thought Myrtle was afraid of the ghosts?"

"Apparently they aren't on her actual piece of land, just in the woods around it."

"Oh," Frank sighed over the line, "that old woman confuses me to no end sometimes. She has so many idiosyncrasies. Not only does she see ghosts, she's so bloody independent I often think it borders on some sort of mental illness."

"She baffles me, too. But she's our friend for better or for worse."

"That she is. So I'll go over there at first light and persuade her to come back to my cabin and stay in one of the guest rooms until her new house is ready to occupy—even if I have to hog tie her and drag her back; although I question her safety even when she'd behind the locked doors and walls again of her own place. Living in a house hasn't saved the others. After Alfred I wouldn't put anything past whoever is behind this."

"I know. But your cabin is a heck of a lot safer than living out somewhere alone in a flimsy tent."

She and Frank made plans for meeting later

Monday and the call ended.

Abigail went to bed, though it took her a long time to capture sleep because she kept seeing Alfred's ghost, if it had been his ghost and not her imagination, and hearing his warning.

She had some odd thoughts before sleep came. Frank had said he'd also seen a shadowlike figure in a store's window and it had spoken to him, too. What was going on? Were both of them becoming as batty as Myrtle? In the store window in town last week and now this. It was almost funny. If what she'd seen tonight was real, that'd make Myrtle not nearly as crazy as they'd always believed. Now that was a frightening thought.

Chapter 11
Myrtle

It sure as hell was dark out, Myrtle mused, as she crawled into the tent and, by the faint light of a tiny flashlight she'd also snatched from Tina's basement, wiggled into the brand new sleeping bag. It was big and fluffy and like the canvas shelter above her and the flashlight it still had the sales tags on it. Tina had liked to buy things she'd never use, whether she had the money or not. Like the tent...Tina never went camping, or not that she'd ever known of, so why had she needed a tent? The woman's house was full of new but unopened things stuffed, crammed and stacked everywhere. Her basement was like a department store. Shelves and shelves of merchandise barely used if at all. Myrtle had gone down there that morning and loaded up on everything she'd need.

She had to leave that house. Tina's spirit, once she'd come home from the sea, kept bugging her. Two days past the shade had suddenly appeared and hadn't left her side for a moment since. She'd stalked her everywhere in the house and jabbered at her like live Tina never had. Evidently death had made her friend really talkative. Imagine that, even the dead could change.

The thing was the phantom never said anything that made much sense. She'd prattled on about long ago meals and long dead friends or other trivial subjects like why did people have to wear clothes or why did cats lick themselves clean when a dunk in the water would do it much more efficiently. The endless talking had driven Myrtle nuts. Then again, perhaps that was her punishment for not going back to the cabin with Tina that night. Tina's ghost was going to try to talk her to death.

Funny thing was, the ghost wouldn't tell Myrtle what had happened to her on the boat, how she had died or who had killed her. And Myrtle tried to ask her those questions all the time at first. It hadn't done any good. As an answer Tina chattered about how she liked the pattern in her kitchen tile, how much she'd spent on bathroom towels and when she bought the bed upstairs and how the salesman had kept flirting with her. Yeah, sure.

Shades. They sure were squirrely. Why they had to bother her all the time she'd never understood, yet they had since she was a child. Sometimes were worse than others and lately it'd been truly bad again. It made Myrtle wonder if something peculiar was going on in the spirit world. It could be something was or could be the full moon made the spirits extra crazy. She had no freaking idea and she didn't really care…as long as they left her alone.

So she had to get out of that house and the idea to camp out on her piece of land that night came to her. It had turned warm suddenly as it often did in May and she'd be fine in a sleeping bag. She could have squatted at Frank's or Abigail's place but she was sick of mooching off people and sleeping in other people's beds. She wanted her own home back and wanted to be there when the big truck brought in the halves of her modular so she could direct the workmen precisely where to put it. Otherwise they'd plunk it down somewhere totally inappropriate. She wanted it beneath the towering oak tree. The one her husband had first kissed her under so many years ago.

Oh, she was aware old people were being picked off like diseased bison trailing the herd, but she'd be careful. Her tent was behind the oak tree and in the middle of a bunch of bushes. No one could see it. It was a small tent big enough for one person. She'd be quiet and only use the flashlight when she had to. Besides, who would think an old woman would be camping out on her empty plot of land anyway? No one. So she reckoned she was safe. And tomorrow bright and early they'd bring out her new home and she'd be there to welcome it. It worked for her.

Unwrapping a candy bar, she munched on it, ate an orange and a chocolate pudding cup; drank a carton of milk. That was a fine enough supper.

Giggling at how she had tricked Frank and Abigail by coming out there alone she switched off the flashlight, snuggled into the sleeping bag and shut her eyes. They'd never find her there. It felt so good to be back on her land. It was where she belonged. There'd been a time when she'd enjoyed sleeping at other peoples' houses and being waited on, but those days were over. Her trailer being burned to cinders had done that to her. As of late all she wanted to do was be back here with all her memories. For some reason, the ghosts, other than her dead husband's every so often, never bothered her on this piece of earth. She felt safe there.

She must have fallen asleep. One minute the sounds of crickets and frogs making their nightly racket filled her head and the next she was startled awake by an unfamiliar noise somewhere outside the tent. Voices. Two of them. It was still dark outside, yet it was that glowing dark right before dawn. She'd slept the night away in the blink of an eye.

Now the voices were closer. There were people whispering and feet crunching through the grass. A pair of light dots bounced around the earth around her. Flashlights. Myrtle was instantly awake. There were people on *her* property skulking around like common thieves or mischief makers. *Please don't let them see my tent.* Good thing before she'd climbed inside she'd laid loose branches over it to hide it from any ghosts that could be lurking about. Leaves and stuff were great camouflage. They'd never know she was there unless she darted out and waved her arms at them in their flashlights' glare. And, of course, she wouldn't do that.

The whispering continued and became louder. It was coming closer. She could make out it was a male and a female by their voices. She recognized the woman's annoying voice. It was the same woman who'd tried to pressure her into selling her trailer before the fire, and most likely the same man with the sour look on his face, with her. The two suits. What the hell were they doing out here this time of night? Up to no good, she thought. She concentrated and listened to what they were saying.

"You sure this is going to work?" The woman's voice. *"You torching her trailer didn't."*

"I was playing it too safe. I didn't really want to outright kill the old crone, but now I don't care. It's like the others. We'll lose that humongous bonus if she doesn't sell...and now that we know she won't cooperate and we have a final deadline, she has to go."

"You're so cold-hearted, Leonard."

"No, it's just business. They're only old people anyway. No big loss. They'd be dying soon enough. We're just helping them along a little sooner, Shelia." A chilling laugh. *"The money's worth it. I'd knock off a hundred old farts for what we're being paid."*

She thought Frank had told her their names were–she fought to recall and finally the names came to her–Scott and Maria? That wasn't their real names then. And they had been the ones who'd burned her home to ashes. The bastards! Now they wanted her dead, too. Wait until she told Frank. He'd make them pay for what they'd done. And Tina? Had they been responsible for her death, as well? She had the feeling they had and listening to them conspire to do away with her now gave her the shivers. It was a shame the big stick she used for defense had burned up in her trailer or she would have jumped out of that tent then and there and smashed them over their stupid heads with it. They more than deserved it.

"And how was I to know the stubborn old witch would rebuild? But I guarantee this will work. She'll probably have them put the new trailer right where the other one used to be. She'll spend the night in the trailer even with no furniture. Old people are so predictable. All I have to do is place the bomb in the ground strategically below the area where the gas lines will be so it'll explode the structure. I'll time it for the middle of tomorrow night. I'll plant the bomb just deep enough so the blast will look like a gas line accident. The earth's all torn up and fresh anyway. No one will notice we put something in it. It happens all the time. A new house and a bad connection and BOOM! And the sheriff is stupid enough to fall for it. Another accident, pure and simple. He won't be the wiser. It'll be the last straw."

"And if the old witch doesn't actually die in the explosion? She escapes again?" the woman questioned.

"Still a win-win. She'll finally sell us her land. I guarantee it. If she doesn't, I'll grab her and take her for a ride she'll never come back from."

"It better work or I'm not going to be happy.

We only need three more lousy parcels of land here to meet our quota. I want to get out of this podunk town and back to the city. This place with all its weird people, mists and woods gives me the creeps."

"It will work. Then we'll visit Tina Thompson's nephew again and get some sort of commitment on paper so when the house is his he'll sell it to us. If it's a signed legal document, the corporation will accept it, since they don't plan on beginning construction for some time."

"Sounds good to me. Let's do this and get the hell out of here. I want to get back to the hotel and order a big fat steak from room service and snuggle up in that soft bed for the rest of the night."

"You going to order me a steak, too? Let me spend the night in that soft bed with you?"

"If do this right and you're lucky, it's a possibility."

The two were moving away from her and Myrtle couldn't catch much more of what they were saying. Something about the third and last property they had to get.

So they were going to snuff her no matter what? So they had another victim in mind? My, my, my.

Then came the sound of a shovel digging into the ground, more whispers and heavy breathing. Myrtle kept real still, listening; her eyelids drooping. She must have fallen asleep or something because suddenly the sun was rising in its full glory and when she looked out of her hiding place the two schemers were gone. She was alone again.

Had it all been a dream? Not likely, she thought. She knew what she'd heard was real.

Scooting out of the tent she searched for where they'd left the bomb and found it only because she knew what she was looking for. She was bending over the freshly disturbed patch of dirt, a little darker than the rest with moisture, when Frank drove up in his truck.

"Myrtle, you had us worried," he said loudly as he strode up to her. "You weren't at Tina's place and after all that's happened lately you know you should be careful." In the new sunlight he was unshaven and looked as if he'd just rolled out of bed. But she probably looked even worse in her rumpled clothes and uncombed hair. So what. At her age she didn't care what she looked like.

"Sorry, didn't mean to upset you and Abigail. I just had to be home, that's all, on my own land. But it's a good thing I was here last night," she pointed to the tent which could now be partially seen under the branches she'd piled on top of it, "because if I hadn't been, by tomorrow night I would have been blown to smithereens."

"What are you talking about?" Frank stopped feet away from her. She could see the relief on his face. Ah, it was so sweet that he cared about her.

Myrtle pointed her thumb at the soil by her feet. "Those two corporate suits that have been buying up all the land around here paid me a clandestine visit a little bit ago. They didn't know I was camping out on my property. I was hid. But they buried a bomb right here."

"A bomb? Why would they do that?" Frank was examining the ground in the area she'd indicated. His expression was priceless. Not many things unhinged the old cop, but she could see this did.

"So it'd blow my new modular home up tonight when I was sleeping in it. *KAPOOW!* Problem solved for them. And me? I'd be in a thousand bloody pieces and dead for sure. Then they could swoop in and steal my land. The S.O.Bs."

Frank, clever as he was, would understand the implications. "It'd look like another convenient accident? A gas line explosion or something?"

"You got it."

"Are you sure it was the same two people from the Lansing Corporation?"

"I couldn't prove it. I didn't actually see them, it was too dark. But I'm pretty sure it was them because I recognized their voices. It was that man and that woman. I'd bet a breakfast at McDonald's on it." She sent him a sly sideways glance above her grin. "I like the sausage biscuits, and I love their coffee, in case you ever want to know."

Frank didn't answer her but stepped away from the uneven dirt as if a nest of poisonous snakes had buried themselves there. "I'd better

261

call the sheriff and tell him to bring out the bomb squad."

"I don't think our town has a bomb squad," Myrtle retorted sarcastically.

"Then he'll have to borrow another town's bomb squad. Either way someone will have to come out here, dig up, and diffuse the thing."

"Better make it quick, Frank," Myrtle quipped, shielding her eyes with her hand, as she looked out at the road in front of them which faced her property. "It looks like my house is here."

And she was right. Coming over the rise of the road about a half mile away was an eighteen wheeler pulling a section of house on a flatbed behind it and there was another truck behind the first one also pulling a flatbed.

"Hot dog!" Myrtle exclaimed and started trundling towards the road. Her arthritic legs were acting up again but that didn't stop her. Pain was all in the mind anyways. She pushed through it as she always did. "It's about time. I've been waiting for this."

When she turned to look at Frank he was already on his cell phone blabbing everything to either the sheriff or one of his merry men. Soon they'd be swarming over the place asking their typical idiotic questions and looking as dumb as always. Mearl's deputies were sure clueless, or, at least, most of them were. They ought to hire Frank. He was worth ten of them easy.

She didn't care about any of that as long as they got rid of the bomb so the people from the modular homes could set up her new house. She couldn't wait to get into it. She'd been too long without one. As much as she liked her rambling she also liked to have a place to lay her head at night away from prying eyes. Some place the ghosts couldn't get to her.

The first truck, with a raucous squeal of airbrakes, came to a stop on the road and she went to meet the man who climbed out of it to explain they'd have to wait some–until the bomb was gone leastways. Once the cops got there and while they waited for them to dig it up she'd sweet-talk Frank into taking her to McDonald's for breakfast. Yeah, that's what she'd do.

Whoa, was she hungry. Thinking about one's own demise could do that to a person.

Chapter 12
Frank

He couldn't believe someone had planted a damn bomb on Myrtle's land and it would have gone off beneath her new home the next night and killed her. He couldn't fathom the gall, cold-bloodedness and greed of those miscreants who were passing themselves off as real human beings and the sadistic game they were playing or the company that would have hired them.

Sheriff Mearl had called in the bomb squad from St. Louis, which was the closest big city, and they'd dug up and defused the bomb. It'd been a mean package all right–a large briefcase of C4 plastic explosives packed in tightly with a timer–and would have done the job ten times over. It would have blown the modular house to kingdom come with Myrtle in it.

The anger inside him, that had been brewing since the beginning of the troubles, and now also thinking of the missing and murdered people, threatened to explode inside him like that bomb would have done.

Frank was going to apprehend those two suits and bring them to justice as well as the unethical corporation behind them. After what Myrtle had overheard the night before, he was almost positive they were guilty of everything shady that had been taking place. Now he just had to find a way to trap them and prove it.

And he had an idea.

Parking in front of Abby's house he turned off the truck and sat there a minute thinking. The sun was lowering into the horizon and the world was awash in a pinkish golden light. It'd been the warmest day, near eighty-six degrees and sunny, so far that year, and it had possessed the first taste of summer. It was a shame its beauty had been marred by bombs and wicked people.

Abby let him in when he knocked and wrapped her arms around him. "I'm so glad you're here. I want to hear about everything that happened today. Every detail."

"And you will."

"Where's Myrtle?" Abby asked, tossing a glance over her shoulder at him, as he trailed her into the kitchen.

"She's settling into her new house and she's as happy as a child with an expensive new toy." Frank ambled over to the coffee machine, poured a cup and sat down at the table. It felt good to sit. It'd been a long day.

"You think that's safe for her after what happened out there today?"

"She's safe enough. The bomb squad got rid of the bomb and Sheriff Mearl, for once, did the responsible thing. He left a deputy to guard over her and her new domicile for the time being. The officer will be stationed indefinitely outside her house in a squad car.

"I also gave Myrtle an extra cellphone of mine I had reactivated today so she'd have a way to call me or the police if she needed help.

Her home phone hasn't been wired up yet."

"That was thoughtful of you, Frank. That old lady has gone through enough. At least, she'll have protection now. I guess she'll be all right."

"We can only hope. I wouldn't put anything past those two yahoos from Lansing. They're pure evil as far as I'm concerned, doing what they've been doing to the old people. It's got to stop."

"Of course it does. What happens now?"

"Like I said, I have a plan. I still have the telephone number from their card and my alias of Frank Stanus I can use—unless they've looked me up and discovered Tina's nephew doesn't really exist. In that case they won't answer the phone or they will hang up on me. If they do answer I'll attempt to lure them out to Tina's house again, the police will be waiting, and they will be taken in for questioning. They won't get away this time."

"You believe that will work?"

"All I can do is try, Abby."

"Good luck and be careful. They might not appreciate being tricked."

"Most murderers don't. But I'll be cautious. My police backup will be hiding upstairs and I'll be armed, as well."

"When are you going to do this?"

"I'll call them tomorrow. I already have it arranged with the sheriff. He's sending out Deputy Stevens to assist me." Frank got another cup of coffee and was eying the pie under the glass cake cover.

Without asking, Abby cut him a slice and placed it on the table before him, along with a fork. She laid a hand over his. "I don't want anything happening to you."

Frank pulled her face down to his and laid a soft kiss on her lips. "I know that, honey. I'll be careful, promise.

"Have you all had supper yet? Where are the kids?"

"We had supper already. I'd just got done cleaning up the dishes before you got here. Nick is at his friend Freddy's house studying for a history test–or so he says–though I think they're calling this girl Nick likes and doing all the other nonsensical things teenagers do. And Laura is upstairs in her room doing who-knows-what. She got home from working at The Delicious Circle, ate quickly and disappeared into her room. If you listen you can hear the music coming through the door. She'll end up going to bed early." Abby smiled. "Her new job is whipping her butt."

"Does she like working for Kate?"

"She loves it and," Abby bobbed her head at a large white bakery bag on the counter, "she brings home left over donuts every time she works a shift. I think she's going to keep the job. She likes the customers, the tips and the sense of being enough of a grownup to bring home a paycheck. Kate's looking for another helper to work the counter and when she finds one it'll lessen the hours Laura has to put in.

Funny thing is, and a new development I never saw coming, Laura wants to learn how to make the donuts so she can help Kate do the baking."

"The girl is growing up and looking towards the future. It's smart of her. You know, working with Kate and learning the donut business from the bottom up might serve her well. It's a nice little job and an easy way to sock money away for art school. Laura still wants to go, doesn't she?"

"She does. And her art teacher is sure she can get an art scholarship to almost any college she wants in two years when she graduates." Abby had gotten herself a piece of pie and was eating it at the table with him. "Her grades and her art are that good. She's saving money for expenses, clothes and things for when she goes. She has great expectations for her future and I know she'll work hard for it, too. She saw what lack of education and poverty did to her parents, her family, and she wants a different sort of life. She wants to be somebody. I'm proud of her."

"Laura will be as great an artist someday as you Abby."

"She's already better than I was at that age, and anything I can do to help her accomplish her dreams, I'll do."

"You've been a good mother to those two, you know. I'm proud of you, too.

"How about we go sit out on the porch swing for a while? It's a warm evening and I crave fresh air. I need porch therapy."

"That sounds good to me."

They spent an hour on the swing, talking and watching the night come in. Birds flew around them and wove their way between the limbs of the budding trees until full darkness took over the night and the birds went to their nests to sleep.

Nick came home and an hour later and Abby tucked the two children into bed, or as much as they'd let her. Goodnights, a smile and quick hugs were all the children allowed.

Then he and Abby watched some television and because it was a school night he bowed out early and went home. It had become harder to leave her and the children. He wanted them with him all the time, not living in separate houses, and wondered how he was going to arrange that. There was one way he could think of and lately he'd been thinking about it a lot. And when this latest crisis was taken care of he had decided he'd attend to it.

*****

Frank was yanked from sleep by the ringing of the phone on the nightstand beside him. He grabbed out at it and brought it to his ear as his half-open eyes read the blurry time on his alarm clock. "Frank here…whoever you are…what the heck are you doing calling me at two-thirty-four in the morning?"

A hoarse whisper on the other end hit him. "Frank, someone's shooting at my damn house! Putting great big holes in my brand new siding! I swear to God I'm going to grab my new stick and go out after them. Give them what for. I'll show–"

"Myrtle, slow down! Do not go outside. You hear me? *Do not*. Where's the deputy?"

"How should I know? I don't see hide nor hair of him but his squad car is still out there." The whispering was now nearly a yell over the noise of the gunshots in the background.

"Are you down on the floor? If not get down there now! I'll be right over." Frank hung up and dialed the sheriff's department.

"This is Frank Lester, we need some officers over at Myrtle Schmitt's new place right now! There's someone over there shooting her house up and trying to kill her. There's one of your deputies out there but Myrtle says she can't see a sign of him. He could be in trouble or hurt." That'd get the cops out there fast enough; probably at light speed.

A moment later he was off the phone, had lunged out of bed, thrown on his clothes, slipped his gun and holster in at his belt and was dashing out of the house.

As he roared up to Myrtle's modular the first thing his headlights captured was the empty squad car. He heard gunshots and flashing his lights, he revved the engine, hit the horn and made as much noise as he could. He wanted Myrtle's attackers to know he was there and wanted them to stop shooting at the house. He prayed to God Myrtle and the deputy were unharmed.

The shooting ceased. The night was silent again. He slid out of the truck and, crouching

down low to the ground, sidled up to the
driver's side of the police car and peeked in.
The deputy, in the dark he couldn't tell which
one it was, was lying on the seat. Not moving.
Frank cracked open the door and, still keeping
down, checked the man. He was breathing, but
he'd been hit. There was blood all over him.
There was nothing Frank could do for him, the
wounds were too extensive and there was too
much blood loss. He needed an ambulance.

Where the hell were the cops?

Frank, huddled close to the ground, brought
out his cell phone and keyed in 911. He told the
person on the other end he needed an ambulance
and gave them the address and his name.
"Hurry," he whispered into the phone, "a police
officer has been shot. He needs medical care
immediately."

He eased his body out of the car and keeping
as low to the ground as he could while still
advancing he made his way towards the house.
His gun was in his hand and he was ready in
case anyone shot at him. The whole scenario
brought back way too many unwelcome
memories of his active duty days. Now he
remembered why he'd retired. He was too damn
old to be scuttling around under fire with a gun
in his hands acting like a young recruit.

As he got to Myrtle's front door he heard a
car screeching off somewhere behind the house.
In the distance he caught headlights swathing
through the gloom and dwindling away.

Then Myrtle threw open the door and

launched herself into his arms. The stick she'd been carrying dropped to the floor at her feet. "They shot up my damn house! There are holes everywhere! Those bastards! I tried to catch them and whack 'em in the head but it was too dark out here and they were too fast for me."

"Myrtle, what were you thinking? You could have been hurt. They could have killed you." The old woman shaking in his arms was basically skin and bones. She'd aged so much since the cruise, Tina's disappearance and Clementine's death. She'd lost some of her spunk, but not all of it. He didn't want to think about what would have happened if she'd come face to face with her attackers, stick in hand, when they had guns. It was a miracle she was alive.

It made him furious that some dipshits were trying to kill her. What had the world come to that even the old ones were being killed off as if their lives didn't matter?

"I wasn't thinking, Frank. I was hopping *mad*! Look what they've done to my pretty new house...it's riddled with bullet holes. Why did they have to do that?"

Frank gently shoved Myrtle into her house and closed the door behind them. He couldn't take the chance her assailants might still be out there lurking somewhere ready to do more damage. Myrtle switched on the living room light. She'd turned it off when the fireworks had begun. That had been smart. The room was empty except for a sleeping bag in the corner on the rug. Myrtle's new furniture hadn't arrived yet. It was supposed to be delivered on Thursday.

"They want you to sell your land, that's why. They thought they could scare you into selling–or kill you. Either way they'd get the land."

"No, they wouldn't. I put everything I own into Abigail's name last year so it'd go to her. Those murderers wouldn't have gotten their dirty hands on any of it and it would have served them right." Myrtle's chuckle was wicked.

Frank was stunned and wondered if Abigail knew about this change in Myrtle's will. Most likely not or she would have mentioned it to him.

"Abigail don't know about her inheritance and you don't need to tell her, neither. I want it to be a surprise."

Oh it will be, Frank thought. "I won't tell her."

"Good. Now what are we going to do about that deputy out there? Is he still alive?"

"Barely. He appears to have lost a great deal of blood. I called 911. An ambulance should be on its way." And right on cue a siren could be heard coming nearer through the night.

Myrtle was aimed for the door. The words, "We gotta go see to him. Come on," no sooner out of her mouth than she was gone. Frank right behind her.

They got to the squad car as an ambulance,

273

lights blazing and sirens wailing and followed closely by the sheriff's car, squealed up in front of it. Two paramedics tumbled out and came running, got the wounded police officer, who Frank finally recognized as young Deputy Warren, out of the squad car and onto a stretcher while Frank enlightened them to what had occurred. They checked Deputy Warren's vitals and slid him into the rear of the ambulance as Frank, Myrtle and Sheriff Mearl watched.

"He's still breathing," one of the paramedics assured them before he got back behind the wheel. "There's a chance he'll make it if we get him to the hospital soon enough. So we're out of here."

The ambulance drove away. Frank knew he'd be checking in on the wounded officer's condition later that night. He might even go by the hospital to see how he'd fared. He prayed the deputy wouldn't die.

Then the remaining three of them went inside Myrtle's house

Sheriff Mearl looked around at the bullet holes in the walls. "What happened here Frank?"

The man was so unobservant he couldn't figure that out?

Yet it was Myrtle who spoke up. "It's those fiends, sheriff, who are tormenting us old folks here abouts. The same ones, I'm sure, who are vandalizing our homes and knocking us off one by one to steal our land. They're scaring us into selling one way or another and this is what happens when we don't sell to them." She spread her arms around. "They either terrify us, burn our houses down, shoot them up like Swiss cheese or knock us off. The Lansing Corporation wants our land awful bad."

"The evil Lansing Corporation conspiracy again, huh? They're killing off our old folks so they can build some secret illegal government lab or something to do something dangerous to us and the town?" The sheriff tossed a scathing look at Frank. "That's pure poppycock. No company can get away with doing such preposterous things. It's ridiculous. This isn't *Under the Dome.*

"Now her," he tipped his head at Myrtle, "I can understand believing that nonsense but you, Frank, you know better. You were once a cop and you live in the real world. Well, most of the time anyway. This isn't some fiction book. This is real life. Corporations don't go around killing people."

"Apparently this one does," Frank snapped. "And what's worse is they're not done yet. There's three more pieces of property they want to purchase and Myrtle's place here is one of them. According to Martha they have to have all three to sell the deal to the Lansing Corporation."

"Martha's in on this, too, huh?" The sheriff shook his head. "I should have known. She's as imaginative as you, Frank. She should write murder mysteries as well."

By now Myrtle was angry. She didn't care

much for the sheriff and never had. She thought he was a lazy officer and a foolish man. Frank usually agreed with her and that night was no exception. They weren't going to get any help from him. He didn't believe them.

"No matter what you think, sheriff, what happened here tonight is real. Someone tried to kill Myrtle and she needs protection. Someone shot the deputy."

"On that I agree. Someone shot up her house and someone shot my deputy." He addressed Myrtle, "You got any enemies, old woman?" There was a smirk on the sheriff's fat lips.

Myrtle just glared at him.

When she refused to answer him, he went on, "It could have been a drive-by shooting."

"In Spookie?" Frank almost laughed. "That's ludicrous."

"Well," the sheriff went on, "or it could have been a bunch of drunken old boys driving around having a little bit of fun or teenagers with their daddy's guns letting off a little steam. Who knows?"

"They shot your deputy," Frank reminded him. "They could have killed him. That's not having a bit of drunken fun. We need to catch these people doing these crimes."

For the first time the sheriff's demeanor changed. His shoulders slumped and the look on his face was resignation. "I agree on that. They did shoot my deputy tonight. They, whoever they are and for whatever reason they're doing this, need to be caught. All right, I'll send another man–two men–out here to guard the house. One of them will be Deputy Caruthers, my best man. He has the experience to better protect Myrtle than Warren had."

Frank felt a sense of disappointment. Caruthers wouldn't have been who he would have picked, but the sheriff was right, the senior officer did have more time on the job. It still wouldn't do.

Then the sheriff did something Frank never would have thought he'd do. He apologized. In his own way, but still an apology. "I admit, Myrtle, I should have taken this all more seriously. We'll do better next time. You'll have protection."

"It's not enough," Frank declared. He'd made a decision. "That's it Myrtle. Pack your bags you're coming home with me and this time I won't take no for an answer. You're in danger here. You've escaped harm twice and three times a charm. Until we catch these criminals, you need to be somewhere much safer. My house."

The sheriff shook his head up and down and muttered, "I think Frank is right. You'll be safer at his place, Myrtle." For once the man was using his brain.

"I don't really have any bags, Frank, except my suitcases from the cruise," the old woman then grumbled petulantly. Frank could tell she didn't really want to go, but she was scared. "Most everything I have burned up in the fire remember? All I got is those things and what I scrounged from Tina's house. I'm even wearing some of her old clothes and, yuck, she had the worst taste, not to mention she was fifty sizes bigger than me. Do I have to leave my new house now? I have so much to do. Heck, leave me a gun and I'll protect myself. I can shoot, you know, and—"

Frank cut her off, ignoring her tirade. "And sheriff, you can send your protection squad out to my cabin. I won't always be there but Myrtle will. They positively have a bullseye on her now and I don't think they're going to back off. That's not their MO. In fact, they could escalate things. We need to find them and deal with this or there will be more murders."

"This was an attempted murder," the sheriff inserted.

Now it was Frank's turn to glare at him. "This time. But I still think the others were murdered."

"That's your opinion. Now Frank, we've had this discussion many times before. Leave the police work to me and my officers. You are *retired*, remember?"

"They've hurt and killed friends of mine, Mearl. I can't just sit back and allow them to keep doing that." Frank could have told the sheriff what he already knew, the knowledge of and the dealings he'd already had with the two suits from Lansing Corporation and what he was planning, but he didn't. The sheriff would interfere in some asinine way, as he always did, and Frank couldn't allow that. He wanted those two reprobates responsible for his friends' deaths to pay for what they did and he wanted to get to the bottom of what the Lansing Corporation was up to. He would settle for nothing less. He owed it to Beatrice, Tina, Clementine and Alfred. The sheriff wouldn't be much help so he was leaving him out of the equation until he had the two killers in his grasp. Then he'd hand them over to the officer with a bow on them.

"Stay out of it, Frank, I'm warning you. If you don't," the sheriff stood to his full height of five foot nine and puffed out his chubby chest, "I'll have to lock you in one of my jail cells in protective custody until this is all over. You hear?"

Frank's smile was contrite. "Whatever you say, Mearl."

The sheriff tossed him a scalding look. "Good. I knew you'd see it my way."

When the sheriff wasn't looking Myrtle stuck her tongue out at him but when he looked at her again she flashed him a sickly sweet smile.

Frank could have laughed, but didn't.

"Now Myrtle," the sheriff returned to business, "tell me in detail what happened here tonight and don't leave anything out."

"Sure sheriff."

For fifteen minutes Myrtle talked and the officer listened; he took notes. Frank was impressed at that. Mearl wasn't usually that conscientious. It must have been the wounded officer that was finally making the man take the situation seriously. The elderly people threatened and dying hadn't been enough and that alone made Frank dislike the man all over again.

The sheriff drove off and Frank, just short of hog-tying her, took Myrtle home with him. The old woman wasn't happy, but he didn't care. She wasn't safe at her place and he wouldn't put it past those Lansing stooges to make a repeat appearance that same night.

Because now they seriously wanted Myrtle dead.

Chapter 13
Kate

The day was almost over as Kate closed up The Delicious Circle. She'd seen Laura off for home and told her she'd see her tomorrow. The girl was working out beautifully and Kate was so grateful she had her. The shop was always super busy and she'd never be able to handle it alone.

Kate was smiling and humming to herself as she walked down the sidewalk, feeling the happiest she'd been in a long time. Her first week and it had gone better than she could have dreamed. Most days her donuts sold out. The townspeople had been generous in their praise and their patronage. It looked as if her shop would be a success. That was a relief as her bank account and her confidence had both needed to be replenished. Taking in the sleepy town bathed in late afternoon shadows, she sighed in contentment. Spookie was beginning to feel like home again. She'd been away a long time before her mother's illness had called her home. Now her mother was dead but she was here. She still had to go on living.

Odd how her reason for returning home lasted just long enough for her to start her business and realize Spookie was where she wanted to get old. She'd spent her childhood here and now someday she'd die here. She hadn't known how much she'd missed the town and its quirky people until she'd come back.

Scrutinizing the shops lining Main Street, some

closing for the night and the people thinning out but still laughing and chitchatting among themselves, she was at peace. Now if only those pesky people wanting her to sell her mother's house would stop calling and nagging her she could begin to recover her full happiness. They were relentless. The woman had had the nerve to visit her at the shop yesterday and further pressure her.

"We'll give you top price, the woman had persisted. *How about two-hundred and fifty thousand? No, well, we could throw in a little more. You know it's not worth that but we are prepared to give you that much for it. The company we work for is exceedingly generous and very anxious to purchase your property."* She didn't buy any donuts, only a cup of black coffee she left half of on a table before she stomped out, pissed Kate wouldn't accept her latest offer.

It wasn't the constant calling and visits that irritated Kate the most, though, it was the subtle threats hidden behind the words and the continual mentioning of how dangerous her mother's neighborhood had become. *"You know the rumor is the area is haunted? Weird things are happening and the residents are mysteriously coming to harm. If I were you I'd unload that money pit of a house and stash the cash in the bank. You have a nice place to live right up there above your shop. Why not live there? It'd be more convenient than running back and forth to that dilapidated house out in the woods. What do you say? Have we got a deal?"* And on and on.

Kate had steadfastly rejected every proposal

and tried to be polite, but she was getting tired of being nice. She wanted the woman and her associate to leave her alone. She *wasn't* selling. Her mother had loved her home and Kate knew she'd want her to live in it, care for it and love it as she had done. Those Lansing Corporation puppets could offer her half a million and she still wouldn't sell.

Then there was the fact that Frank and Abigail had warned her of the corporation and its agents. They didn't trust them and believed that in some way they might be involved with the crimes occurring around her mother's neighborhood. So she had to be careful.

Tonight for the first time in a week she was driving to the house to gather the clothes and things she needed. Frank had also warned her to stay away from it but she needed those things. She'd decided what harm could it do if she drove out there before dark, got what she wanted and quickly left? In and out. What harm? It wasn't as if she were staying the night or living out there. She trusted Frank and Abigail enough to heed their advice and hold off on that until it was safe again. How long would that be? She had no idea.

Should she let Frank know where she was going? When she was in her car, she keyed in Frank's number. She got the message prompt and said she was heading out to the house to snatch up some things but she wasn't going to linger or stay. "I just wanted to let you know I was going out there. Call me back when you get this."

Hesitating, she thought: *I should wait until he calls back at least. I shouldn't go out to the house alone. Wait. Am I a child or something? I can take care of myself. No one's going to bother me. I'll only be there a handful of minutes. I'm going.*

When she got done at her mother's place she'd drop by Abigail's for a visit before she called it a night and returned to the shop. It would be nice to sit in Abigail's cheerful kitchen, drink coffee and chat for an hour or two. Kate liked being there with the hustle and bustle and the kids. Their cat, Snowball, for some reason she could never understand, seemed to like her. The minute she entered the house the cat would be either rubbing all over her or would be in her lap. Because of the creature, Kate had begun to think about getting a kitten herself.

She'd also get an update on the Lansing Corporation case and if Frank and Abigail had discovered anything else of importance. As Abigail, Kate wanted the mysteries and murders solved. She wanted justice for her mother and the others.

It was a gorgeous warm evening. The woods along the way were full of birdsong and soft sunlight. Kate loved the scenic route to her mother's house and always had; loved being out in the country, driving past the trees and fields that smelled of wildflowers and spring planting.

There was something wrong. She knew it as soon as she stood on the porch and unlocked the front door. She felt a presence…a strong presence around her as she entered the house. As if someone were entering the house right beside her. It was eerie and unsettling. Then she received another shock.

The living room was bare of everything…furniture, television, wall decorations, rugs, accessories and her mother's collection figurines. The mess was gone. Everything was *gone*. It was cleaned out as if the owner had not only died but had moved out all their earthly belongings in one sweep. Only dust balls and shadows had been left behind.

The other rooms were the same. The kitchen was empty, even the refrigerator and stove were gone. She roamed through the rest of the rooms. In her mother's bedroom, where were her mother's things? Her bed, dressers, her personal items, jewelry and clothes were gone.

Where were the things Kate had brought from the city and her personal items? All were gone as well.

"What the–"

Her first thought was those two knuckleheads from the Lansing Corporation had done this. They'd brought out a moving van and cleared out her house without her permission or had hired someone to do it. How dare they! But then the doubts crept in. Who in their right mind would completely clean out another person's house without their knowledge, consent or a bill of sale? There were laws against that, weren't there?

Unless they were thugs plain and simple and didn't care what laws they broke and this was just a strong-armed tactic to get her to sell? Perhaps they weren't representing a corporation at all? They were burglars…just cleverer than normal burglars–or serial killing psychopaths? Everything Frank and

Abigail had been telling her about the disturbing incidents that had been occurring came back to her. And suddenly, standing in her plundered and empty house, she was finally seeing her mother's death in a different light. Were Frank's doubts about her mother's passing not being an accident closer to the truth than she'd believed?

It was at that exact moment her cell phone in her pocket rang.

"Kate? This is Frank. I got your message. What's up?"

"I'm at my mother's house and you won't believe what's happened here. Someone cleared it all out. I swear. All my mother's belongings, furniture, every last little thing, are gone! My stuff, too. The house is totally empty!"

"What are you doing at your mother's house? Are you alone?"

"Yes, but–"

"Kate, you shouldn't be there by yourself. After what's happened, it's too dangerous. If someone emptied the house, they're probably watching you right now and at this point I wouldn't put anything past them. What's another dead body? Another opportune accident? I want you to leave now, you hear? Get out of there."

"Okay, I'm leaving. I only came by for the rest of my things and they're gone, too. I'm going."

"Good. I'm on the road and heading your way. But go now." Frank hung up.

Something rippled through the air around her and, poised in the guest bedroom's doorway, a chill raced along her skin, an electrical charge that raised tuffs of hair along her arms and lifted the hair away from her skull. Someone or something was standing beside her, she could feel them, but when she looked, there was no one there. Again.

There was a whisper in her ear. *Leave.*

"Mother, is that you? Are you here? What are you trying to tell me?" Kate sent out her own whispers, tears rimming her eyes. How she missed her mom.

Then she heard the ruckus behind the house. Someone was shrieking and screaming out in the woods. The cries, so primal and terrified, sliced through her body like a scalpel. It sounded as if someone was being tortured or murdered. She couldn't tell if it were a man or a woman or something else. Her senses were alert and straining, her heart was a drum in her ears, but she couldn't comprehend the sounds she was hearing. Were they from the living or the dead?

She ran into the kitchen and looked out of the window above the sink. The evening shadows had gloomed up the woods and she couldn't see anything past the perimeter of the yard. Nothing moved, yet the horrendous outcries continued. Suddenly they were closer, on the side of the house and all around.

Behind her someone hissed in her ear: *LEAVE NOW! You are not safe here.*

An urgency in the ghostly voice triggered her survival instinct and she sprinted for the front door and ran out towards her car. Her vehicle's wheels spun off the gravel as she left the driveway and they hit the road.

She was about a mile away from the house when she met Frank's truck speeding from the other direction. He swerved off the road and drove up beside her; waved her to the shoulder.

"Are you all right?" was the first thing he asked when he came up to the open window.

"In what sense?" Her laugh was caustic. "I've just had the strangest experience. Not the strangest of my life, but close."

Frank seemed openly relieved. "You can tell me and Abby all about it. We've been invited there for supper if you'll come?"

"Of course I will. Supper sounds like just what I need. Live people sitting down around a real table eating food. I was going to stop by Abigail's anyway. I'll meet you there."

His truck stayed close behind her car. If she hadn't of known better she would have thought he was worried about her safety. She guessed a cop never changed whether he was retired or not.

*****

"Someone cleared everything out of your mother's house? Everything?" Abigail's eyes showed her surprise.

They were in the kitchen ladling out bowls of the chili Abigail had made. Kate had already told the story to Frank out in the front room the minute they'd gotten to Abigail's place, before he ran out again to get Myrtle. She was staying with him at the cabin and no way was she going to miss out on dinner at Abigail's. Frank would be back with her soon.

Before supper Kate gave the details to her

friend. "Every last stick, pot and pan, bed and blanket, stove and refrigerator, memento and all her important papers. My stuff is gone, as well. There's nothing left there at all. I still can't believe it. It's lucky I had most of my clothes and necessities in the loft. I was only returning for what was left. Odds and ends. I just want to find out who did this despicable thing and get everything back. There was a lifetime of my mother's possessions and valuables there. Things I can never replace. I don't know what to do now about it. I called the sheriff as Frank advised and reported the crime. The sheriff behaved as if he didn't believe me, so I told him to go take a look at the house for himself. That'll make him a believer.

"Along with everything else that's happened out there, I finally see what you and Frank are getting at. Something is really wrong and someone is behind it. Someone is doing these awful things."

"When the kids are in bed Frank will tell you what we've found out. I don't like speaking of these things in front of them. They don't need to know."

"I understand that. I can wait. I'm still digesting what I saw today myself."

Abigail handed her a glass of milk and they took their chili and drinks into the dining room where the others waited for them, including Myrtle.

They had supper and it was calming to have the normalcy around her; Abigail's cat on her lap. They talked of her first week as a business owner and Laura regaled them with lively anecdotes of her first week as an employee.

"Laura's turned out to be an excellent worker.

I'm teaching her how to make the donuts next week. I'm so happy I have her."

"And I love working there," Laura admitted. "Except those donuts have already added ten pounds on me. I'll have to be careful in the future." She'd patted her tummy and smiled. "But they sure are yummy. I can't wait until I can make them. They're really works of art as far as I'm concerned. Kate has also promised I can be creative with some of the older recipes. I want to try my own variations eventually. I also think sugar cookies, sometimes decorated for the individual holidays, would sell well. People love sugar cookies. Oh, and cream puffs. My mother had the most divine recipe for them. The puff pastry melted in your mouth. I'd like to make them in her memory.

"And I think Kate should add some of those round tables of hers outside under a brightly colored awning. So when the weather's nice people can eat their pastries and drink their coffee or hot chocolate outside. I also feel we should decorate the front windows more. Fill them with pretty teapots, cups and other eye-catching accessories and trinkets in a bakery theme."

"See, she has creative plans," Kate had noted. "She's an artist in her own right."

It was an awkward evening. Everyone pretending everything was normal when nothing was.

The kids went to bed and the grownups sat around the kitchen table. Outside the night had fallen and Kate was sure glad she wasn't anywhere around her mother's house and she was with other people. Just remembering and speaking about what had transpired at the empty house gave her goosebumps.

"Maybe it was your mother's spirit warning you at the door and up in the bedroom to leave because you were in danger," Abigail said softly after she'd spoken of the experience, "and Myrtle's ghosts you heard in the woods doing the same?"

Kate had looked at her and remained silent, her mind fighting against the reality of dead people speaking to her. She had never believed in ghosts before. Well, now she wasn't so sure.

"I'm not surprised at this latest stunt, though. It fits the escalating pattern. I'm so sorry they stole your and your mother's possessions," Frank had said. "They want you to sell, Kate. This was done on purpose so you would."

"I'm not! The house is still there and so are my memories. I don't know what I'll do with it now, but I'll be damned if I sell it to those crooks. What have you learned that might help us stop them?"

Abigail and Frank, taking turns, disclosed what they knew.

Frank reported how he'd tried often enough to get in touch by telephone with anyone at the Lansing Corporation who would speak to him, but, though his friend Charlie had gotten him phone numbers, no one was answering any of them; which he found unexplainable. He knew someone was picking up the calls but not talking and after twenty or thirty seconds the line would go dead. "How can a corporation do business if they don't answer their phones? Unless there's some secret phrase, a pin number I should have punched in, or something else, that I needed? But I'll keep trying, Kate."

Myrtle threw in her harrowing experience from the other night when someone had trespassed on her land and planted a bomb. A bomb! The old lady was still spitting mad and embellished her story some. They let her. Abigail said she did that a lot.

All of it scared Kate. She could easily have also been a victim and she could be laying in the funeral home right now as her mother had so recently been.

"Yesterday I was going to lure them out to Tina's house again and have the sheriff detain them for questioning," Frank spoke after Myrtle was done with her story, "but Mr. Lethgrow telephoned me before I could call him and asked for another meeting tomorrow at noon. He said they'd be out of town on other business until then. Now I know what they were doing." He sent a look Kate's way. "I agreed. Obviously, my cover hasn't been blown yet."

"So you're really meeting them again tomorrow?" Kate's was looking through the night window. There was the smell of rain heavy in the air and the wind had picked up. A storm was coming. She could barely keep her eyes open and knew she'd be going back to town soon. Four in the morning, when she started making the donuts, arrived really early. She needed to get to bed.

"I'm going to try. They've proven slippery before so I wouldn't put it past them to somehow rabbit away again. I've met the type before and if they even get a whiff of a trap they won't show up.

If they do, Deputy Stevens will be somewhere else inside with me waiting for them. This time I'll get them to tell the truth. The nice guy gloves will be off."

"Good luck, Frank. Be careful."

Abigail and Frank were holding hands and she smiled at him. "Yes, be careful. If they are behind all this, they're dangerous."

"I'll be fine. I know how to handle criminals, remember? But, Kate," Frank directed the words at her, "you also need to be cautious. Even with you living in town above your shop I wouldn't put it past them to try to get at you there. Call me or Abigail if anything comes up or even if you suspect you're being watched or stalked. Don't answer your door at night unless you know who's on the other side. And if either one of those two suits show up again at your place of business, call me pronto."

"You instead of the police?"

"You'll get a quicker response from him," Abigail told her. "Believe me."

"Okay, you two, I'll be extra cautious, as well. I'll lock my doors and keep a big stick by my bed." She winked at Myrtle, who winked in return and gave her the okay sign.

After that Kate said goodnight and drove to town with Frank's truck behind her. He waited until she got inside and then he went home.

It was good to have such caring friends and to be welcomed in as warmly as she'd been by the town. Again she realized how fortunate she was. With all that had and was happening to her at least she had those lifelines.

Now if only Frank and Abigail could solve the mysteries of her mother's and the other people's deaths, stop the madness, all might yet be well. And if they couldn't, she worried what the Lansing Corporation would do next. They still desired her mother's land and she refused to sell it to them. Would they now try to kill her, too? The thought they would made her paranoid and every noise made her jump, every shadowed corner seemed to be filled with killers…if she kept going like this she'd end up a basket case.

She just prayed it would be over soon. She had a life to live and she didn't want to be looking behind her with frightened eyes every moment of it.

Chapter 14
Frank

Frank made coffee at Tina's. He'd bought donuts at The Delicious Circle when he'd driven through town and was eating them. When the two arrived from Lansing he figured if he was drinking coffee and eating pastries in the kitchen it'd make him look more at home in the setting. It'd keep them from suspecting anything for as long as he needed them to. He wanted to get them into the house without any problems. Bait the trap. Slam shut the trap. This time they weren't going to escape.

He was ready for them. His old duty gun was snug in the shoulder holster under his jacket and he had another gun in the drawer behind him. Deputy Stevens was hiding upstairs, waiting and listening until Frank voiced the code phrase–*it's a beautiful day*–they'd agreed on, before he'd show himself. His squad car was down the road in another driveway; partially concealed by a wall and bushes.

Twelve o'clock came and around five minutes after the two suits were at the door.

"Time to play the game," Frank murmured as he went to let them in. Mr. Lethgrow hadn't said exactly why he'd wanted to meet Frank that particular day, but since it had fallen in line so well with Frank's own plans, he hadn't questioned it. He'd find out soon enough.

"Good afternoon, Mr. Stanus. Good to see you again." His visitor stuck out his hand and Frank was forced to take it. It was a cold hand. Frank disengaged as swiftly as he could and not tip the man off that he disliked him. The man was alone which didn't make Frank happy. He'd wanted both snakes caught in the same trap and he wondered where the other snake was. Out doing more malicious mischief somewhere? He wouldn't doubt it. At that moment he was grateful Myrtle was stashed at his cabin and Kate was in her shop surrounded by people. Both were safe or as safe as they could be.

"Same here, buddy." Frank had put on his good old boy façade. It was best to continue the act until the last minute. He led the man into the kitchen. "Donuts on the table if you'd like some?"

"Er, no thank you. I already had breakfast." The man was observing him closely. It must be the suit coat. Today Frank wasn't dressed like a country bumpkin. He was dressed like Frank, the ex-cop. The jacket hid his gun.

Frank pressed his back against the sink and leveled his eyes at the man. "What did you want to see me about? I mean, you know the lawyer told me the other day I don't have legal right yet to sell this house and land to you, as much as I'd want to, until the investigation into my aunt's death is officially closed and she's legally declared dead. Bad news, sorry." Frank released an eagerly furtive smile. "Heaven knows I could use the money. But we're going to have to wait."

The man had a briefcase hanging from one hand and now he laid it on the table and flipped it open. He took out some stapled papers. "My company has found a way around that…or the next best thing. These papers, when you sign them, will be a binding pre-contract of a sort."

"A pre-contract? Never heard of that."

"It's unusual, of course, but a signed copy of it will appease the company I work for." The man put the papers in Frank's outstretched hand. "It simply states you will sell us the house and land for the price listed there as soon as it is legally yours. It's like we're taking out an option on it. That's all. You do know what an option is, don't you?"

Frank played dumb. "Nah, not really, but I trust you. So what's the price?" Frank hid his true reaction. He didn't believe the document was legal, but he could be wrong. He'd have to ask Martha about it. She'd know.

"Read the top paragraph. It's there."

Frank whistled. "Heck, that's a dang sight more than you even offered before." He let his steady gaze meet the other man's again. "I have to ask, why does your company want this worthless house and piece of land so much anyway?"

He could have sworn the other man's eyes narrowed, but it was hard to tell. The man had beady eyes to begin with. "Does it matter? I thought all you cared about was the money?"

"I do. But I wasn't born yesterday and there's got to be an interesting reason. I'm curious to know, is all. Is there oil on the land, or gold, or something?"

The man shrugged. "Not that I know of. The corporation I represent wants it. That's all I know and it is all I need to know. I'm just their agent." A phony smile. "I assure you this is entirely legal. All you need to do is agree and sign the papers and, as you can see on the second page, I'll present you with a hefty signing check to tide you over until the real deal is done. Right now. Right here. I have the check in my pocket with your name on it and everything." He patted his suit where Frank supposed he had an inner pocket.

Frank attempted to look greedy, but couldn't do it. It was time to spring the trap. Enough of this playing around. But first he had to ask, "Do you think your company wants this land," he spread his hands out to indicate Tina's place, "bad enough to– let's say–make me think it's haunted, or to empty or burn this house down or perhaps to even kill me to get it? Maybe plant a suitcase bomb beneath it so it'd blow up and I would be more amiable to selling…if I were still alive, that is?"

Frank would have expected shock but wasn't surprised when the man's face reflected anger and then a little, just a little, unease. The man's deceptive expression reminded Frank of almost every criminal he'd ever caught in the act or every one who'd ever suddenly known the game was up. They'd been caught. It was the face of someone guilty.

"I really don't know what you're talking about, Mr. Stanus."

"Oh, sure you do." This is when Frank fully became the cop he had once been and all pretense fell away. "Since I believe you and your partner, Miss Smith, are behind some if not all of the criminal incidents and deadly accidents that have been befalling the elderly citizens around here. Things like the so-called neighborhood hauntings, vandalisms, Tina Thompson's disappearance off the cruise ship, Beatrice Utley's, Clementine Kitteridge's, Alfred Loring's untimely deaths and Myrtle Schmitt's trailer burning down and her new one almost blowing up? We both know you and Miss Smith are behind them. You wanted their land for the Lansing Corporation and were willing to do whatever–*whatever*–had to be done, vile as it was, to achieve that."

"You're insane," the man exclaimed, but there was nervousness in his eyes that gave him away. He seemed to reassess his options and blurted out, "No reputable corporation like Lansing would stand for such shenanigans, much less murder. They're a Fortune 500 company worth billions. They'd never condone such despicable acts."

That's when Frank got it. The Lansing Corporation hadn't ordered the crimes committed in their name, most likely weren't even aware of them. It'd all been this man and his accomplice who'd thought up and carried out the horrible things that had been done. But why?

"No, that's true, and a respectable company wouldn't condone such criminal acts." Frank had moved away from the sink and placed himself strategically near the door, now he edged in front of it. "You haven't been doing any of them on their orders, have you? They were absolutely your idea or your partner's. But why? Tell me that? Why are you tormenting and killing these people?" Yet Frank thought he already knew that answer.

Lethgrow had moved towards the door as well, but seeing Frank was blocking his exit, he stopped. "You are a real nut case, Stanus. I think our conversation is over. I'm leaving."

"I hit the nail on the head, haven't I? *You're* doing these things, not the corporation, and without their knowledge? For money? Is that why? You're ruining and snuffing out people's lives for *money*?"

Lethgrow glared at him, his rage now barely controlled. "Who the hell are you, mister? You're not the gullible simpleton you pretended to be when I first met you." The man's right hand went to his waist and slid under his suitcoat.

"I wouldn't pull a gun on me, partner. You will regret it," Frank cautioned. "And I have a confession. I'm not Frank Stanus; not Tina Thompson's nephew, either. I'm Frank Lester. I'm a retired Chicago homicide detective who lives in Spookie and cares about its inhabitants. The old folks you hurt and killed were my friends. The cop you shot in the squad car was a friend. By the way, he's going to live, though one less murder charge won't matter. Four murders and an attempted murder on a police officer will send you both away forever."

"If all this is true, aren't you taking a big risk with your own safety, Frank Lester ex-cop?"

"Not really. I have my own weapon and I know how to use it. And I'm not here alone."

Lethgrow's eyes glanced upwards. "There's someone else in the house?"

Frank nodded his head, shouting out, "It's a beautiful day!" And a moment later Deputy Jacob

Stevens was standing in the doorway to the kitchen, his gun drawn and pointing at Lethgrow. He stepped forward and with his free hand took possession of the pistol Lethgrow had hidden in his waistband under his suitcoat.

"You can't prove a damn thing," Lethgrow taunted them coldly. "As far as you know I'm just an agent buying up land for my bosses."

"I disagree. I'm pretty sure we can prove your illicit involvement and we will," Frank assured him, "in time. We have a witness to your bomb burying and, I'm sure, if we dig deeper we'll find more proof on the other offenses. Possibly finger prints on the bomb briefcase that will match yours or your partner's or one of your shoes will fit the plaster cast impressions we got from the dried mud shoe prints down by Alfred Loring's creek. Who knows, we might have enough evidence to send both you and your partner to the electric chair."

Frank gestured at Deputy Stevens as he pulled out his own gun and lowered it at Lethgrow. "You can go get your car now Jacob, I'll watch him until you get back. Then you can take him into custody and transport him down to the police station."

The deputy left the kitchen and for five minutes or so Frank was alone with Lethgrow. He tried to grill the man, he asked him questions, but Lethgrow refused to respond, as he stood silently defiant, his face blank. Heaven knew what he was thinking: probably how to kill Frank and get the hell out of there. Frank wasn't about to give him the opportunity, so his eyes never left him and the gun stayed pointed at his chest.

When Deputy Stevens returned he informed Lethgrow, "I'm placing you under arrest Scott Lethgrow." Then he read him his rights.

Frank asked Lethgrow, "Where is your companion, Miss Smith, now? It'll go easier on you if you just tell us. Before she commits another crime or hurts another victim."

"I have no idea. We're not married. She's a liberated woman and goes where she wants to go, when she wants to."

"She must have a cell phone. Call her and ask her to meet you here."

"I'm not going to do that. Do I look stupid?"

"Have it your way." Frank sighed and cocked his head at the deputy. "Jacob, you can take him to the station now for questioning. Sheriff Mearl is waiting for both of you. I'll be there soon after. There are some things I need to check on first."

Frank whispered sideways to the officer. "Watch him closely. Don't let your guard down for a moment or he'll escape."

Deputy Stevens handcuffed Lethgrow and took him out to the squad car.

Frank was putting the key into the truck's ignition when his cell phone rang.

It was Abigail. "Frank, you better get over here. I'm at Kate's donut shop. I think, by your description of her, that woman you're looking for is here right now."

Frank was instantly alarmed. "What is she doing?"

"She's talking with Kate at the counter and she looks irritated as hell."

"We have her male associate in custody and he's on his way to the police station. I didn't know where she was, though, so this is good news. Keep her there if you can."

"I'll try." Abigail hung up.

Frank drove at a high rate of speed to town. He had a lump in his stomach, his cop's danger instinct was screaming again, and he only knew he needed to get there as soon as he could.

Chapter 15
Abigail and Myrtle

As Abigail dropped her cell phone into her purse she saw Myrtle coming into The Delicious Circle. Wasn't she supposed to be in hiding at Frank's place? That woman! With her eyes never leaving Kate at the counter arguing with the woman in the expensive looking gray suit, she got up from the table and went to head off the old lady.

"Myrtle, what are you doing here?" Abigail had taken her arm and guided her to the table where she'd left her coffee and a plate of Laura's sugar cookies.

"Ooh, cookies! Can I have some?" Myrtle begged excitedly but her hand was already on one by the time Abigail said she could. "And I want some coffee, too. A big, big cup. With cream and sugar."

"Answer my question. What are you doing here?"

Myrtle gave her a pout. "I was sick and tired of hiding out at Frank's cabin. I got lonely. Hungry. So I thought I'd take a chance and come into town and get some donuts. Lucky me. You were here, too. Good thing as I forgot my money at home."

"It isn't safe for you here." Abigail's voice was sharp, her gaze still on the woman at the counter.

"Oh, I'm safe enough." Myrtle's eyes had zeroed in on the case of donuts behind her and her voice lowered to a whisper, "I brought one of Frank's guns. It's in my purse here." She patted the brand new orange bag she had hanging from her shoulder. It clashed with the mauve checkered summer dress, also new, she was wearing. The dress was, as usual, a size too large and hung on her small bony frame. Her hair, sticking out everywhere, had a shiny children's barrette holding it down on one side of her head. At least she didn't have on any make-up, no cerise lipstick, which made her look somehow younger. She probably hadn't gone shopping for cosmetics yet.

"You have a gun in your purse?" Abigail was stunned. "Please, please, say you have the safety on?"

Myrtle huffed, "Of course. I've known how to use a gun since I was a child. My daddy taught me when I was ten. Frank has such a large, excellent collection of them I didn't think he'd miss just one. I picked the biggest one I could fit into my purse. A Colt Python. Beautiful weapon. This time when I come across those two bomb-planters I'll be ready. I'll shoot their butts off." She chuckled and seemed pleased with herself.

Abigail stole another glance at the bomb-planting woman at the counter. *Oh, oh.* Wait until Myrtle sees her. Yikes, she could see the headlines now: *Crazed old lady shoots woman suspect in donut shop. Woman dead. Old lady in jail. Donut shop shot up.* That could *not* happen. Good thing Myrtle's back was to the counter and she hadn't seen who was up there. Not yet anyway.

"Keep that gun in your purse," she hissed at her friend. "And don't go shooting anyone, you hear? You don't have a gun permit. It's illegal."

"But I–"

Myrtle didn't have a chance to finish before Laura

was at their table. "Hi Myrtle. What can I get you?"

Myrtle, swallowing the last of the cookie and directing a harsh glare at Abigail, mumbled, "A large coffee and three of those yummy glazed donuts. Oh, and a chocolate-covered cake donut, too, please."

"Sure Myrtle. Going to get them now.

"And do you want anything else Abby?" Laura had her order pad open, her pencil poised, and a smile on her lips. She was a happy little worker bee. Her copper hued eyes were shining and her long hair was pulled back in a high ponytail so it'd stay off her neck. Outside the sun had heated up the earth to nearly eighty-seven degrees and it was warm in the shop.

"No, thanks Laura. I'm fine. I just need to say something to Kate."

She swung around to Myrtle and grabbing and lightly pinching her hand, said, "I'll be right back. There's something I have to do. You stay here at the table…don't leave. Don't call attention to yourself, you hear?"

"Yeah, yeah," Myrtle groused.

Laura scurried off to get Myrtle's donuts and Abigail got up and worked her way through the customers and tables to the counter where Kate was still quarreling with the pushy brunette; the woman Frank wanted her to try and detain if she could. She had no idea how she would do that, but something would come to her, it always did.

"Ma'am," Abigail sent Kate a conspiratorial look that she hoped said *play along*. "I would like another of those crème horns, please? I saw the girl you have waiting on the tables was busy so I thought I'd come on up and get it myself. You're so crowded today. Business seems to be so good. You must be delighted."

The woman in the suit beside her sent a casual glance her way–her pale shade of green eyes were arrogant and chilly–and that glance dismissed her as quickly. She wouldn't know she and Kate were friends or Abigail hoped she wouldn't.

Kate, with a return look of full understanding and relief, replied, "I am. It's been better than I ever could have hoped for. The town's embraced me and my donuts with open arms, er, mouths." A nervous smile that had more than one meaning behind it and Abigail caught. "Another crème horn coming up." She stepped away, moved down to the glass case furthest from her, and took a crème horn from it as the woman she'd been arguing with waited, drumming her polished nails on the counter, impatience on her lovely face.

When the crème horn was on a paper plate and Kate leaned over the case to hand it to her, Abigail turned her head so the woman couldn't see and whispered near her friend's ear, "Frank's on his way. Keep her here if you can." Smiling, she carried the crème horn back to the table.

"What's up?" Myrtle wanted to know. "I saw you say something secret like to Kate. I see that woman who came to my trailer and helped plant that bomb up there hassling her. We should call the sheriff right now and have her arrested before she tries to blow this place up. She and her friend belong in jail.

"Or better yet, I'll just shoot her in the legs so she

can't get away." The old woman's eyes were flashing with self-righteous anger, her small fist silently thumping the table; her other hand inching towards her purse.

"Shhh, you're not going to do that, and keep your voice down," Abigail told her. "Don't you dare bring that gun out, either. I know who that woman is. Frank just called me and said he took her partner into custody. He's on his way here now to get her, too. We're supposed to stall her. Keep her here. So don't make a fuss or let her see you. It might scare her off."

Myrtle did something she rarely did. She did as she was told and fell quiet. She gave Abigail a thumbs up and devoured another cookie. She kept stealing looks behind her, though, her one hand lightly lying on her purse.

Laura brought Myrtle her donuts and coffee.

Abigail watched Kate at the counter with the woman. She was smiling now and so was the woman. Excellent. Kate was trying to keep the woman there. Probably telling her what she wanted to hear. *Well, perhaps you are right. Perhaps I will sell you my mother's house. I do have this shop to care for. Donuts to make. How much did you say your company was offering? You do know the house is in need of a lot of repairs....*

Abigail intercepted Kate's look and, behind the brunette's back, gave her the same thumbs up Myrtle had given her. *Frank please get here soon.* Should she call the sheriff herself and make sure they knew one of their suspects were at Kate's shop? They could send out a squad car and an officer from right here in town. *Frank's coming. Just hold on.*

And that's when it happened. The woman in the gray suit abruptly stopped talking to Kate, looking around and caught Abigail staring at her. A frown settled on her mouth. Then, without another word to Kate, she pivoted on her high heels and marched out the door.

Abigail jumped to her feet and dashed to the bakery's front window. The woman was walking briskly towards a black Chevrolet across the street. No, she couldn't leave. She'd disappear down the highway and escape. Again.

That's when Myrtle came hurtling past her like a revenge banshee, out the door, and into the street. A gun held out before her in her hands.

Abigail was close behind. "Myrtle! Don't! *COME BACK HERE MYRTLE!*"

The day had gotten even warmer and the sun above hotter. Abigail heard someone else coming in her wake and looked over her shoulder to see it was Kate. And Laura. Both of them had dashed outside to see what was happening. Laura was standing on the edge of the sidewalk, one foot in the street.

What was happening was Myrtle had the woman trapped in her car, the gun aimed at her through the open car window. The vehicle was running but not moving yet. "Don't you drive away, you murderess!" Abigail and half the town could hear what Myrtle was shouting at the woman. "We have questions for you and you're coming to the police station to answer them. You and your bomb-making, friend-stealing, murderer boyfriend. I know it was you two who planted that bomb on my place, most likely burned up my old trailer. Did you kill my friends Tina, Beatrice, Alfred and Clementine, too? I bet you did. You have that guilty smirk on your face. The sheriff wants to talk to you. Get out of the car, girlie. Now. We're taking a stroll down the street to the police station."

Myrtle was shaking the gun in a jerky sideways motion at the woman in the direction of the station. Her face was a mask of righteous determination.

But the woman didn't listen to her. Instead, she shoved down the acceleration pedal, made an obscene hand gesture at Myrtle, and the car took off.

Myrtle shot the gun. Once, twice, three times. By the sound of it she hit the car every time, but the vehicle didn't stop. It did a wild U-turn in the middle of the street and went in the opposite direction because there was a group of townies in the road gawking at the goings-on.

The car picked up speed and was rocketing all over the road and straight at Laura, still standing on the sidewalk.

Abigail screamed, "*Laura watch out! WATCH OUT!*"

Myrtle had hobbled into the road by then and pointed the gun at the advancing car. Three more shots rang out and the car, when the windshield shattered, swerved just enough to the left that it missed the young girl.

Shaking, Abigail ran up to Laura, grabbed and held her. "Thank God you're okay!" She looked up in time to see Frank's truck ram into the woman's runaway car further down the street. They weren't going fast but the car got the worst of the deal. Frank's truck stopped it dead.

Frank hopped out of his vehicle and, a gun held in front of him, ran up to the wrecked car and dragged the woman out. She didn't seem to be hurt. She was cursing and yelling, but he gripped her arm forcefully and aimed the gun at her. "That's enough, Miss Smith. I'm making a citizen's arrest. You were behaving in a manner that was dangerous to the people here in town, driving erratically and recklessly, so I'm placing you under arrest. There's no sense in fighting it. You're coming with me to the police station and you are going to answer some questions we have for you. Your associate Mr. Lethgrow is already waiting there for you. So come along."

"You don't know anything, you idiot. You have no proof we were involved with any of the things that happened. You have no proof! And you purposely crashing into my car like a crazy person…and that old witch with the gun shooting at me like she was some out-of-control vigilante? My lawyer will crucify both of you. How dare you! You're the ones who will be in jail, believe it, not me." The woman was viciously indignant and behaved as if she were completely an innocent party.

Abigail had to admit, she was quite the actress.

"Shut up and start walking," Frank snapped at the woman. "It's not far."

Since the police station was a block away he herded her off the street and escorted her down the sidewalk with everyone staring at the procession.

As they moved past her and Laura, Myrtle ambling up to join them, Frank looked at her and said, "I'll be at your house later tonight, Abby, and I'll tell you all about it. When the cops arrive tell them what happened here and that they can find me at the station. Oh, and please, can you call a tow truck for me and have my truck taken to Ratledge's Body Shop on Highway 37? He'll know what to do with it."

"I will, Frank." Abigail met the apprehended woman's haughty stare and smiled devilishly at her. The woman grimaced in return. Oh, well, so much for being friends.

Then Frank and his prisoner were gone.

The police cars arrived for the accident and Abigail, who knew all of the officers, explained what had occurred and then she called Ratledge's to come and drag the truck away. She didn't bother with the Lansing woman's vehicle. She didn't care what happened to it. The police would have it towed away somewhere and impounded.

Samantha showed up and wanted the scoop on what had happened for the newspaper's next edition. Abigail, back at Kate's shop and over another cup of much needed coffee, caught Kate up on what was happening and what Frank had found out about who was really behind their problems.

"You mean those two agents from Lansing Corporation caused all those hauntings, vandalisms and deaths because they just wanted those old people to sell their houses and land? That's appalling."

"It was appalling. But we figured it out and Frank set the trap. The two people responsible are both in custody. There shouldn't be any more hauntings, disappearances or *accidental* murders. The culprits are behind bars for now. It's over, thank God."

Kate had sat with them for a time, divulging what she and the Lansing woman had been discussing and listening to what Abigail had had to say while Laura worked the cash register, but then had to go behind the counter to start doling out donuts and cookies and smiling at her customers. And they all wanted to know what the commotion had been about. Knowing Spookie, the news would be all over town by sunset.

Abigail thought about Kate's mother and how she'd died, how the others had died and she was so relieved the killers had been caught. Kate and Myrtle would have been next, she was certain of it. They had saved a life and perhaps more than one. She hoped both killers would get what they deserved. The company, too, if it was involved and deserved it.

Myrtle had stayed for a while after the excitement, as well, boasting about how she had saved Laura from being run over by shooting the woman's car up. Abigail had given the old woman her due. She had saved Laura and again she found herself thanking the old lady for someone's life. Last time it had been her she'd saved. She'd invited Myrtle for a celebration supper later in the week. It was the least she could do.

Myrtle was gone now. One minute she'd been there yakking away about her exploits at the table with her, Kate and Samantha, and the next she had wandered off. Heaven only knew where. Down the street probably bragging about what she'd done to anyone who would listen and then off to her new home now that the coast was clear and the danger was gone. Myrtle had said something earlier about furniture, and a stove and refrigerator, being delivered.

Abigail had prudently and discreetly taken the gun away from her after the cars had crashed and put it in her own purse. She'd give it to Frank when she saw him that night. No one had mentioned the gun, or asked about it so Abigail hadn't offered the information, either. So far. Eventually someone in the police department would notice the bullet holes in the woman's car and ask and then Abigail would have to let Frank handle it. He'd think of something to get Myrtle off the hook. He usually did.

"So the corporation was behind all this?" Samantha closed her notebook and had slid back in her chair. She had a paper with exciting news in it to get out so she wasn't staying long.

"That's to be decided, yet. All we know is the two, Mr. Lethgrow and Miss Smith were representing the Lansing Corporation but we don't know how involved the company was with what actually went down. Frank and his friend, Captain Bledsoe of the Naval Intelligence Service, will eventually put all the pieces together. I guarantee it. I'll keep you updated as I find things out."

"Thanks." Samantha exhaled a sigh. "I'm only glad this nightmare is over. The town was really becoming spooked. There for a while everyone believed there were ghosts haunting us all. Doing destructive things. Scaring the bejesus out of us. People were beginning to talk about having a town exorcism or something. Nice to know it was, as usual, just evil people."

"Evil all right. Tormenting and killing old folks for their property as if they didn't even matter. I hope they both go to prison for a long, long time."

"Me, too," Samantha concurred. "The trial should be fascinating and I'll be there covering it all for the Journal." Samantha got up and left.

Abigail got up, too, and after saying goodbye to Kate and Laura she walked out into the street. She had to get home to make supper. Laura would be off work in two hours. Nick was probably already home waiting for her, along with Snowball. It'd been a day and she was tired. Home sounded so good. She couldn't wait to hear from Frank, find out what Lithgrow and Smith had had to say for themselves. Now that should be a neat tale or two.

At least the mystery of the ghosts was solved. As usual, there weren't any.

It was as she was passing by Stella's Diner and saw her reflection she glimpsed the dark figure again. The shadow man. The darkness swirled around him and slowly lightened until she could see him clearly. This time she recognized who it was. Alfred. It was Alfred.

He was smiling now. *Thank you*, his lips formed the words and she heard them in her head. Then he was gone. He had turned into a puff of smoke.

She spun around and again, of course, there was no one behind or beside her on the sidewalk and she felt a shiver as hot as the day was.

Abigail found her car, got in it and drove home. Apparently the day had been more trying than she'd originally thought. What she needed was her home, her children and her cat. And later, Frank of course.

At least now the old people in town were safe. Myrtle and Kate were safe. That finally gave her peace of mind.

*****

Around nine-thirty Frank rode over to her house on his motorcycle. The children were in bed. The two of them sat out in the warm June night on the front porch and Frank summarized what had ensued after he'd taken Lithgrow and Smith in for questioning.

"First off, turns out Lithgrow and Smith aren't their real names. They are really Leonard Britton and Shelia Mathis. The sheriff ran their fingerprints and that's how we discovered their false identities. They each have extensive criminal records and backgrounds. Britton's even been in prison a time or two for criminal assault and Mathis has been in jail for burglary and check forging.

"When Britton was a young man he was in the army. That's where he learned how to make bombs."

"Did they admit to what they've been doing?" she asked.

"They sang like cornered birds after we presented the evidence we already had against them. I admit, though, I did exaggerate some of that information so they'd confess. But, regardless, we had enough with Myrtle's testimony to charge them for attempted murder and I'm sure we'll find more proof for the other crimes as the investigation proceeds.

"I called the Lansing Corporation's headquarters with a special telephone number Britton gave me and learned that, yes, the two were officially working for them to procure the land they desired, but that–under no circumstances or agreement between them–had the Corporation sanctioned any of their dirty tricks, harassment or killing of the prospective sellers. They were shockingly horrified at the crimes."

"It was all those two, huh?"

"It was all them. And with Captain Bledsoe vouching for the company's respectability, I tend to believe Lansing might not have condoned the dirty tricks and the murders at all and didn't even know about any of them. They're probably not guilty, other than for hiring the wrong people to represent them, that is. Of course, there will be a trial and the Lansing Corporation will be expected to testify under oath about all of this. I, myself, think Britton and Mathis alone are responsible for the crimes. It could be they did only act out of greed and without permission from Lansing."

"For the money?"

"For the money and the obscenely huge bonus they were promised if they procured the land by a certain date; in this case, by July. They wanted that damn money so badly in the end they murdered for it. So as far as I'm concerned, they belong in prison or sitting in the electric chair."

"So they did burn Myrtle's trailer, clear out

Clementine's house, plant that bomb beneath Myrtle's new modular home…and they did kill Beatrice, Tina, Clementine and Alfred?" Even as she said those words she still couldn't believe anyone could be as cruelly heartless as to murder for the reasons they murdered for. It made her sad what people would do for money.

Frank answered in a distraught voice, "I believe so. But Britton and Mathis haven't confessed to any of the actual murders yet. They're trying to come off better than they are. But they will eventually. None of those deaths were accidents. They arranged all of them. I'm sure of it. And we'll get the complete truth sooner or later…in writing. At least those two assassins are behind bars where they won't be able to do any further harm. The old people of Spookie are safe tonight and that's what matters."

"That's what matters, yes." She took Frank's hand in hers as the swing rocked to and fro. The sky above was a panorama of black velvet dotted with twinkling stars. The breeze was soft feathers on her skin. She could hear the crickets and frogs singing their night songs. For the first time in weeks she felt content knowing the town and her friends were safe. The danger was over. All was well. For now.

She and Frank talked more about the case and other things in their lives for a short time as the moon rose above them. It was getting late and both of them were weary. Abigail had agreed to help Kate at the donut shop early the next morning while Laura was at school. She enjoyed helping Kate. The next morning being a weekday the shop wouldn't be real busy and the two friends would have time to visit and chat. Thinking of Kate made her remember something.

"Frank, are we still having that get-together on Saturday night? You know the barbeque and playing cards afterwards?" she wanted to know after Frank had yawned for the third time. They'd be parting soon, their beds calling. The get-together had been planned weeks ago and she'd almost forgotten about it until earlier in the evening when she'd smelled barbeque on the evening air. Now she remembered to ask him. Myrtle had told her a couple days ago if she had her stove by then she was making her famous deviled-eggs.

"With those two in jail and the mystery of the ghosts and murders most likely solved, I don't see why not. It'll be a sort of celebration. Another mystery solved."

"And a celebration of your new novel being released soon, right?"

"Ah, you remembered." Frank seemed pleased.

"Of course. I'm so proud of you. Your third published book.

"About Saturday, is it all right if I invite Kate to come over? I see her tomorrow so I could ask her then."

"Sure. The more the merrier. You know how I love a crowd."

She could see his grin even in the gloom of the porch. There was just enough light from the room behind them. It was then it hit her. She loved Frank and had come to depend on him. The kids respected and loved him. He was a major part of her life and she couldn't imagine the future without him. Staring at him in the dark, she felt her lips curve up into a smile. *She loved Frank.*

"So are you ready for our next adventure, Abby?"

Laughing this time, she answered, "Our next adventure? Let's see…we've solved a thirty year old missing person's mystery, a serial killer mystery and now a ghosts/land-grab/old folk's murder mystery. What could top those? Aliens in city hall? Vampires in the town square? Dinosaurs running rampant in the streets of Spookie?" She laughed again.

"Who knows?" Frank stood up and brought her to her feet with him. "We'll have to wait and see. Right now, though, I'm going home, but I will see you tomorrow at Kate's. I've gotten addicted to her donuts and coffee and I love watching you bustling around waiting on the customers. You're so cute."

Abigail gently shoved him away. "Cops, waitresses and donuts. You just like the free donuts I give you."

"That, too. Goodnight Abby. See you tomorrow." He kissed her one last time and left.

Abigail waited until he was gone and went inside. She had a stack of bills to take care of and the latest recorded episode of *Supernatural* to watch before she hit the bed.

Because tomorrow was another day.

Chapter 16
Epilogue
Abigail and Frank

It was August. The air was a hot, muggy blanket that smothered the land, but on it there was the sweet scent of rain. Perhaps a storm was coming in later that night. The summer had been uneventful, calm even, in every other way. No ghosts in old ladies' basements, women disappearing off cruise ships or unexplained murders. For that Abigail was grateful. She liked it when her days were normal and routine.

She'd begun a new commission painting the outside of Johnny's Pizzeria. The proprietor wanted a wall mural of people eating a pizza at a table and an outside garden around them. It was an ambitious undertaking, painting a brick canvas fifteen feet high by twenty-five feet long in the ninety degree sun, but the wall was shaded part of the day and that had made it bearable. She liked the idea that people driving into Spookie would see her artwork as they drove down Main Street. So she worked hard to make sure the mural was a good one. It was coming along splendidly and she hoped to have it done by the weekend. Life was good.

Laura had worked the summer at Kate's Delicious Circle bakery and she'd learned the secrets of how to make the donuts and run a business. On top of it, the girl had saved a decent amount in her bank account for college in two years. In September Laura would be a high school junior.

Nick had spent most of the summer out of town with two of his siblings, William and Penny, at his Aunt Bessie's. He'd spent the sultry days splashing water in the local lake, turning brown, and playing with his brother and sister. Abigail had missed him, but had been happy he was happy. He'd be home next week. School would begin three weeks after that in September.

It was past suppertime. Laura was out with some of her girlfriends at the ice cream shop using up the last of the summer vacation.

Abigail was waiting on the front porch swing for Frank as the evening shadows slipped in. Finally it was cooling off and the breeze felt good on her skin. She had a slight sunburn from painting in the sun some of the day though she'd worn a hat and sunglasses. By tomorrow night she'd be as red as a tomato if she wasn't careful. Long sleeves and pants might help that, though.

Frank rode up on his motorcycle around eight o'clock and she was excited to see him. He'd spent the last three days in court testifying against Leonard Britton and Sheila Mathis and she couldn't wait to hear what had happened. He'd kept her up to date day by day but that afternoon the verdict had been expected to come down and she hadn't heard the final news yet.

"How did it go today in court?" she asked as soon as his boots hit the porch steps.

"Just the way we wanted it to go." He kissed her and sat down beside her, his arm going around her shoulders.

"And how was that?"

"They found them both guilty of every charge. They left fingerprints in the right places and their ultimate confessions did the rest. Britton had an extensive criminal history behind him. He's been in prison for assault and various other heinous crimes numerous times. The story that went around the courthouse was he'd had a deprived, abusive childhood at the hands of a grandmother. He was sent to live with her at the age of ten when his parents both went to prison for drug offenses. Which explains his hatred of the elderly. Apparently his grandmother was a real nut case and used to lock him in closets and starve him when she thought he'd done something wrong. Of course, he was always doing something wrong in her eyes."

"You think that's a good excuse for growing up and killing old people for money?"

"I don't. A person can rise above whatever their childhood does to them. In the end, everyone is responsible for what they do in life, how they live as adults. Britton, I believe, is a common psychopath. He makes excuses for everything terrible he does, feels little or no regrets, and always blames someone else. Mathis was just the brains of the duo. But she is as bad as he is; another psychopath. In court she didn't look one bit sorry for what they'd done. Brought her down a peg, though, jail has. Her hair and make-up looked horrendous." A soft chuckle.

"Tina's death they couldn't tag them with. No evidence there. But three murders were all they needed to convict them. Their finger prints were found at Beatrice's place, on a stick they used to bludgeon her in the basement, and both their shoes matched the imprints found in the mud where Alfred's body was dumped. Same with Clementine, Britton's DNA was found under her fingernails. She must have put up a fight."

"But Clementine's body wasn't autopsied and she was cremated?"

"Well, I had a friend of mine down at the medical examiner's office take some samples when Clementine was in the funeral home," Frank confessed, "but before she was cremated, just in case. Turns out I was right to do that. Don't worry, I had Kate's permission.

"Anyway, they'll be sentenced sometime next month. Britton will most likely get the death penalty and Mathis, possibly. She wasn't the one who actually murdered the old people, he was, but she was an accomplice. At the least she'll get life."

Abigail clapped her hands. "Justice has been served. Thank goodness. How about the Lansing Corporation? Were they implicated or vindicated?" Thunder crackled somewhere in the sky far away.

"As I believed, they didn't have a clue what Britton and Mathis had done. The two had acted on their own, greedy and impatient for the money and the bonus. Lansing was cleared of all wrong doing, except hiring the wrong people to work for them. That alone isn't a crime.

"And wait until you hear this. One of their vice-presidents, Mr. Vincent, was in court to testify on behalf of the company and after it was over he waylaid me outside the courthouse to inform me their board of directors had decided, in a show of good faith and regret for the unauthorized crimes Mathis and Britton had perpetrated on our populace, to gift the houses back to anyone in the survivors' families who wanted them and to donate the remainder, the unclaimed land, to the town to do with whatever it wishes. They have forfeited all claims and they are not going to build their new facility here."

"Well, that's generous of them. I wonder why they'd do such a thing? They must be losing a great deal of money."

"They are. My take on that? They don't want the negative press. It was bad enough to be dragged into this whole mess and they want their part in it forgotten. What better way than to pull up stakes and walk away from it? Clever, if you ask me. They're a vast syndicate and the money is a drop in the bucket to them. They won't miss it. Some of the land won't be claimed. It'll go to the town and I wonder what we'll do with it. Any ideas?"

Abigail thought about it. "You know the town could resell the homes and land and use the money to improve the landscaping along Main Street? Or it could fix the roads or renovate some of the municipal buildings or some of the land could be turned into a town park?"

"All excellent ideas." Frank hugged her. "You should present them to the city council at the next town meeting."

"I just might," she commented. "I'm only tremendously relieved it's over and behind us."

"I tried to get an address or an operating telephone number for Lansing from Mr. Vincent, but he said he wasn't allowed to give out that information, smiled, walked away, and was instantly picked up and whisked off in a shiny ebony limousine. The number Britton had given me months ago no longer works, it's been conveniently disconnected."

"Ah, that company *does not* want people to know it exists or where it's located," Abigail concluded.

"Tell me about it. Even my friend Charlie can't get a lock on their location or what they do. It's so hush-hush and high security. I think it's tied into our secret government. Maybe it handles the interplanetary alien problem or some such thing like in those *Men in Black* movies."

"There you go again, Frank, with your hidden government and alien conspiracy theories."

"Hey, there is a secret government, you better believe it. And they're most likely hiding all manner of nefarious secrets from us. Darn, I really wish I could have followed the bread crumbs back to Lansing somehow. I'm dying of curiosity as to what the company really does."

"I bet you are.

"Was Myrtle at court today?" Frank had told her the old woman had attended every day of the hearings and had testified earlier in the week about the night she heard and saw Britton and Mathis planting the bomb on her property.

"Every day. We often, well always, had lunch together. Tacos or burritos in this little hole-in-the-wall next to the courthouse. She was on this Mexican food kick. I paid of course."

"Of course. How was she?"

"Like Myrtle. Eccentric and a model of high fashion." Frank had an affectionate grin on his face. "You know she was wearing high heels and a hat today with her bright green dress. The hat looked like a flower garden. She didn't look half bad, but kept tripping in her heels. That woman, what a character.

"Oh, and when she was on the stand, after her testimony was finished, she treated everyone in the courthouse to a booming rendition of Perry Como's song *Funny How Time Slips Away*. She said it was in honor of her dead friends Tina, Beatrice, Clementine and Alfred. It brought tears to everyone's eyes. They even let her finish the whole song. Let me tell you, it was an event."

"She's something, all right. But she's a good friend, a courageous lady, and I believe she saved Laura from either injury or possibly death when that Mathis woman swerved onto the sidewalk and almost ran her over. If Myrtle wouldn't have shot your gun at the car, it might have run Laura over. Now I owe that woman not only for my life but for my daughter's as well." Abigail hadn't forgotten how Myrtle has saved her the year before from the Mud People Killer by whacking him over the head with a stick in Abigail's bedroom. "She might be a scrawny little thing, yet she's fearless."

"Yes, she is. You should have seen her on the stand. For once she made perfect sense and behaved as if she knew what she was doing and saying. She sounded amazingly normal. It almost makes you wonder if her dottiness is an act."

"I think so. I figured that out years ago. Myrtle likes people to think she's a little nutty. It's a cover. She's a lot smarter than she portrays herself."

"I think so too," Frank echoed. "You know I got the sheriff to drop the gun charges on her. I blackmailed him by saying I'd never tell a soul he never took any of the crimes against the old people seriously. That and Myrtle is so old no one would put her in jail for something like saving someone's life, even if she was illegally packing a gun."

"That was good of you on both counts. I'd hate to have to visit Myrtle in jail. Think of all the food we'd have to bring her." She laughed.

"And Myrtle seems so tickled with her new modular home and furniture. She couldn't stop talking about it. She's thinking of planting flowers in the front and fruit trees in the backyard. She wants me to build her a deck in the rear, too. She's on a roll.

"Oh, and I almost forgot. You know when I left that old woman today at her place she said something you'll get a kick out of."

"Don't tell me…she's already got another mystery for us to solve?"

Frank chuckled again. "How did you guess?"

"I know Myrtle. She loves to feed us troubles to solve. It's what she lives for…that and trying to push her way in and help us solve those troubles. It's like a hobby to her. What is it this time?"

"She wouldn't spill the beans. Said she'd tell us all about it tomorrow when she comes over for supper. Here."

Abigail laughed. "She's invited herself to supper again?"

"Yep."

"I can't wait," Abigail said, "to hear what she's come up with now."

"Me, either. Whatever it is, I bet it'll be a doozy."

"I bet."

They became silent for a time as the day drifted away. The sound of thunder in the distance grew louder. There was lightning dancing on the murky horizon.

"Rain's coming and coming soon. Feel the temperature dropping?" Abigail shivered.

Out on the lawn the mists had crept in. It was like a churning wall working its way across the grass towards them. Spookie and its infamous fog. Abigail shook her head, thinking about it. "The fog's getting really thick, Frank. You ought to go home before it gets any worse and before the storm hits. The roads out to your place could be treacherous if you wait any longer."

For an answer Frank pulled her closer. "I'll go in a few minutes." His voice had fallen to a husky whisper. He turned towards her and kissed her. A long lingering kiss.

"I hate having to leave you, Abby. I hate it more every day. We need to be under the same roof, in the same bed, every night. Together. I need you to be a part of my daily life, all the time. I love you."

Abigail held her breath. She could sense the tension in his body and hear the excitement in his voice. Something wonderful was about to happen. Something she'd been waiting for for a very long time.

"Frank?" Her heart was racing and her face felt flushed.

Then after three long years of being each other's friend and lover Frank spoke the words she'd been waiting for. "Abigail Sutton…will you marry me?"

Even in the dimness under the porch she could see the ring he held in his fingers. It sparkled in the faint light like a tiny star in his hand. He'd slipped from the swing and was on his knees holding the ring out to her. "Please marry me. I love you more than my own life. I love the children. I want us to be a family. Together. Forever."

Abigail knew her answer but her happiness froze her words. Tears trickled down her face. "Yes," she finally whispered. Then louder, "Yes, I'll marry you Frank Lester. I love you, too. I think I have for a long time."

The ring was slipped on her finger and Frank got up from his knees and drew her into his arms. His embrace was gentle and sweet. He kissed her again as tears streamed down her face. She could feel his love because it surrounded her like the night and the fog.

"How about an August wedding, Abby?" he breathed. "I don't think I could wait any longer. I've waited long enough."

"But it's already August now."

"I know," he countered. "I don't want a long engagement. I don't want any engagement. Both of us know how quickly life goes. We don't have all the time in the world any more. Marry me in August."

"Then August it is. Is next week soon enough for you? How about on my birthday, August the eighteenth?"

"It'll do fine."

Abigail's thoughts were whirling around so she could hardly catch them. But she was so happy her tears wouldn't stop. Frank wiped them off her cheeks and kissed her lips again.

"What kind of wedding shall we have, Abby?"

"A simple one," she answered, smiling up at him. "Just us, our family and our friends from Spookie."

"Well, we have a lot of friends, you know. Everyone in town will want to be there. You think my cabin will hold them all?"

"No, let's not have it at your cabin…let's have it here at my house where it all began. Where we solved our first mystery together from those scraps of paper I found inside these walls. We can put up a tent for the guests in the backyard and Father Mac, I'm sure, will do the ceremony."

"You can arrange all that in eight days?"

"I know I can. Martha and Kate will help. The children will help. And where will we live after the wedding?"

"We can decide that later, Abby. We have a little time."

The rain, a soft curtain of water, began to fall.

"Very little," she said as they got up from the swing. But she laughed. They'd work it out. They always did.

She lifted up the finger with the ring on it and watched the diamond sparkle. A wave of memories of her first husband Joel rushed over her and for a moment she felt sadness, but it passed quickly. That was her past; this was her present and future. Frank was her future. How she'd loved Joel, but Joel had been gone for years and she had a life to continue living.

The most astonishing thing was that she'd found love again when she never believed she ever would. She'd found Frank, Laura and Nick and all her friends in Spookie. She'd found a new life and joy in spite of the occasional mysteries, dangers and murders. And she knew how truly blessed she was to have a second chance at life and love in a town she'd grown so fond of; with friends she'd grown to care about. Now she'd have it all. At last.

"I'll see you tomorrow." She walked Frank to his Goldwing, where he swung his leg over and settled onto its seat. She didn't care that it was raining. She didn't care about anything but the happiness she had as Frank smiled at her. "I'll be at Kate's in the morning serving out coffee and donuts and showing off my beautiful ring." She let go of his hand. Sending him home alone was hard, but soon they'd never be apart again. What was a week?

"I'll see you tomorrow and every day after that for the rest of our lives, my love." He kissed her and she watched him drive away into the foggy, rainy night. Then she went into the house and up to bed.

She looked around her home as she moved through it. So much had happened since she'd bought the fixer-upper and made it hers three years ago. Only three years? It felt like a lifetime ago. Now it was also Laura and Nick's home. She loved this house and wasn't sure she could leave it if Frank wanted them to live at his place. Maybe she wouldn't leave. Maybe she and Frank and the kids would live here?

She caressed the walls with her hand as she climbed upstairs to bed. No, Frank's cabin was much bigger and a far better place to raise a family. Out in the woods where the air was fresh and clean. They should live there. It was the smartest move.

She could rent her house out to someone who would love it as much as she had. She wouldn't have to sell it. She'd never have to sell it if she didn't want to.

Stop thinking about it. Tackle it tomorrow in the light of day. Things were always clearer in the morning. Sleep was what she needed.

In bed, in the moonlight from the window, she stared at the ring Frank had given her. It seemed to glow and sing to her. Its song was so full of future promises. She couldn't wait for her new life with Frank and the children to begin. But now sleep, sleep.

Because tomorrow would be a big day. She and Frank had so many people to tell about the mystery they'd solved and about their coming wedding. There was so much to do and she so much wanted it all to begin…another chapter of her new life with Frank and the children in Spookie.

*****

If this is the first of my Spookie Town Murder Mysteries books you've read, be sure to check out

the rest of the six book series, as well as my other twenty-three novels, here:
https://tinyurl.com/ycp5gqb2
All six of the Spookie Town Murder Mysteries, as well as my other twenty-three novels, are also available in Audible audio books here:
http://tinyurl.com/oz7c4or

About **Kathryn Meyer Griffith**...

Since childhood I've been an artist and worked as a graphic designer in the corporate world and for newspapers for twenty-three years before I quit to write full time. But I'd already begun writing novels at 21, over forty-nine years ago now, and have had twenty-nine (romantic horror, horror novels, romantic SF horror, romantic suspense, romantic time travel, historical romance and murder mysteries) previous novels and thirteen short stories published by legacy publishers since 1984; since 2012, though, I have self-published all of them.

I've been married to Russell for over forty-two years; have a son, James, two grandchildren, Joshua and Caitlyn, and a great granddaughter; and I live in a small quaint town in Illinois. We have a quirky cat, Sasha, and the three of us live happily in an old house in the heart of town. Though I've been an artist, and a folk singer in my youth with my brother Jim, writing has always been my greatest passion, my butterfly stage, and I'll probably write stories until the day I die…or until my memory goes.

2012 EPIC EBOOK AWARDS *FINALIST* for my horror novel **The Last Vampire**-*Revised Author's Edition* ~ 2014 EPIC EBOOK AWARDS *FINALIST* for her thriller novel **Dinosaur Lake**

*All Kathryn Meyer Griffith's books here:
http://tinyurl.com/oqctw7k
*All her Audible.com audio books here:
http://tinyurl.com/oz7c4or

Novels & short stories from Kathryn Meyer Griffith:
Evil Stalks the Night, The Heart of the Rose, Blood Forged, Vampire Blood, The Last Vampire, Witches, Witches II: Apocalypse, The Nameless One short story, The Calling, Scraps of Paper (Spookie Town Murder Mystery #1), All Things Slip Away (Spookie Town Murder Mystery #2), Ghosts Beneath Us (Spookie Town Murder Mystery #3),Witches Among Us (Spookie Town Murder Mystery #4), What Lies Beneath the Graves (Spookie Town Murder Mystery #5), All Those Who Came Before (Spookie Town Murder Mystery #6), When the Fireflies Returned (Spookie Town Murder Mystery #7; out in Dec. 2020), Egyptian Heart, Winter's Journey, The Ice Bridge, Don't Look Back, Agnes, Before the End: A Time of Demons, The Woman in Crimson, Human No Longer, Four Spooky Short Stories Collection, Forever and Always Romantic Short, Night carnival Short Story, Dinosaur Lake, Dinosaur Lake II: Dinosaurs Arising, Dinosaur Lake III: Infestation, Dinosaur Lake IV: Dinosaur Wars; Dinosaur Lake V: Survivors.

My Websites:
Twitter: https://twitter.com/KathrynG64
My Blog: https://kathrynmeyergriffith.wordpress.com/
My Facebook author page:
https://www.facebook.com/KathrynMeyerGriffith67/
https://www.goodreads.com/author/show/889499.Kathryn_Meyer_Griffith
https://tinyurl.com/ycp5gqb2

Kathryn Meyer Griffith